SANTA CAT

BEHIND THE LACE CURTAINS

1856 - 1926

Margaret Koch

OTTER B BOOKS

Santa Cruz, California

Santa Cat: Behind the Lace Curtains, 1856 - 1926

A Contemporary California Fiction paperback original published by Otter B Books.

ISBN 1-890625-04-3

First Printing: August 2001

All photographs in the text and on the cover
come from the Margaret Koch Collection
at the archives of The Museum of Art And History.
Cover designed by Amanda Tennent.
Manufactured in the United States of America.

Foreword

Santa Catarina was a quiet, peaceful kind of town that almost seemed to want to hide itself in a fold of the California coastline.

A town where waves broke on pale sand beaches.

Where tall redwoods marched back into sloping mountains.

Fertile valleys were tucked away between gentle foothills.

It was a town that developed from clusters of Ohlone brush huts to squat Spanish adobes to Yankee fur traders with their muzzle loaders to covered wagon settlers with their horses and oxen. A town that welcomed civilization.

Judge William Mills put it this way: "We're a gen-u-wine town now, boys. We got us a real safe to lock our tax money in, instead of putting it in that box under Sheriff Dawson's bed."

That was Santa Catarina in the 1850's — a town referred to more casually by its residents as Santa Cat.

CONTENTS

MADAME PEANUTS

When Madame Peanuts and her girls rode the stagecoach into Santa Catarina in 1856, their presence was a well-kept male secret until one of her customers was unlucky enough to collapse and die during a visit. It happened in one of the upstairs bedrooms of the farm house the Madame rented from a Portagee. The unfortunate customer was Jed Oldham, livery stable owner and prominent citizen of Santa Catarina, a small California coastal town usually referred to as "Santa Cat" by its residents.

Jed expired of a heart attack while on top of one of the Madame's girls. The unhappy girl screamed for help and several customers who were similarly occupied in neighboring bedrooms, hastily pulled on their pants and rushed to the rescue.

They lifted Jed off and luckily, Irving Parks, the only undertaker for miles around, was downstairs having a drink at the bar. He went up immediately and made a hasty professional appraisal of the situation.

"Don't seem like he's breathin'," he announced.

Sheriff Jim Dawson, who was also downstairs at the bar that night, had to notify the victim's wife. He could hardly lie about the location, although he softened the details as much as possible, telling her it happened in the bar. But the real story got around with lightning speed. The widow shortly sold and left town.

The whole thing was a severe shock to some of Madame Peanuts' regulars. Particularly the older men. The threat of a heart attack seemed to cool the ardor of the male population for several weeks.

Sheriff Dawson was philosophical. "Well, boys, I can't think of a better way to go, if you gotta go."

Irving Parks reflected, "He never knew what hit him."

A young lumberjack said, "Aw hell, that was one in a million shot — wouldn't happen again in a hunnert years."

When business dropped off for several weeks, the Madame thought of moving back to San Francisco. But she paid another month's rent to the Portagee landlord and business began to pick up again.

The house sat back from the dirt crossroads, one of which ran back into the hills to a string of lumber mills. The other road went along the coast to Carterville, a farming center. Her place was handy. Customers could tie their saddle horses or their buggies to hitching racks out back, out of sight, a real convenience for the more prominent members of Santa Cat society.

At first, no female feathers were ruffled, because the good women of the town were busy raising kids, keeping house and attending church. But the wives and mothers of Santa Catarina, who called themselves ladies, were unaware of Madame Peanuts only briefly. It was a topic husbands naturally never mentioned.

The Madame might have plied her profession inconspicuously for some time if it hadn't been for the unfortunate mishap of Jed Oldham which had thrust her place of business into the limelight. But she was a practical business woman. And as a sideline, Madame Peanuts raised lap dogs she sold in San Francisco. She didn't deliver the dogs herself, but sent them up with a man who worked for her. None of the Frisco ladies knew that the dogs they prized so highly had come from a whore house. They were pretty little things, all white and fluffy, and Madame Peanuts always tied dainty ribbon bows around their necks before sending them off.

The dogs were in a chicken coop near the house, and their yapping could be heard at all hours. That didn't always please the Madame's guests. Once, old man Gaff even tried to get his money back by claiming that the yapping got his mind off his performance.

"Them dogs is a bother," he complained. "A man can't even get his pecker up with all that racket going on."

But the Madame knew she had a corner on her business; she could do as she liked. She kept what she considered a high class place at the crossroads, in spite of the rough customers who made up the bulk of her business. If a patron got too drunk at her bar and became obnoxious or started a fight, she called in the six-foot Swede, Olaf, who worked for her. He had hands like hams and shoulders like a stevedore. His appearance was all that was usually needed to settle matters.

As far as the dogs were concerned, nuisance or not, they were to play a part in saving the Madame's business before long. That is, after the wives and mothers of Santa Cat learned about the whore house.

The Madame herself was a small woman with dark hair, dark eyes that flashed fire when she got mad, and the shadowy suspicion of a moustache above her upper lip. When she smiled, a couple of gold teeth showed. Her name was not Madame Peanuts, of course, although everyone called her that and she accepted it. She usually had a pocketful of peanuts that she nibbled on. No one knew her real name. Names were not important in her business. In fact, they could be a liability. There was a rumor that she was French and was married to the Swede, but she was close-mouthed about herself. Even her girls didn't know anything about her except that she ran a good house, fed them well, and treated them fair and square.

She kept three girls most of the time, although they came and went. Sometimes she had four or five. The girls traded around. When they got tired of country life, they went back to San Francisco to work for awhile. So a customer never knew whether or not the girl he liked would be there the next time he went.

Shortly after Madame Peanuts settled in the house, her clientele included not only the loggers, farmers and mill workers, but a good number of the male members of the local Temperance Lodge who wore dark suits with vests and gold watch chains instead of rough work clothes and boots.

Undertaker Irving Parks complained once. "Madame Peanuts, it's a hell of a note, I sure liked that Big Mabel and now she's gone."

The Madame didn't blink an eye. "She's working in Frisco now, Peters, and if you don't like what's offered here you can go up there."

The trip to San Francisco took two or three days, depending on if you missed the boat at Alviso and had to wait over. The stagecoach part of the journey was dependable, but the boat — well, you never knew.

Parks thought about that and decided to make do with what was available. He was shortly seen with a drink in one hand and the other hand exploring up under one of the girl's skirts.

Madame Peanuts' place was fair-sized for its day. Ten years before, in the 1840s, it had served as a stagecoach stop where horses were changed and passengers could get something to eat and even spend the night. She rented it from a Portagee who spoke English only when it was to his advantage. When anyone asked him why he rented out to a whore house, he took refuge in "No spik! No spik!" He was a businessman too. He knew the place was too far out of town for a family with school-age children, too small for a hotel and too far from the coast for a resort. But it was perfect for the Madame and her girls.

When business was brisk on a Saturday night, customers had to sit at the bar and wait their turn. They could be heard complaining.

"Hurry up dammit! You don't need all night!" Or "What

in hell are you doing up there? You'll wear that girl out!"

That was when the liquor flowed freely and tempers got short, but Madame Peanuts was making money. She sold cheap booze she bought from a fellow with a 'still back in the forest, and she charged customers double what she paid for it. She poured most of the drinks herself and she could squeeze a lot of drinks out of one bottle of corn liquor. As for the bottles, once in awhile she bought some good stuff at the store for special customers like the Sheriff, and when those bottles were empty she saved them and filled them with the cheap stuff. She filled and re-filled. A bar customer might see the label and think he was drinking some pretty fancy stuff when all he was getting was rotgut from the 'still.

She refused to add on any more bedrooms, knowing that more rooms could cut down her bar business where patrons waited for a girl and a room. The bar was about ninety percent profit, all hers, but she split with the girls on the bar, too. If she hadn't, the girls might have left for Frisco.

One girl put it plainly: "Ain't nothin' here but trees and lumberjacks and most of 'em tromp all over your feet when they dance."

Indeed they danced, if it could be called that. Loggers' boots kicking and stomping, splintering the rough wood floor in the barroom. They danced and drank and raised hell, giving the bedsprings a vigorous workout, besides.

Everything was going along fine, the dogs were selling well, the girls were not complaining too much, the moonshiner was sending a steady supply, and Madame Peanuts was making money, when disaster struck. Disaster in the form of Sheriff Jim Dawson. He appeared at the door one June evening when the dance floor, bar and bedrooms were particularly busy. A sometime customer himself, he wasn't wearing his badge. He usually left it off when he visited. Madame Peanuts greeted him with a big smile, showing her gold teeth.

"Come in Sheriff. What can we do for you?"

Her smile faded when be pulled out an official-looking paper and announced that she had to close down her business within ten days.

"What the hell you talkin' about, Sheriff?" she demanded. "You know I run a good clean place here. I don't cheat nobody. I don't put up with no rough stuff."

Sheriff Dawson frowned. "I know — I know. But I gotta close you down, Madame Peanuts. I'm sorry as hell about it, but that's the way it is."

"Why?" she asked. "We're way out here where we don't bother nobody or nothin'. You know that."

He nodded. "I know. But we got a club in town. The no-booze bunch. Women. They want you closed down. Worried about their kids growing up with a — a influence like this, close to town. So I gotta close you. You know how women are," he finished lamely, not mentioning that his wife was one of them. But Madame Peanuts probably guessed. She had been in business other places and was nobody's fool. She also knew when it was foolhardy to argue.

"How long do I have?"

"Oh I reckon about ten days, give or take a couple. That's on this paper Judge Mills wrote. I can maybe hold it off a little longer. I'll see what I can do. By the way, is Edna here?" He figured he might as well kill two birds with one visit as long as he was there.

"She's busy but she oughtta be free in a few minutes, Sheriff. I'll tell her you're here. Sit down and let me pour you a drink. On the house."

Madame Peanuts knew when she had lost, but she could lose gracefully.

The Sheriff sat and had his whiskey neat, out of a good bottle, because he was a special customer. She served it to him in a fancy glass. "Everything's on the house tonight, Sheriff," she said, just to let him know she held no grudge.

After awhile Edna came downstairs, followed by a logger who headed for the bar. Edna was a big-busted Norwegian farm girl from Minnesota who hated farm life and had run away at age sixteen, about five years earlier.

Edna's blonde hair and blue eyes were striking, but they were secondary to her physical attributes which were outstanding, even in Madame Peanut's place where physical attributes were important.

The Madame got Edna aside and explained the situation to her while Sheriff Dawson finished his sipping whiskey. He prided himself on being a gentleman, even in a whore house, and besides, he liked Edna. She was a cheerful girl who liked to laugh, and she had those big — he couldn't bring himself to say the word, but those were what he liked and didn't get at home. Mrs. Dawson was a thin woman, flat-chested, poorly endowed, you might say.

Edna came over and sat on his lap with her ample chest barely below his chin. The buttoned neck of her dress was cut low and promised everything the Sheriff had in mind. In her own way, Edna was a business woman too. She knew how to display her assets.

For politeness' sake the Sheriff asked her if she wanted a drink. She shook her head and ran a fingertip around one of his ears. He smiled. Then she leaned closer and nipped his ear gently. Nothing unladylike, just friendly, friendly and waiting. After several minutes he said something to her, they got up and went upstairs. Edna was already unbuttoning the neck of her dress. She knew what he liked. The Sheriff was a methodical customer. He always started at the top and worked his way down.

For a few weeks, the closing of THAT PLACE at the crossroads mollified the female Lodge members, but the men of Santa Catarina were anything but pleased.

"What're we going to do?" Undertaker Irving Parks wanted to know.

Another complainer was Jesse Hayes who owned the Mercantile Store.

"Jim you can't let this happen," he fumed at the Sheriff. "You've got to do something about it! Those damned women!"

Judge William Mills shook his head when he heard

the complaints.

"I'm sorry boys," he said. "But the women — you know, it's gettin' so this ain't a free country any more."

But Sheriff Dawson just grinned. He had been doing some heavy thinking.

"Boys, I got me an idea. But it's going to take a little time," he said.

For a short time things were quiet in Santa Catarina with the wives congratulating themselves and each other on getting rid of "That woman" and "That place". They also were having more success in dragging their husbands to the Temperance meetings.

Then, one day, a terrifying piece of news began circulating through the back fence gossip grapevine. No one knew where it had started. But the wives and mothers were horrified. It seemed that "That woman" — Madame Peanuts — had decided to go straight. She was planning to raise the dogs as her sole business and she was going to move into Santa Catarina. Right into town. And there she'd be, under the noses of the decent wives and mothers. It was a thought too awful to consider. They would probably run into her everywhere — except church. The Mercantile Store, the butchershop and maybe — oh terrible thought — even church, if she really reformed.

Then another rumor joined the first: she was considering the purchase of the vacant house on Riverview Avenue, one of the best streets in town. Judge Mills and his wife lived there. So did several other town fathers of prominence who had been customers at Madame Peanut's place of business. Even the Judge had indulged once in awhile.

The rumors came to a head one day with the appearance of the Madame herself, in her buggy, with the Swede handling the reins. It was about noon, a time when ladies who resided on Riverview were likely to be home for the mid-day meal. Madame Peanuts sat regally beside the Swede, resplendent in a purple velvet cape and matching velvet hat with a long, white ostrich plume.

The Swede tied the horse to the hitching post at the edge of the street and gave the Madame a helping hand down from the buggy. She stood there for several minutes, looking up at the empty house and giving neighbors a good look at herself. By then, Mrs. Mills who lived across the street, and Mrs. Parks who lived next door, were behind the lace curtains at their windows. They had never seen Madame Peanuts before, but they knew instantly who she was.

They watched, fascinated, horrified, glued to their curtain lookouts, as the Madame made her way slowly through the garden, around the house, and out back to the half-acre where she would be raising the dogs. She and the Swede spent a lot of time on the back lot, pointing at and discussing various features of the property which included a carriage house and a chicken coop. Finally they went inside the house.

About then, Irving Parks came home for his noon meal and walked into an hysterical scene with his wife. He had noticed the horse and buggy next door but had no idea it was Madame Peanuts.

Mrs. Parks was so upset she could hardly speak. "That — that woman! She's over there — she's going to buy that house and — Oh, Irving, you've got to do something to stop it!" Mrs. Parks was a very heavy-set woman and she was panting with rage. "I won't live next door to that — that —" she moaned. "Where are my smelling salts? I feel faint."

Parks got her smelling salts from the parlor mantel and attempted to calm her. By the time he had her quieted down with a promise to "do something", he forgot all about his noon meal and fled back downtown. He walked swiftly, his hat pulled low, hoping that Madame Peanuts wouldn't pass by in her buggy and maybe speak to him. He considered it a narrow escape.

At the vacant house,, the Swede and Madame Peanuts came out, got into the buggy and clip-clopped slowly around through the adjoining streets before heading out of town. They left a wake of troubled neighbor women who gathered in little knots to discuss the impending disaster.

"She can't come into town — she just can't," moaned Mrs. Parks who had long suspected her husband's purity.

"The nerve of her!" stormed Mrs. Hayes. "Think of the children! If she buys that house my children will have to walk right past her place every day to get to school. I won't have it!"

"Flouncing herself right in our faces like that!" Mrs. Mills said.

They decided that the Sheriff must be told in no uncertain terms that he must make "That woman" raise her dogs somewhere else — out of town. She must not be allowed to purchase the vacant house on Riverview and he must talk to the owner about that too!

"The best street in town," sniffled Mrs. Parks

Mrs. Mills being the Judge's wife, was chosen to head a delegation to the Sheriff. That very afternoon.

Sheriff Dawson, who knew all about the rumors and the visit to the house, acted surprised and a bit hurt when the ladies showed up at his office.

"Ladies, he reminded, "you asked me to close her down and I did. Now, if she wants to go straight and raise dogs, that's her business and there's nothing wrong with it. I can't ask her not to raise dogs. And I can't keep her out of town if she's so disposed and she's got the money to buy the house. Dogs is legal business and this is still a free country, ladies."

The women shuddered at the news — the very thought of Madame Peanuts let loose in town — their town! They went home after laying down the law to Sheriff Dawson, making it clear that his job was in danger if he didn't do something. It was up to him, and he better act!

Two evenings later, in the line of duty, Sheriff Dawson was sitting at Madame Peanuts bar, sipping a fancy glass of whiskey. She hadn't moved out yet, nothing had changed, except the girls were gone, to Frisco.

When the Sheriff had closed her down, a few weeks before, she had merely locked the front door and put up a CLOSED sign out by the front gate. Wise in the ways of towns and sheriffs and human nature, she had gone on paying the rent and raising her dogs. And she wasn't surprised when Dawson came riding out on his saddlehorse to tell her she could stay.

"But don't start everything up right away," he cautioned. "Don't be too hasty gettin' the girls back here. But I sure miss that Edna," he added.

Business at the crossroads gradually shifted back the way it was before the good women of Santa Cat started their reform movement. The rumors died down. And the female residents of the town were spared the sight of "That woman" walking their residential street, living in their pristine neighborhood and breathing the same air.

Madame Peanuts took the Sheriff's advice. She waited a decent interval, then sent a note to San Francisco by way of the Swede when he went up to deliver some dogs. Her spelling wasn't the best, but she got the point across: *send me three gurls fast and Edna if she is ther. I need her bad. I ow a dett to the sherif.*

THE SONS OF THE GREAT GRIZZLY

"We're a civilized town nowadays," Judge William Mills declared during an informal gathering over Madame Peanuts' bar in 1858. "Just lookit at what we're doing. We're building a schoolhouse — an honest-to-God schoolhouse with two storeys and a cellar. We're puttin' up a town hall — all solid red brick. And we're talking about a bank. A real bank. We've got us a hotel too — the Catarina House. Boys, I think it's time we started a lodge. A place where we can go evenings to socialize. Have a horn or two. Play a little cards." He looked around as a thought struck him. "We can't always come out here — it ain't a far piece from town, but it ain't always handy."

His drinking friends listened respectfully, nodding, their heads.

"You mean a bank? A real, honest-to-God bank?" asked Jesse Hayes who owned the Mercantile Store. At present, Hayes was keeping the town's money in a safe in his store. Before Jesse got the safe, delivered by stagecoach from San Francisco, the town's money had been locked up in a wooden box nailed to the floor under Sheriff Bill Dawson's bed. After strenuous objections from Mrs. Dawson, the money went into Hayes' safe.

Judge Mills continued: "With all the developments we're doing, it's only fitting that us men have our own lodge."

Someone spoke up. "How about a branch of the Masons or the Knights — something like the lodges we had back east? You know...."

The Judge interrupted. "That'd take months to get the papers and all. And it'll cost money. No, boys, I'm in favor of starting our own lodge. Here we are. Pioneers in Californy, you might say. It oughta be something connected to the state."

True, they were pioneers. Many of them had gone through hell and high water to reach the golden state. They jolted across the prairies in covered wagons, spent seasick months sailing through mountainous ocean waves, and suffered sore rear ends from riding mules across the Isthmus of Panama. They knew what hardship was. Once in the golden state, they had shoveled their way through tons of rock and gravel while freezing their feet in ice water, pursuing gold that often wasn't there. Now, in Santa Catarina — called Santa Cat by less reverent citizens — they had found a different kind of gold. Great forests of redwoods to cut, hills of limestone to mine and ship out to less fortunate parts of the world, and in the valleys around Santa Catarina, fertile river-laid soil in which crops and orchards thrived.

Fortunes were being made by those disillusioned miners who felled the redwoods and sliced them into lumber for houses and buildings; others who dug out the limestone and burned it, creating a powder that made cement.

It was time for some fun. A lodge was the answer in this town of three thousand. (They didn't count the Indians or the Mexicans, although they did plenty of the work around Santa Catarina.) So it was decided. A lodge. But a lodge needed a meeting place and a symbol. Some important decisions must be made. They gathered around the Judge to offer suggestions for a symbol.

"How about a covered wagon?" someone offered. An idea that was immediately turned down. Someone else said a seagull would be nice — Santa Cat was on the Pacific Ocean. Finally, the Judge spoke up.

"What lodge symbol could be better than the old grizzly bear?" he asked. "Cussed mean, brave as all get out, and tough as nails."

The men cheered. Grizzly bear it was. Unanimous.

The fact that they had hunted, killed and exterminated the bear almost to extinction, didn't bother them. The grizzly was on the Great Seal of State, wasn't it, the Judge reminded them. That was good enough for their lodge.

Later, a handful of the town's most prominent citizens got together at the Judge's home to make more weighty decisions. The Judge wasn't really a judge, but carried the title due to his claim that he had "read law with a lawyer back home in Tennessee." He also had presided at an impromtu early-day trial for a Santa Cat horse thief who, shortly afterward, dangled from a sturdy oak tree. And from that day forward, Judge William Mills was called Judge and recognized as such by one and all.

Besides the Judge, the founding committee included Lewis McLaren, the only lawyer in town and a close friend of the Judge; JesseHayes, who owned the Mercantile Store; Sheriff Bill Dawson, Doctor Leslie Coburn and Irving Parks, the town's undertaker.

There was a brief discussion about inviting Pete Bonadelli, who owned the main saloon in town.

"We oughtta ask him," suggested Irving Parks, whose mind was on the possibility of acquiring liquid refreshment at a healthy discount. "He can bring the likker."

"The wimmin will screech bloody murder," Jesse Hates said. As a businessman with many women customers, he was particularly sensitive to their whims and fancies. "They'll never put up with it."

"Ohho! Now wait a minute! What is this goin' ter be, anyway? A female institution? I thought we was going to have a lodge for us men," Lawyer McLaren protested. He was the only man present who was not married.

"Sure we are!" the Judge said. "But the women — you know how women are — or maybe you don't know. As soon as they hear about this they'll want part of it — just to keep an eye on us. In fact, I'm sorry to say, Mrs. Mills is already talking about it," he added heavily.

"Shet!" That was Irving Parks.

"We'll keep it separate," the Judge said. "We don't have to meet with the women except maybe for some special occasions."

"Count me out if the wimmen are in, Jesse Hayes said. "It's enough to try to please 'em down at the store without having them in the lodge too. Why, they wouldn't let us play cards or lift an elbow. You know that! Lookit the Temperance Society! They wimmen run it and they'd turn this lodge into the same kind of shivaree if we let 'em in."

"We can have different meeting nights," the Judge said.

"And a locked cupboard," the Sheriff said.

"But what about a meeting place?" Doc Coburn. asked.

It was true that the earliest part of pioneering was done with and Santa Catarina was growing, with a few New England style houses being built to replace the earlier Spanish and Mexican adobes. There were two main thoroughfares, Plaza Street which had board sidewalks in front of the Mercantile Store and the Sheriffs office, and Wave Street which fronted Pete Bonadelli's saloon and Mack Pierson's blacksmith shop. They were streets that had evolved from wagon tracks, but now they were smoothed down and graveled over. Santa Catarina was beginning to look like an American town instead of a Mexican adobe settlement.

It was the older part of town where the melting ruins of adobes stood, in which the Sons of the Great Grizzly finally found their meeting place. There were still a few intact adobes remaining and they settled into one of them, but not without some grumbling.

Jesse Hayes was the most outspoken: "It's a damn shame that red- blooded pioneer Americans have to conduct their meetings in a mud hut where some greasers or Indians lived just a coupla years ago," he commented.

But the men were safe there; the women wouldn't even consider using it. And the old adobe was adequate.

There was a crippled wood stove for heat and coffee — one leg was propped up on flat rocks. There was a cupboard with the doors missing; the men hung a curtain over it. The second room was large enough for meetings. The men knocked together some benches to sit on and a couple of rough tables for card playing.

"I guess it'll have to do," Hayes said.

Lawyer McLaren then reminded Hayes that it was pure luck that the town condemned the adobes and removed the Mexican families who were living there. All more or less legal, by stretching a point or two, but McLaren didn't go into that. Besides, this adobe, the largest still standing, was the only available building in town outside of Temperance Hall which was in the final stages of construction. They all agreed that Temperance Hall was out. In fact, they hadn't even considered it as a possibility.

So it was the old adobe, built years before by Spanish settlers. And some of the few remaining descendents of those early-day Spaniards looked on and disapproved. "Those men using that adobe don't know from nothin'," proclaimed Jose Posada, who spoke good English. "That was our first real town building in Santa Catarina." However, the Spanish population in Santa Cat had dwindled to a mere handful with the arrival of the Yankees, and there were few left to protest the takeover.

By the time the Sons were organized, with bylaws, a meeting night set, and dues, there were twenty-four members signed up, including a couple of lumber mill men and several farmers who lived out of town. They also asked Saloon Pete to join. He was considered a definite asset and he was so busy running his saloon and making corn liquor on the side, that he probably wouldn't come to many meetings.

Those first meetings when the lodge was being organized, were guaranteed to be lively ones. The members were strong characters to begin with. Opinionated. Stubborn, most of them. Especially when it came to electing the first officers. Some of them thought they didn't need officers, but Judge Mills overruled that notion.

"We need regular officers," he said, "or we won't ever amount to much." He had a private hankering to be the first president. Since the horse thief hanging, he had taken to wearing a black suit and a white shirt with a black string tie. He let his gray hair grow a little longer. Mrs. Mills said it made him look more distinguished, more judge-like, but she complained about having to iron his shirts with a sad iron heated on her wood cook stove.

"We need a president," the Judge said, looking around expectantly.

Sheriff Dawson had a more elaborate suggestion. "How about a Grand Grizzly? That sounds good to me. Any old lodge can have a president."

So the lodge was organized with a Grand Grizzly and a Vice Grizzly. The Judge suggested that the other officers should go by the regular titles, as otherwise the names would get too cumbersome.

"The officers oughtta have some badges or medals or something — you know — those things that hang around their necks. They all do. Even in Italy," Saloon Pete suggested.

No one could think of what kind they should have. Ribbons and medals? Where would they get medals? Send east for them? No one was making medals in California. Sending east would take months, maybe longer, and cost a lot of money.

Then one of the farmers, Orrin Call, had a practical inspiration. He removed the matchstick toothpick from his mouth. "Lissen! I got some bear claws left from that old grizzly I shot a year or so back. What's better'n that? Real grizzly claws. I threw 'em out when I skinned the bear out behind the house. But they're still there. I'll get 'em — they ain't hurt none — good as new."

Judge Mills brightened up. "Yes! Some of the wimmin can sew them onto ribbons or such — they'd probably be tickled to do that for us. Make regular doodads for the officers with real bear claws. That's fine."

Mrs. Mills and several other wives volunteered, privately laughing about it among themselves, saying it was a crazy idea, but they did it to please their men. The Grand Grizzly had claws on a red ribbon to hang around his neck. The Vice Grizzly's were sewed to a blue ribbon and the lesser officers all had green ribbons with fewer claws sewed to them. The claws were arranged to hang from the ribbon ends like fringe.

"Them look right smart," commented Farmer Call, pleased with himself. "Who woulda thought those claws would ever amount to anything? That ol' bear never knew what hit her. Did I ever tell you how I laid fer her? Got her with one shot — right between the eyes? Right square between the eyes, boys."

Call was long-winded and prone to brag about killing what he claimed was "The last grizzly b'ar in the Santa Catarina mountains." But since he had provided the claws, the Sons had to listen to him out of politeness, although most of them had heard his story several times before.

When Call finished his seemingly endless monologue, the members agreed unanimously that it would now be appropriate to "crissen" the new lodge with a horn or two of whiskey, all around. Saloon Pete had thoughtfully provided liquor and tin cups. The Sons circled around the Judge, lifted their cups together and announced "Here's to us — Sons of the Great Grizzly!"

The Grizzly Lodge began to flourish with weekly meetings on Monday nights. The most official business conducted was a more or less formal march of officers into the room, wearing their bear claw regalia. But the real business was cards and drinking, with an occasional after-Lodge excursion out to Madame Peanuts' establishment beyond the edge of town. Everything was going along fine until the wives began to ask questions.

"What do you do down there every Monday night?" Mrs. Judge Mills asked. (She preferred to be addressed that way.)

"What? Hmph." The Judge was nonplussed for a moment, although he had known that such questions were bound to come up. "Well, my dear, we — we discuss business. The improvement of Santa Catarina. Things like that."

Mrs. Mills was looking doubtful. The Judge added hastily "Some of the members indulge in a harmless game of cards — no gambling, you understand." But that wasn't the end of it. Other wives started to ask questions. A few even imagined they noticed whiffs of liquor on their husband's breath after Lodge meetings. The men could see trouble ahead. They talked it over.

"What'll we do?" Asked Undertaker Irving Parks, "Mrs. Parks is askin' too many gol'darned questions."

"Yes, and the ladies are already planning to organize a woman's Grizzly Lodge, too," the Judge said.

"Tell 'em to tend to their own business," growled Lawyer Lewis McLaren, the only bachelor among them.

"It ain't that easy — you don't understand wimmen," Irving Parks said.

"And I don't aim to," McLaren answered.

Parks laughed. "Jest you wait! Some pretty little schoolmar'm will smile and bat her eyes at you and you'll be a goner."

"Nope. I plan to stay single."

They all laughed at that.

"But down to business, boys," Jesse Hayes said. "What're we goin' to do? T'other day, a passel of women talkin' about it in the store. Things is gettin' serious. Next they'll want to be comin' to our meetings to find out what's goin' on."

They all had a drink while they thought that over. Then Judge Mills spoke. "Some kind of charity," he mused. "That's the answer. They can't find nothing wrong with that."

"The Temperance Society is sendin' money to a missionary someplace," suggested Irving Parks.

"Nope," the Judge said, "That's too far away. It's gotta be something right here in Santa Cat. Something they can see. How about that widow woman — her man got killed in the woods a couple of weeks ago. I heard she's got a bunch of young'uns, too. We could have a chivaree — no, not that — but something like that to raise money for her."

"Not here," someone said hastily.

"Maybe a barbecue — how about a bull's head barbecue? Ain't had one of those for a spell," someone else suggested.

"Yeah, a good old-fashioned Mexican bull's head barbecue. We can get Jose Ortiz to do the cookin' — we dig the holes and furnish the fixin's," the Judge said.

Joseph Perry, the town's butcher shop owner, spoke up: "I'll furnish the bull's heads — cheap."

And so it was decided. A trio of members volunteered to dig the holes where the bull's heads would be buried to cook for hours in nests of oak logs and coals. Other members volunteered their wives for potato salad, baked beans and coffee.

"We can charge four bits a head," the Judge decided.

"I'll set up a lemonade stand," Saloon Pete offered, then added with a wink "with a little extry for the men folks."

"Boys, it sounds good. We oughtta get forty-fifty people anyway. And we got a real honest-to-God thing we can tell the wimmen about," Irving Parks said.

Project decided, business done, members recessed to the card tables and the shelves behind the curtain where the whiskey supply was kept.

The wives received news of the project with mixed emotions and a good deal of doubt.

"Do you think they really mean it?" Mrs. Parks asked the Judge's wife over the back fence.

"I'm planning to make the potato salad, a washtub full. Saving my bacon grease and I'll have to get more vinegar from old man Jenkins — he's got apple trees," Mrs. Mills said.

"I'm lined up to make pies," Mrs. Parks said. "Good thing I put up those blackberries last summer."

"But the plans for this here thing — men aren't any

good at making plans for something like this," Mrs. Mills said. "You know what I think — I think us members of the food committee oughta go to the next Grizzly meeting to make sure things are going along all right."

"The men never invited us to do that, Mrs. Parks said. "They just want us to fix part of the food."

"We'll just surprise them," Mrs. Mills said. "Drop in after we get the dinner dishes done and the children down for the night."

And that was how a committee of seven wives, including leaders of the Temperance Society, happened to go to the next Monday night meeting of the Sons of the Great Grizzly. No advance warning.

The ladies could hear sounds of revelry before they knocked at the door. But even so, the actual scene that greeted them was not what they expected. Two poker games were in full swing with a pile of coins on each table. Gambling! And even worse, tin cups of something that was not coffee were everywhere. The ladies sniffed. Liquor! No doubt about it.

The men looked up, startled. Judge Mills dropped his cigar — it landed in his cup of whiskey. Irving Parks, who was just lifting his cup to his mouth, spilled it down his shirt front. Jesse Hayes said "Shet!" The others were speechless, paralyzed.

Mrs. Judge Mills, who had led the little delegation of women into the lodge hall, sniffed again and said "Well!" Then she turned on her heel and led them out again. "That was a mistake!" she snorted as they headed for their homes, all in a state of shock.

Some of them were saying things like "I can't believe it!" and "I had no idea!" and "I couldn't believe my eyes!" and "What do we do now?"

"We talk to our husbands when they get home tonight," Mrs. Mills said with steel in her words. "It's our duty to lay down the law to them!"

Some serious discussions took place that night in a number of homes in Santa Catarina and it was a thoughtful group of civic leaders who left their homes to go to work the next morning. Several of them gathered at the Judge's office to discuss the situation.

"What in hell are we goin to do?" mourned Irving Parks. "They saw everything! They're raising hell!"

"We're going to do what we have to do — get rid of everything and invite the women to a meeting to prove it," the Judge advised.

"Do we *have* to do that?" Parks said. "What's the use of havin' the Grizzly Lodge if we can't do a little drinkin' and card playin' now and then?"

"Let a little time go by — we'll get it all back in a couple of months, after things settle down," suggested the Judge.

"Them women won't forget it that quick," predicted Jesse Hayes.

"Well boys, I got another idea," the Judge offered. "We'll build us a lodge hall. I got a lot out on the edge of town — far enough so the women can't bother us. We're right under their noses, here."

"I got a pile of redwood lumber down to the store — I'll donate it," Hayes said. "I'll throw in the nails too."

"I'll give twenty-five dollars toward it," Lawyer McLaren said.

"If we all pitch in we can build it inside a month," Parks said.

"I'll donate the lot, the Judge said. "And about that bull's head barbecue — we better put that off until things cool down at home. Mrs. Mills was pretty upset over the whole thing."

They all nodded.

The Judge spoke again: "Parks, you get rid of the cards — hide them in one of your coffins if you have to. Saloon Pete can take back the liquor — temporarily, for the time being. And we'll invite the women to our next meeting. All nice and clean."

"Will they believe it?" Parks doubted.

"They'll be glad to — especially when we go to the

Temperance meeting and declare our sins," the Judge said.

"Oh hell no! Not that!" Hayes protested.

The Judge held up his hand to silence the protest. "It's a cheap price to pay, boys, and it's a hell of a lot better than trying to live with an impossible woman."

They all saw the wisdom of that. And that's what they did. The men went to the Temperance meetings and bared their souls. Penitent. Solemn. Serious. The women quieted down. The new lodge hall was built — with a concealed liquor cupboard that had a secure lock. The cards and dice came out of the coffin down at Irving Parks' undertaking parlor. And in three months the Grizzlies were back in business.

Their new lodge hall was even closer to Madame Peanuts' establishment. "Very handy" as Judge Mills observed.

BROTHERS

There was only a handful of Mission Indians left around the Santa Catarina Mission in 1860 when the Culver brothers arrived from Massachusetts with a small sack of gold coins, to set up their general store. They had owned and operated a store back east and they knew the business. But they found conditions very different in the new state of California.

Pete Culver, the older of the two by four years, was the boss and he was known to have a shrewd head for making a dollar. Joel, who was twenty-two, mostly followed Pete's orders without question; his blue eyes were gentle and his voice was soft.

The Santa Catarina Indians who had not been killed by renegade whites, or alcohol, had fallen easy prey to diseases introduced by the invading white settlers. Measles, smallpox, influenza, diphtheria, to name the worst.

Mountain Man Ole Gustavson, who had killed more than his share of Indians while coming west a few years before, summed it up in a few words:

"We don't gotta do nothing," he trumpeted. "Just give 'em a good case of the clap or measles. They'll die like flies." And they did.

The Indians had homes, huts built of branches plastered with mud for warmth in winter, and they had branch-roofed shelters for shade in summer. Their structures were efficient and entirely suitable for their way of life in the mild California coastal climate. But they were looked upon as untidy clutters of trash by easterners like Pete Culver.

Wise in the ways of weather, the Indians always chose sensible sites near water for bathing and drinking but they avoided the coastal flood plains where a sudden downpour could wipe out their villages. Neither did they settle on the beaches, open to wind and storm, or under the great redwood trees back in the mountains where dampness and shade struck to the bones even in summer. They knew better. They knew the seasons and they paid periodic visits to the beaches to gather kelp and shellfish, sea birds and their eggs. They trekked regularly back into the redwoods to collect cones, roots, berries, and to hunt small animals.

For hundreds, perhaps thousands of years, the Santa Catarina Indians had survived in their village near the San Carlos River, a stream named by the first Spaniards to settle the area. There was only one thing wrong with the Indians' choice of village location. It was a prime site for a town. When the Yankees arrived in their covered wagons and sailing ships, the Indians with their brush huts and sweat houses were in the way of progress. Alfie Lewis, the blacksmith, Joe Trimmer, who had horses, and Pete Culver with his vision of a general store, got together and gave the remaining village families twenty dollars to move out. The money was divided between five families and paid for approximately fifty acres of land.

"All fair 'n square. We paid 'em," commented Alfie, who later became a town father and a leader in the Sons of the Grizzlies Lodge.

Four of the Indian families moved back into the hills, several miles from Santa Catarina which began to gradually creep into the newly acquired property as more covered wagons rolled in. Alfie opened his blacksmith shop in a rough shed he put up; Joe Trimmer's livery stable began to take form and the Culver brothers paced off measurements for their store.

One of the Indian families didn't leave, and instead

remained just beyond the boundary of the acquired property, much to the annoyance of Alfie Lewis.

"Them Indians sure ain't goin' to help the looks of the town when we get it built up here," he growled.

The family had tried to build a house that looked like a white man's place, and they patched it together with odds and ends of boards instead of the branches and mud they would have used normally. They were the Cazadors, who had adopted a Spanish name and Catholicism when the Franciscan padres first arrived in the Santa Catarina area. There was the family patriarch, the grandfather, his son Luis, and granddaughter Gracia. The missing family members had fallen victim to one of the smallpox epidemics that swept through the Mission population at intervals.

Gracia Cazador was seventeen, slim and dark with lustrous hair and eyes as deep as midnight. She could read and write, having been taught in the Parochial school at the Mission, and she dressed neatly in hand-me-downs from the Ferris family. She did housework for them.

When Gracia heard about the property sale she objected strenuously.

"It's not enough. It's not fair. It's the same as if they stole the land from you," she told her grandfather.

But the families had accepted the twenty dollars and they shrugged their shoulders, saying they could not fight the white men. They had put their marks on the white man's paper and that was that.

After the deal went through, Pete Culver went back to the adobe where he and Joel rented a sleeping room, and bragged about it. Joel had kept out of it, leaving all business deals to Pete. But Joel had some doubts when he heard the details.

"Twenty dollars? That's not even a dollar an acre. That don't sound fair to me when you consider it's prime business property — right on the river and the flat."

Pete chopped him off. "They took the money and glad to get it. Put their marks on a paper with a couple of witnesses. All fair 'n square. Legal. It's done. Them Indians wasn't doin' nothing on that land — just squatting on it. Now you and I'll build our store there and Lewis is already puttin' up a shed for his blacksmith shop and Trimmer plans to fence part of it for his horses. He's goin' to build a barn, next. Don't that sound like things are goin' to move ahead, boy? Now all we gotta do is get our lumber and start work."

"Yes, well, there's a couple of lumber mills handy to town — the Garver mill is nearby."

Pete snorted. "Huh! I talked to them already. They're too high. I'm goin' up in the woods tomorrow to do some dickerin — I'll get it cheaper and get 'em to haul it down here, to boot."

The next day, Joel, who would be doing most of the building, began to lay out marks for a mud sill foundation. He also talked to Gracia's father, Luis Cazador, about helping him with some of the heavy work, much to Pete's annoyance.

"Why do you bother with that ignorant savage?" he said. "He's not worth two-bits a day."

Joel looked at him, then said: "I know you're the head of our business, Pete. And I listen to you. But I'm goin' to be doin' the building and I need help for some of it. Luis is a good worker. I'll pay him myself if you're thinking about the two-bits."

"Why don't you hire a white man?" Pete muttered as he went out.

Joel had watched the Indian families leave their land and he felt pity for the women's ragged dresses and bare feet, and for the men's air of hopelessness. But he knew it would be useless to expect understanding or sympathy from Pete.

The redwood lumber and roof shakes arrived from the mill in a horse-drawn wagon, nails came in a barrel on one of the sailing ships that frequently put in at Punto Malo, two miles up the coast, and work began on the Culvers' building. Joel began to lay a log foundation and showed Luis Cazador how to use the tools. He was pleased to see that Luis learned fast.

Pete Culver was not eager to dirty his hands with the work of building. He saw himself as the boss, in a white shirt and black string tie, behind the counter when it was built. Indeed, so did Mary Layton envision him when she smiled sedately at him as she passed the tent where he had set up his temporary office. She found reasons to pass by, often. Pete took notice of the smiles, the brown curls straying from beneath her bonnet, and the fact that she was the daughter of Henry Layton. Henry was the proprietor of the stagecoach station and the adjoining adobe house where Pete and Joel rented a sleeping room. Layton not only owned the whole layout, he had a finger in other Santa Catarina developments. There were plans for a wharf which was badly needed for the sailing ships which visited ports on the California coast. Layton was a man of vision, a prospering man. And so it was that Pete Culver began to court Mary Layton with matrimony in mind.

Joel worked long hours on the store; it must be finished by winter and stocked with the hundred and one things necessary for pioneer life in a raw, new State. California was only six years old, although sailing ships had called at its makeshift ports for a number of years, bringing a variety of goods, sometimes even luxuries, to the early Spanish settlers. Now, with more Yankee settlers coming every month, it would be handy to have a store in town where a man could get a shovel handle to replace his broken one, and a woman could buy a sack of beans and a length of cotton percale.

So Joel worked on steadily, helped by Luis Cazador, and occasionally by Pete whose conscience didn't bother him too often. Joel got to know Gracia when she brought her father's mid-day meal to the job. At first, he paid her scarcely any attention. He worked single-mindedly, hammering and sawing. Gracia barely glanced at him. She was shy, and besides, the priests at the Mission had warned the Indian girls about men. White men.

One day Joel was hammering wall studs into place when she appeared with the usual basket of lunch for Luis.

Joel glanced up, his hammer hit the nail a crooked blow, the nail flew off the two-by-four and hit Gracia's hand. She gave a startled squeak of pain and dropped the lunch basket.

Joel dropped the hammer and took her hand to look at it. "I'm sorry! It's my fault — the nail...," he began to apologize.

"It's nothing," she said, trying to hide her hand behind her back.

"Let me see," he insisted.

Luis Cazador, who was standing by, picked up his lunch and went over under a tree to eat, while Joel and Gracia became acquainted.

"When we get the store built and stocked, I'll have some liniment to put on cuts," Joel remarked.

She laughed. "Never mind. I know what to do for it — it's that little bush growing right over there on the river bank." She pointed.

"Honest?" Joel was surprised. "Why it — it's wonderful to know about things like that," he said.

"My people have used it for many years," she said. "My grandmother taught me about plants."

"It looks like a weed to me," he said with a smile.

"See that other bush over there — we make a cool drink from the leaves for hot days." She pointed at another plant.

Joel was genuinely interested.

"I'll make some and bring it tomorrow," she promised. Then, shy again, she said, "If you would like to taste it."

"I would like to very much," Joel said, and that was the start of the friendship between them.

In a few weeks the, store building was nearly finished. It was one large room in front, lined with shelves, and two rooms in the rear for storage and living quarters. The shelves would hold everything from canned goods to bolts of cotton fabric. A black iron stove came by wagon from Yerba Buena to sit in the middle of the large room. Joel made a couple of benches. Barrels of staple foods lined one,wall. Pete moved a sturdy chest of drawers into one corner to serve as desk and cash register.

Finally, Joel could look around and feel pleased with the result of his labors. "It begins to look like a real store," he said.

Pete nodded. "You just wait and see. This state's goin' to amount to something some day, with all that gold they're finding up north."

"Maybe we oughta be mining," Joel suggested.

Pete shook his bead. "Listen boy, we ain't miners. It's hard, dirty work and you gotta have a lotta luck besides. We'll be here in business when all the gold's gone. You wait and see. This town's goin' to grow."

Pete busied himself ordering special stock from the East Coast, to be shipped out to California on an early fall sailing vessel. He also made a week-long wagon trip to Yerba Buena and brought back merchandise.

"Had to pay dear for it up there," he said with disgust. "Everything's sky-high up there. A lot cheaper to order from the East by ship."

Most of the Santa Catarina village residents were curious about the new store. They watched its progress from stacks of rough boards lying on the dirt, to the finishing of the shake roof. A couple of farmers even came from down Carterville way — about ten miles by wagon track.

"Reckon we're goin' to have us a real good business," Pete said.

More merchandise arrived on a sailing ship which anchored out in the bay near Point Malo. Merchandise intended for Santa Catarina was loaded into row boats, then ferried ashore through the waves and dumped up on the sand. Joel and Luis Cazador reloaded it all into a wagon and hauled it to the store.

Business began to thrive. Pete took pains to order scarce items like pins and needles and thread, sheets of foolscap paper, canned goods and staple foods as well as shovels, axes and wire. Once the store was built and the stock inside, Pete turned the clerking over to Joel and began courting Mary Anna Layton in earnest with a view to early marriage. That made it necessary to find or build a suitable house for his bride-to-be. There weren't many available houses in Santa Catarina. The two or three that were empty were either melting adobes or decaying shacks fit only for fleas and woodrats. Property titles also were so entangled as to cause fights which sometimes erupted in bullets.

"I don't know what to do except build us a house out behind the store," Pete said. "There's plenty of room. Dammit Joel, Mary Anna and me want to git married. I never figured on that when you and me left to come west. Thought I had me plenty of time. Years. You got to tend the store while I work things out, boy."

Joel didn't mind waiting on customers and tending the store. When old Mrs. Farley bought more than she could carry home in her sack, he had Luis Cazador deliver her order. Luis carried everything in a large basket on his back supported by a tumpline that circled his forehead. Joel paid him in dried beans and an occasional slab of salt pork.

Everything went well. The older women in town liked the arrangement and the surviving members of the Cazador family were eating well, until Pete discovered Joel weighing out beans for Luis one day.

"What the hell you think you're doing, boy? We're not in business to feed those Indians."

"He works for them, Pete. Does a lot of chores for us here at the store." Joel went on to try to explain. "You know, Pete, there's only one old priest left at the Mission and he can't do much for them. There's even talk of closing it down and using a visiting priest from San Juan or Monterey."

"How do you know so much about it? We ain't Catholic," Pete growled.

"Oh, I hear things," Joel said. He didn't say that Gracia Cazador kept him informed. He went on weighing out the beans but after Luis left with them, Pete lit into him again.

"I tell you Joel, we ain't running a feed station for them savages. You got to stop it here and now!"

Joel didn't answer; he knew it was useless. But he

continued to hire Luis Cazador for delivering and doing odd jobs, and he paid him in food. One day, when Gracia came to the store, Joel, who pitied the destitute Indians, went even further. She came to buy cotton fabric for a dress. Joel got the bolts down off the shelf, there were two patterns, one brown, one blue.

"Then we have this percale, too," he said, unrolling a length. It was dark red with flowers on a blue ground.

She looked at it and held it up. He could tell she liked it best.

"How much is it?" she asked.

Joel thought quickly. The percale cost more than the calico. "Same price," be said casually.

Gracia gave him one of her rare, shy smiles. "I need four yards. I was afraid it would cost more than the other. Here. This is all I have to pay for it." She put some coins on the counter.

Joel measured the yardage, cut off a generous four yards, rolled it up and handed it to her. Then he gathered up the coins. "Got thread for it?"

Her smile faded. "Oh. I forgot."

"Here." He handed her a spool. "Only color I've got."

"But I can't pay for it." she said.

"Never mind. It's not much."

"Thank you, Mr. Culver. I'll pay you next week for the thread." She took it and went out.

Joel put the bolts back on the shelves and turned to find Pete standing there.

"How long's that been going on?" Pete demanded. "My Gawd, Joel, she's an Injun! You gave her that percale — and the thread! How can you lower yourself to the gutter that way? I'm marryin' a white girl in a coupla months and I won't stand being disgraced by you! I won't have a squaw man for a brother!"

Something in Joel snapped. He went up close to Pete and looked at him. Then he slapped his face. Hard. "I'm leaving," he said. "I'll get my things and clear out tonight. I want my half of the business. I'll let you know where to send it." He walked out of the store and left Pete standing there.

Pete made a move to follow him, then stopped. "All right, if that's the way you want it!" he yelled. To himself he muttered "He'll come crawlin' back in a coupla days."

Two months passed. Joel had settled in Carterville, ten miles down the coast by rough wagon road. There wasn't much communication between Santa Catarina and Carterville, even in later years when the valley surrounding Carterville became a rich fruit growing center.

Joel lived in a tent at first, then after Pete sent him his share in gold coins, he built a small store on a lot he bought. Luis Cazador had followed Joel to Carterville and had constructed a native shelter for himself of branches plastered with mud. He continued to do odd jobs.

Carterville might as well have been a hundred miles from Santa Catarina instead of ten. The wagon road between the two settlements wound back and forth over sand dunes that dragged at the wheels, through creek shallows deep with mud even in summer, and over steep hills dotted with scrub oaks that overlooked the ocean. It was a full day's journey by wagon or horseback.

As the years passed, Santa Catarina thrived as a lumber shipping point, a wharf was built, Pete married Mary Anna Layton and became a pillar of the newly founded Liberty Methodist Church and one of the town's leading businessmen. After a decade of prosperity, he donated one of his downtown lots to the town so a city hall could be built there. A colony of Italian fishermen also settled to build boats and harvest the riches of the Pacific. Santa Catarina was gaining a reputation as one of the best vacation spots on the Pacific coast.

At Carterville, farmers who had discovered the fertile river flood plains of the valley planted grain fields, then orchards, and shipped their apples and plums to Yerba Buena — which had become San Francisco — by sailing ship.

Joel enjoyed a modest success with his store but never

got rich because he always seemed to be taking care of someone who was hungry, or cold, or had no place to live. A sack of flour here, a pound of beans there, a slab of salt pork — it all added up. But he lived comfortably with his Yankee wife and seven children and was content.

Luis Cazador worked for Joel until he was too old to work any longer, then spent his days dozing in a chair on the store porch. Gracia had fallen victim to one of the diptheria epidemics that swept through California periodically in the 1870s.

Pete died first. When Joel showed up at Pete's funeral in Santa Catarina, none of Pete's family knew who he was. At the church he heard one of Pete's daughters whisper to her mother "Who is that man? Sitting over there? What's he doing here?"

SANTA CAT'S FINEST — 1863

Judge William Mills was worried. The late-day stagecoach passenger and mail service from San Francisco had brought some unsettling news. A letter. Addressed to the Court Authorities of Santa Catarina. The Judge had served as Mayor for a few years and now was serving as Santa Catarina's legal authority, the reigning court judge. He had never studied law, but since the day many years before, when he had led a posse that tracked down and hanged a horse thief, he was known as Judge Mills. Stealing a man's horse was an offense equal to murder in California in 1854.

Now, nine years later, with the horse thief's bones mouldering in a shallow grave, the Judge was looked up to as a highly respected leader by the approximately two thousand Yankee citizens of Santa Catarina. Not counting Indians, of course.

Everyone in the town knew that the War Between the States was being fought in the eastern states. Battles raged in Maryland, Virginia, Tennessee, Pennsylvania, Georgia, Mississippi and Kentucky. But those places were thousands of miles away from California. No one expected the war to explode in what was being referred to as the 'golden state.'

The letter was from the War Department and it started quietly at first, with the news that President Abraham Lincoln wanted to free the slaves. The Judge snorted. California had already done that in 1852. The next sentence caused the Judge to frown:

"General Ulysses Grant has failed to take Vicksburg and there is a grave danger that the North will lose the War...."

The further he read, the more he frowned. He usually lit a cigar and strolled back to his office to read the mail at his leisure. But today he took off at a brisk walk, the open letter in his hand. The news from the East used to be eight or ten days late reaching Santa Catarina, having come from St. Joseph, Missouri, to Sacramento by Pony Express, then to San Francisco by river boat, and finally to Santa Cat on the Butterfield Overland Mail Coach. The Pony Express had been done away with in 1861 when the newly-developed telegraph system linked California to the Eastern states.

On this particular day, the coach driver himself handed the letter to the Judge saying "Orders to give it to you myself, Judge.

As the Judge went up the plank sidewalk, Irving Parks caught up with him.

"Bad news, Judge?"

"It don't sound good the Judge said. "The south is winning and all-hell is going to break loose up in Frisco."

"How so?" Parks wanted to know. "Why, we're a couple thousand miles from all that ruckus back East. And what's that about Frisco? It ain't any closer to the war than we are."

The Judge shook his head. "This here letter's from Sacramento. There's a senator stirring up trouble — name of Gwin. He's a southerner. He's got a bunch together — call themselves the Knights of the Golden Circle or some such."

Irving Parks swore. "They oughtta be hung! Anyway, we haven't got slaves. We freed 'em back in the fifties. Hardly know what a nigger looks like out here, anyway."

"This Gwin fellow — his bunch will likely spread down to Frisco." The Judge waved the letter at Parks. "We're likely to get trouble right here in Santa Catarina. Listen to this, Parks. He figures it's kind of an army of his own. They march around and — by God! — it says here they even fly the

Confederate flag!"

"No!" Parks said.

"Yes, they do. And this letter says us northerners should raise a company or two down here in case we're needed — we can be called out. That is, if Gwin gets any ideas about taking over California for the south."

"Count me in," Parks said. "We can get the Sons of the Grizzlies in it too — bring it up at the meeting tonight."

"Good idee," the Judge agreed. "And I'll just stop by the newspaper on my way back to the office. Get Ferguson to put a story in."

"Is he northern or southern?" Parks asked.

"He damn well better be for the north," the Judge growled "if he knows what's good for him."

"So far he's been level-headed about things," Parks said. "Puts out a pretty fair weekly."

The Judge had stopped walking and was reading the letter again. "It says here that the California government has passed an Act allowing money for us if we organize," he said. "'Fifty dollars a month for rent for a meeting place to hold drills and such.'"

"The Grizzlies' hall," Parks said.

The Judge nodded and continued. "Two thousand dollars for every county that raises a cavalary company of fifty men. And eleven dollars a month for every man-jack that joins up. Hell, Parks! We can't afford to let that go by. Most of us got horses — or can get one."

"I'll go buy one if need be," Parks said. "We gotta defend the Union."

"We'll get it all underway tonight at the Grizzlies' meeting," the Judge said. "Reckon there'll be Temperance fellows that will want to be in on this, too."

"How about the Mex?" Parks wanted to know.

"There'll be enough of us without them," the Judge said. "Of course if the fighting breaks out here we might need them."

"Better get a couple of them into it just to be on the safe side," Parks said. "Hernandes and Delgado."

The Judge approved. "Good. We'll get it going tonight."

There was a strong undercurrent of excitement when the Grizzlies met that evening. Word had spread about the two thousand dollar payment to the county and the eleven dollar monthly payment to each cavalryman.

"And fifty dollars a month to meet in this hall," the Judge announced. "Boys, we got to support the Union. We all got guns and most of us have a horse." He looked around the hall. "I don't think we got a southerner here, do we?"

The answer was a shouted "NO!" from the membership. If there was a southern sympathizer, be was keeping very quiet about it.

Plans were made for the Judge to write an official letter to the War Department and to the Governor in Sacramento. Members talked excitedly about what they would do "if those damned southerners ever come down here and try to make trouble!" Members without horses made spur of the moment deals with members who had horses to sell and there was much talk about guns and saddles and swords.

The Judge rapped for silence and waited for the excitement to die down. "We got another problem with this," he said. "We need uniforms. Where do we get them?" The members looked at each other. Uniforms. Uniforms cost money. "And they got to be blue," the Judge added firmly.

Jesse Hayes who owned the Mercantile Store stood up. "Your honor, I can order outfits," he announced. "Get 'em cheaper through the store. Sell 'em to you wholesale — all the best shoddy — rewoven wool."

"How much?" the Judge asked.

Hayes thought for a moment. "Off hand — plain dark blue coat and pants — about fourteen dollars I reckon. That's a close guess."

The members weren't happy with that. There was a ripple of low talk, much shaking of heads.

The Judge rapped again. "How about just getting the coats?" he asked. "We can wear the pants we have."

"I can do that for — oh, say, about six-fifty or seven dollars," Hayes said.

"That sounds more like it," the Judge said. "Then we'll get our womenfolk to sew on braid or whatever we need on the sleeves."

Hayes counted the members present. "Thirty six," he said. "I better get a couple extra just in case."

"Don't order yet," the Judge cautioned. "We got to get more members for this cavalry before we're legal."

Hayes looked at him. "I'd like some money on this, Judge. It's a fair-size outlay for me."

Before the meeting ended, each man agreed to put two dollars down with the balance due on receipt of his coat. Plans also were discussed for a parade down Surf Street to introduce the cavalry to the town officially.

"We can wear our coats and get the town band to march and play," suggested Sheriff Bill Dawson.

"Might scare the horses," someone said.

"Hell man! If you can't hold a horse in, you oughtta fall off!" the Sheriff said.

It took a month for the legal recognition of the Santa Catarina Cavalry to arrive from Washington, D.C. by way of Sacramento, and for the coats to arrive from San Francisco by way of stagecoach. It took another week for the wives to get together and figure out how they were going to decorate the coats. Yellow braid on the sleeves for the enlisted men. Officers got sleeve braid and some on the collar as well.

"Mighty smart looking," the Judge observed. He claimed the title of Captain and his coat was lavish with braid. Mrs. Mills had labored long and diligently with her needle.

"I reckon it'll do," Irving Parks said. He was second in command.

The men had met to wear their coats and plan the parade.

"Don't you think we oughtta practice some, first?" someone asked.

"We'll get plenty practice," Parks said. "By law, we're

required to meet regular to march and shoot. What do you think we're getting paid for, anyway?"

The parade was set for Sunday afternoon, a day when stores and businesses were closed, and late enough not to interfere with church.

"Since it's our patriotic duty, nobody can complain about a parade on Sunday," observed the Judge.

There had been stories in the weekly Santa Catarina Wave and a lot of talk. Everyone in town knew about the cavalry and the parade.

"A parade will be a fine way to get the town behind us," the Judge said. "Every man-jack wearing a pistol and a uniform coat."

"What're we supposed to do? Just ride our horses down Surf Street?" asked Attorney Lewis McLaren. "Don't you think that looks kind of tame?"

"Tame!" the Judge exploded. "Maybe you don't want to ride with us?"

"Oh no — I was just thinking...."

"Don't think! Just get your ass on your horse and and try to look like a real soldier," the Judge growled.

On the day of the parade, the riders gathered early out behind the ruins of the Santa Catarina Mission where there were open fields and a corral. They planned to practice riding in two lines abreast; they wore their pistols and some had muzzleloading Springfield rifles in boots strapped to their saddles. A few had fortified themselves with bottles of whiskey which they passed around freely. Jeb Parsons brought his bugle. Someone had remembered to bring the American Flag and the California Bear Flag. Irving Parks took the Bear Flag and the Judge carried the American Flag.

The Judge bellowed "Fall in, men!"

Jeb raised his bugle and blew a loud blast. The Judge's horse was not accustomed to a bugle blowing five feet from his ears. He reared suddenly, catching the Judge unawares, the Judge fell off and landed in a mixture of mud and manure but managed to keep the flag upright. He got up, swearing and brushing off his pants.

After more bugling and some shouted orders by Irving Parks, two straggling columns of horses and riders formed behind the Judge who was back in his saddle. They practiced riding around the field for a few minutes at a slow walk, with the Judge leading and Irving Parks bringing up the rear. The Judge was just about to shout orders to speed up and trot, when one of the riders who had been helping himself to a bottle, yelled "Hell! This ain't no fightin' bunch!" He pulled out his pistol, aimed at the sky and pulled the trigger. Before the blast died away, horses were neighing in panic, jumping and bucking, men were hanging on, sliding or falling off, swearing and yelling.

"What son of a bitch did that!" the Judge yelled. "I'll nail his hide to the barn door!"

The guilty rider was in such a hurry to shove his gun back into the holster that it caught — and went off again. The bullet went through his boot.

He began to moan. "Ohhhh — my foot!" and half slid, half fell from his horse.

"Serves him right, the damned fool!" the Judge said.

Irving Parks stopped to assess the damage to the foot; the wounded rider left to find a doctor. The others, who had dismounted, got back on their horses and headed for Surf Street. It was time for the parade.

The ten members of the town band were waiting in their red jackets and caps. So were the Ladies' Aid group and the Women's Temperance Club, both wearing white dresses. There was even a small group of older Grizzlies who figured they were too old to enlist or who didn't care to get on a horse. They hobbled along with their canes and walking sticks, waving the Bear Flag. Surf Street, the town's main thoroughfare, was lined with spectators young and old.

The two lines of cavalrymen headed the parade with the Judge and Irving Parks leading, each with a flag. The women's groups were next, then the Band with other small platoons like the Grizzlies, bringing up the rear. They marched to a single muffled drum beat. The Band was not to play until they reached the adobe that served as Court House. Mayor Lester Jenkins was to make a speech. He was waiting on the steps, suitably dressed in tails and top hat.

As the marchers arrived in the street in front of the old adobe, they filed into place, forming blocks, and waited for everyone to arrive. When everyone had come and they were all standing in place, waiting, the Band members raised their instruments and blasted out a lively military march.

The cavalry horses, unused to such ungodly noises, and already having been spooked once by the pistol shot, went wild again. Suddenly there were horses jumping and plunging and rearing with men swearing, women screaming and everyone on foot running, trying to get out of the way. It was total disaster.

The Band music dwindled off as the musicians scrambled to safety. The Mayor took one horrified look and retreated into the Court House. Twenty minutes later, the cavalrymen, some afoot and some still mounted, found themselves alone on the street.

Irving Parks whose horse had run off up the street, looked up at the Judge who was on his horse but was having quite a struggle staying there.

"What do we do now, Judge?" Parks yelled.

"Go home you damned fool!" the Judge yelled back.

For days, the parade was the main topic of conversation in Santa Catarina. Remarks and opinions varied widely.

"We are so fortunate that the Judge wasn't hurt — or worse," Mrs. Mills told her friends. "It was all in the line of duty — for the Union, you know. He has such a clear sense of duty."

"Irving never should have got on that horse — he's no rider," his outspoken wife commented publicly. "Why, he might have been killed!"

"A bunch of damn fools trying to look like fighting men," growled Attorney McLaren who had been bucked off. "I learned my lesson. To hell with the eleven dollars. It ain't worth it!"

"I had to move real lively to keep from gettin' kilt," one of the older Grizzlies said. "Lost my walkin' stick too. Never did find it."

"That's the last time I will ever march with those men! I smelled likker on them!" came from one of the Temperance women.

"No wonder they fell off their horses," commented one of the Ladies Aids. "It was no place for a lady. They can march by themselves from now on!"

The final word came at the Grizzlies' next meeting. "Well boys, it was a bust. Guess we'll just have to practice by ourselves and forget parades for awhile," the Judge said. "But we'll be ready if those damn southerners come down here and try to make trouble!"

"Trouble! We got enough already. My wife is giving me hell for gettin' on a horse," Irving Parks said. "And it irritated my piles — they're killin' me!"

And that was the end of parades for the Santa Catarina Cavalry.

THE LAST WORD

Louie Poletti didn't plan to spend his old age as a second-hand junk man. He had thought of other ways to keep busy and make a dollar or two... as a crew member on one of his friend's fishing boats during the salmon season, or maybe doing a little gardening for the wealthy families of Santa Catarina.

But the second-hand business just kind of grew on him after his wife, Luisa, died. He had to make a living and that wasn't easy for a man in his seventies in Santa Catarina, not even in 1874 when eggs were fifteen cents a dozen and a slab of bacon cost forty cents. His new career came about because of his prolific vegetable garden and Luisa's furniture.

There was a general business slump in California and it hit hard in Santa Cat — as the natives called the little coastal town — when the limestone mines closed. Louie had worked in the mines all his life. He and Luisa could get by because they were frugal and had saved a little nest egg. They owned their small cottage which was located on Seaview Avenue which was considered one of the town's good streets. True, the modest clapboard structure looked out of place there sitting between two tall, stately Victorians, like a brown sparrow between two peacocks. But it was theirs, clear and free.

Louie was thin and gray, never a big, husky fellow. When he lost his job as tally man, keeping records of loads

of lime rock at the mine, they could still get by because
Luisa cleaned house for a couple of the wealthy families.
They pinched pennies and raised vegetables in their small
backyard. Their cottage was badly in need of a coat of paint;
it hadn't been painted for twenty years or more, but their
neighbors didn't complain about it too much. Just once in
awhile. Often enough to upset Luisa.

"Some day, when we can afford it, we'll paint the
house," Louie would say to her. He even mentioned it to Joe
Perry, one of the next-door neighbors who was critical. But
there were no jobs to be had, although Louie searched
diligently and inquired everywhere. Painting the house was
out of the question, even when Joe Perry's pointed remarks
became more frequent.

"You know, Poletti," Joe Perry would say, "a run-down
lookin' house drags down the others around it. Ruins
property values."

Perry's house, which was on the north side of Louie's
house, was two-storey with a small tower at one corner. It
was painted pale gray and looked quite elegant. A tall hedge
separated it from the Polettis. On the south side, a reclusive
elderly couple lived in another, smaller Victorian which was
painted a spotless white. A white fence, built by the couple,
ran between their Victorian and the Polettis.

Then, suddenly, Luisa died. One June morning she
was herself, going cheerfully off to work with her mop and
bucket. The next morning, she was lying in bed, cold and
still.

For a few days, Louie was so busy with the funeral
and church people calling and bringing food, that he was in
a state of animated shock. They had no children, no relatives
except a few who lived in Italy. But when the funeral was
over and things quieted down and Luisa was in the ground
at the Catholic Cemetery on the hill, Louie had to face facts.
He had no money after paying the undertaking parlor and
the grave digger. He moped around the little house which
had always seemed so cozy for the two of them, and now
was so empty. He carried buckets of water to the vegetable

garden, then quit when he thought about paying the water bill at the end of the month. Santa Catarina, although a small town, prided itself on its water system that ran down the main streets in hollowed redwood logs buried in the ground. Louie lived on early squash and string beans from the vegetable garden and Mason jars of tomatoes and peaches that Luisa had preserved. After a few weeks, the supply of preserved fruits and vegetables began to dwindle but the squash vines in the garden were loaded. He almost groaned; he was getting tired of squash. He thought about a fish dinner. He could fish for Cod off the rocky cliffs along the ocean. Then he remembered he would need a license. Two dollars. He quit lighting a lamp at night; the kerosene can was almost empty. So he went to bed at dusk. Fortunately, it was summertime. He could get by without firing up the wood heating stove in the tiny parlor. But he still liked to heat up his squash dinners and make coffee, so he scrounged vacant lots for pieces of fire wood. Coffee. Another worry. His supply of coffee beans was running low.

Louie was too proud to ask the church for charity. The priest had conducted Luisa's rosary and burial service without asking for a penny. And Louie wouldn't ask his neighbors or friends for help.

He thought about selling the house but with money so tight and hard times in the job markets, no one in Santa Catarina was buying houses. Besides, it might take months to sell it. And where would he live if he sold it?

That was when he sold the first piece of furniture. He was desperate. The Water Company was waiting, he was out of coffee and kerosene. Then, one day, Mrs. Perry happened to be out in her garden when Louie was weeding the squash in his. He tipped his hat to her and the next thing he knew, Mrs. Perry was leaning around the end of the hedge admiring his squash.

"My! You certainly have a fine looking vegetable garden, Mr. Poletti. Just look at those squash. I wish Mr. Perry would put in a vegetable garden for us, but he says he's got all he can handle with the butcher shop."

Louie straightened up and wiped his hands on his trousers. "Could you use some?" he asked. Then he picked a couple and passed them over to her. After all, he had more squash then he could eat and he was getting awfully tired of them, anyway.

"How kind of you," she said. Then, after hesitating, she went on. "Mr. Poletti — I don't like to bring up personal matters so soon after your — your loss, and all. But — with Mrs. Poletti gone — if you ever decide to get rid of that corner whatnot, I wish you would let me know." She paused again, then plunged ahead. "I took a fancy to it once when your wife was kind enough to ask me in one day, for a cup of tea."

Later that day, after a cold washup (he couldn't spare the wood to heat the bath water on the kitchen stove), Louie began to think about the whatnot. He went into the parlor and looked at it. The few trinkets Luisa bad collected over the years were on the shelves. Three sea shells. A piece of glass she picked up on the beach one day. A puffed-up red valentine heart made of satin. Louie had given it to her shortly after they were married. A couple of faded daguerreotypes — her family in Italy. All the things were dusty, he noticed. So were the carved shelves of the whatnot.

"I ought to clean it off," he said to himself. Then he thought, *No, I won't. I'll sell it if she wants it. I don't need it. I'll never miss it.*

He removed Luisa's collection and put the articles away in a bureau drawer. And the next day he approached the ornate front door of the Perrys' Victorian house, rang the handbell and made what he believed was a grand deal. Mrs. Perry gave him ten dollars for the whatnot — and later bragged to her husband about her bargain. "It's worth twice that," she told him.

Louie could eat meat again. He walked downtown to Perry's butcher shop and bought twenty five cents worth of pork chops and another fifty cents worth of beefsteak. Enough for two or three meals. Another two-bits went for kerosene, and that evening he feasted on chops by lamplight.

He even considered spending a couple of his precious dollars for a cord of firewood but thought better of it. He could walk down to the beach and pick up driftwood. Carry it home in a sack. Free.

He looked around the parlor. There was that slippery horsehair chair he never sat in. Didn't like it. Uncomfortable. Stiff. He wondered if Mrs. Perry .....

That was the beginning of a whole new career for Louie Morinetti. He gradually sold off most of his furniture, keeping only enough for his own comfort. Bed, table, chairs, the wardrobe where he hung his one black suit and his work clothes. He sold a bureau, a mirror, a footstool — word had got around to Mrs. Perry's friends and she notified them when there was a piece of special interest. Several ladies wanted some of Luisa's good dishes; he sold all of them and kept only the cheap, everyday stuff.

Next, he was getting inquiries about pickets for fences. He made a deal with a mill at the edge of town and soon he had a pile of pickets in his side yard with a sign advertising "Fence pickets — Cheap." The pickets led to pieces of used tools and machinery: saws, grinding stones for sharpening knives and axes, wagon wheels, buggy springs, a cider press that was broken but he fixed it, a sewing machine, some roofing shingles from the mill, harnesses, a lot of odds and ends that people brought and left. Some wanted a dollar or two for their goods, others traded for something that was there. Some left their articles on consignment and when they sold, Louie kept part of the money.

The yard in front of Louie's cottage had been planted to lawn, but now it blossomed with all kinds of junk. The lawn gave up and died. There were piles of old books covered with canvas to keep off the fog and rain. "Louie's Place" became a catch phrase in Santa Catarina for anyone who needed a tool, part of anything, or something real cheap.

Louie was eating meat regularly, and he had a small leather sack almost filled with quarters and dollars and fifty cent pieces. He hid it in a box under his bed. Louie didn't need much to live on and business was fairly good.

He discovered that he liked to barter; it was a challenge.

Just when things were going well, they started to fall apart. Louie had just finished eating a most satisfactory dinner one evening when he heard someone knocking at his front door. He opened it to Joe Perry who was not looking happy. Louie sensed trouble immediately. Joe was a heavy man with beefy arms and fingers like sausages — the sausages that hung in his butchershop window. He came right to the point.

"Louie you gotta do something! That mess in your yard out there — " He motioned over his shoulder. "We can't have that. It's spoiling the whole neighborhood."

Louie gulped. This was something that, in his joy at making a decent living once again, he hadn't really considered. He had thought of it, yes, but he had pushed the thought out of his mind. He didn't know what to say. Finally he nodded. "I'll clean it up."

Joe said "Fine," and left.

The next morning Louie went out to see what he could do. He spent the day moving the piles of roofing shingles to the side of yard, away from the Perry's, and next to the neighbor's fence on the other side. They seldom ventured outside, maybe they wouldn't notice. They were Mr. and Mrs. Harold James. Mr. James was a bookkeeper at the Mercantile Store; he left for work early and returned home late. His wife was a semi-invalid. Louie piled the roofing against their fence; it was still on his own property, but the way things were going... he shook his head. No telling what might happen. At least it was not so noticeable there. And the Perry's couldn't see it.

Next, Louie got busy and straightened up the pile of tools and machinery parts. He covered it all with old sheets he no longer needed or used.

I can uncover them when people come to look them over, he told himself. He worked all day and when he was finished he looked the front yard over, critically. The lumps of machinery covered with sheets weren't exactly attractive. But at least the stuff was out of sight. He went to bed and slept soundly that night.

The next day a farmer arrived with a water pump he traded for wagon wheels and buggy springs and he threw in a dollar and a half, to boot. He looked everything over before he left.

"You've got a right handy business here, Poletti," he said. "I'll be back. Got me a plow and a barrow I don't need no more. I'll bring them, next time."

The rest of the day was busy, off and on. It was the evening that turned into a disaster. Louie was polishing off a beefsteak and thinking about bed when he heard a noise that took him to the door. He opened it to a flare of light. Firelight. The pile of shingles and posts and pickets was on fire. Sparks were flying high into the night.

Louie ran for a bucket, then to the garden faucet. He carried bucket after bucket to douse the flames but it was too late. He could smell kerosene. Someone had done too good a job. By the time be had the fire out, most of the shingles and pickets were a total loss and the heavier posts were badly burned. Worst of all, the garden fence, which really belonged to Mr. & Mrs. James, was badly scorched. Louie groaned. He would have to replace the burned portion of fence. He cleaned up the mess as best he could, and finally got to bed.

That wasn't all. The next morning early, there was someone banging and shouting at Louie's door. He got his eyes open and hobbled to the door in the long underwear he slept in. An irate teamster greeted him and shook his fist under Louie's nose. "Look out there!" he yelled. "Look at that street! I cain't git my team and wagon through it!"

Louie looked. Someone had carried pieces of that machinery out of Louie's yard and had thrown them into the street. There were saw blades, sledge hammers, lengths of pipe, sheets of tin, grindstones, window sashes, a couple of bedsteads, a wagon bed and harnesses strewn on the street. Louie could hardly believe his eyes. He pulled his overalls on and laced his boots with shaking hands, and hurried outside. With the teamster's help, and a lot of cursing, they got the street cleared and the machinery back in Louie's yard.

The teamster whipped up his horses and left, yelling "Don't you never let that happen again!"

Louie sat down to a cold beefsteak breakfast, then went out to clean up the mess in the front yard; he and the teamster had thrown everything back in a jumble. He was hard at work when Joe Perry came out of his house, on his way to the butchershop. He stopped and looked.

"What happened, Poletti?" He smiled a little. "My, my. Looks like you got some trouble. Too bad about that fence getting burned. Young hoodlums playing a prank, I'll bet." And off he went, to work.

Louie went inside and sat down to think things over. He didn't for a minute believe that young hoodlums had set the fire and thrown the machinery into the street. It was obvious that his business wasn't going to survive. At least not in his front yard.

He put on his jacket and set out to find a new location. It took him two days to find a place he could afford to rent, a suitable site, next to the property owner's house so Louie wouldn't be robbed blind when he wasn't around. An Italian fisherman had the ideal location, at the side of his house, a vacant lot where he spread his fishnets out to dry and be mended.

"Plenty room," he said. "Two dollars a month."

Louie took it, but before he could move everything, piece by piece, in his wheelbarrow, he awoke one morning to another episode of trouble. Again, pieces of machinery were blocking the street in front of his house. Angry passersby were complaining and there was a man in a buggy waiting to get through. Louie trundled load after load in the wheelbarrow and it took him five days to move everything to the new location.

Joe Perry came out one evening to express his approval. "Finally come to your senses, Poletti," he said. "This ain't no place for a junk business. The ladies don't like it. Spoils the look of things."

Louie paused. He was raking the empty front yard. Then he said "I aim to paint the house next. Fix up, some. Always meant to, never had the money."

Joe Perry nodded. "Glad to hear it, Poletti."

Two weeks later, Louie's paint supplies arrived at the Mercantile Store. Paint supplies were limited in Santa Catarina; they had to be ordered from San Francisco to get the color Louie wanted.

One bright fall morning, Louie began painting his house. Joe Perry came out on his way to work, took one startled look and burst out with "Gawd Almighty!"

He turned, went back inside to get his wife and they both came out. She looked, threw her hands in the air and started shouting at Joe. "Now look what you done! You sure fixed it, you did!"

Louie was putting on a coat of bright yellow paint. Easter egg yellow. Not the mellow yellow of railroad buildings and depots. Instead, it was a yellow that shouted and demanded the attention of every passerby. And that wasn't all. Louie was painting the window frames a brilliant blue. The front of the house was almost done. It was quite a sight.

Louie went right on painting that day, ignoring the curious stares, the snickers, the indignant remarks. He whistled a happy little tune as he worked.

"I think that burned fence would look nice painted blue too," he said to himself as he worked.

THE HONEYMOON

Santa Catarina, California, was a quiet little town back in the 1880s. A church-going town both Protestant and Catholic, referred to as "Santa Cat" by the less reverent. Life went on at a horse and buggy pace; everybody knew everybody else's business, or most of it. And although he was a newcomer to town, Professor Robert Pudley thought he was getting an intellectual girl when he married Miss Ella Elizabeth Worthington.

An incredible combination of beauty and brains, he was blissfully convinced, when he looked into her blue eyes. The perfect mate for a school principal just a few credits away from his Ph.D., although he already claimed the title. During several years' teaching in the Eastern states, Professor Pudley had observed that beauty and brains were seldom wrapped in the same package.

Miss Ella saw the Professor as a prime matrimonial catch in a town with woefully few prime catches. A step up the social ladder, too. Miss Ella's mother was of a similar mind. In fact, she had met the new arrival in town before her daughter did.

"He is a very cultured gentleman, my dear," she assured Ella. "He gave the program at the Woman's Church Social — he read his favorite poetry. He told us that poetry is his favorite pastime."

"Poetry?" For a moment Miss Ella found it hard to

believe in a town full of lumberjacks, fishermen and farmers. And she wryly visualized the Professor as a thin, wispy man with thick eyeglasses and a celluloid collar. That is, until she saw him at church the following Sunday.

He was actually a hearty specimen of manhood, and Miss Ella's imagination had run away with her. Her heart had beaten faster at the thought of being held in those muscular arms. She couldn't see his arms, of course. He was always properly and impeccably dressed. But she could imagine them, and she did, every time she saw him. Which was every Sunday, at prayer meetings every Wednesday evening, and sometimes at choir practice on Friday evenings. Professor Pudley had a pleasing baritone voice as well as the conjectured muscles. He occasionally filled in for the choir's regular baritone.

Miss Ella herself couldn't carry a tune in a bucket. But she could play the piano without hitting too many sour notes, and sometimes she volunteered to play the church's little foot-pump organ when Amanda Swithin, the regular organist, couldn't make it.

Not only did Miss Ella volunteer, but now she urged Amanda to take more practice evenings off.

"You've put in so many hours for so many years, Amanda dear," she said sweetly. "And you've done such a wonderful job. I don't know what the church would do without you. But you must get weary at times, and I really don't mind spelling you, to give you a little rest."

Amanda was only too glad to get some relief, and Miss Ella was delighted to get further contacts with Professor Robert. She preferred to call him that. She didn't really care too much for his last name. Pudley. Ugly, she thought. So she began calling him Professor Robert and he began calling her Miss Ella. Their friendship grew.

One Friday evening, when the choir had finished a particularly rousing rendition of *Onward Christian Soldiers* and practice was over, Miss Ella allowed a tiny copy of *Sonnets from the Portuguese* to fall from the reticule in which she carried a handkerchief and a small bottle of smelling salts. The book fell, unobserved, on the carpet behind the organ bench. Professor Robert was nearby but he was in serious conversation with the church deacon. The other choir members were filing out to go home. Miss Ella left the book where it had fallen. As she started up the aisle, she paused by the two men. Clutching her reticule by the drawstrings, she opened it and said plaintively, "Oh dear! I believe I have lost my little book."

Professor Robert turned to her, "A book? A book?"

"My *Sonnets"* she said softly. "I had it when I came in tonight and now it's gone."

"Well, we'll just have to look around," the deacon said. "It must be here."

"I'll be glad to look, sir," Professor Pudley offered quickly. "If it's here, I'll find it."

Of course he found it. As Miss Ella had intended all along. It was just another version of the old handkerchief drop.

"Oh, you found it!" she cried with delight. Although she had never cared much for poetry, she had made up her mind to pay more attention to it from now on. She had had to search through the bookcase at home for quite awhile to find a book small enough to fit into her reticule. The *Sonnets* fit perfectly.

"So you are fond of the *Sonnets?*" he asked when he handed the book to her.

"Oh yes! They are so inspiring," she bubbled, vowing privately to read the little book from cover to cover when she got home.

That was the beginning of what soon blossomed into romance. They began meeting at least once a week in Miss Ella's parlor to read poetry. Professor Robert did most of the reading, because, as Miss Ella told him: "There is something about the masculine voice...." She never quite said what it was, but the way she looked at him when she said it made things clear. Her ignorance of poetry was never exposed because he made the choices and did the reading.

"We have so much in common," she told her friends.

"She's a wonder," Professor Robert announced to anyone within earshot. "She actually has a brain in that pretty head of hers."

They took long walks together, sometimes along the seashore, for Santa Catarina is located on the Pacific Ocean in a setting of rocky cliffs, dashing waves and white sand beaches. Sometimes they walked in the hills back of town, through redwood trails, among the ancient trees that filled the air with fragrance.

As the months passed and Miss Ella did learn quite a bit about poetry, their conversations began to center on plans to marry and establish a home.

Riverview Avenue would be lovely, she suggested delicately. That is, if he thought so too. There just happened to be a rather large home for sale on Riverview which she admired one day as they walked past.

"Of course you must make the decision," she said. "Our home must be suitable for your purposes and your career."

How could he not think the Riverview home suitable when he was looking into her azure eyes under that soft cloud of pale gold curls. He arranged to buy it.

As for Miss Ella, when she looked up into his gray eyes and thought about the intimacies of marriage, she could almost forget that she didn't much care for his name. A name that soon would be her name. Pudley, Ugly. But she would adjust to it.

Once or twice during their courtship, she had a hint that marriage was going to include more learning than poetry and love. They happened to be walking on the beach, the tide was out and their way took them past an eroding cliff. That was when the Professor spied something embedded in the cliff which claimed his immediate attention and elicited an air of excitement Miss Ella hadn't seen since he read Walt Whitman's *Leaves of Grass* to her.

"What is it?" she asked. She could see nothing but rock. Wet rock. He was digging it out of the cliff with his penknife. "Look at that! It's a fossilized chiton — very old —

it could be, oh, perhaps a million years or more." He held it for her to see, although damp sand and drops of water were dribbling down, threatening her skirt and shoes.

She looked at it as he pointed out the ridges in the large, sow-bug-like shape, and she made little noises that she hoped sounded like she was interested. Privately she wondered how he could possibly be so enthused over something that looked like a dirty old rock. Privately she also had always considered the earth to be not nearly that old. A million years? Hadn't the new Reverend at the church announced something like — about eight thousand years?

"I must add this to my fossil collection for the school," the Professor said. "I was going to tell you, my dear, that I will be teaching science next year as well as serving as principal. Burdon is leaving and it's next to impossible to find a qualified science teacher who is willing to come out here. They all think Santa Catarina and this part of California is the ends of the earth as far as culture and education are concerned."

He proceeded to wrap the fossil carefully in his handkerchief to carry home.

"Robert, I don't know anything about fossils," she said in a sudden burst of candor.

"You'll learn, my dear, you'll learn," he said tenderly. "After all, you are marrying a science teacher as well as a principal. I taught science in New Haven before I decided to come west."

A science teacher. A man who read books she would never understand, even if she wanted to, which she didn't. The poetry was enough. And he was a man who, no doubt, would drag home all sorts of oddities, and she, like any dutiful wife, would have to pretend she was interested. A man who obviously regarded his collection of fossils on an equal footing with rubies and emeralds. She hadn't even known that he had a fossil collection until that day.

Miss Ella frowned a little and shuddered as she wondered if he collected snakes and spiders too. There seemed to be a whole integral part of Robert Pudley's life about which she knew nothing, except that his parents were dead, he was an only child with a few relatives back East, and — he was in love with her. She looked at the small diamond twinkling on her left hand and decided that none of it mattered anyway. Hadn't Mama said that when a man married, all he thought about for months was getting to bed. She had blushed to hear it at the time, but now she reconsidered. She was probably worrying about unimportant things. If that was true — and Mama should know — Robert would forget his fossils when he climbed into bed next to her. She shuddered again, deliciously this time, and she observed how handsome he looked with his dark hair slightly windblown. His hat had fallen off during his pursuit of the chiton fossil.

And yet, as they strolled along, there was a new thought nagging at her brain. "Robert," she said tentatively. "Do you really think that — that fossil can be that old? A million years?"

"Oh yes. Easily. Maybe older."

"But Reverend Whittley said — I believe I heard it right — that the earth is something like — eight thousand years old. And, as you know, dear, he is considered a very learned man. How can that be?" As she said it, she hoped she hadn't gone too far.

"Ella, the man knows nothing about science and geology," he answered patiently. "He should keep to his religion and leave the earth alone. Oh, yes, he's sincere. And he preaches a good sermon. He knows his Bible. But as far as science goes — no." He turned to her. "Now don't you worry your pretty head about it, my dear."

She wanted very much for him to take her in his arms and reassure her, but he couldn't. He was carrying the handkerchief-wrapped fossil in both hands as if it were a precious crystal chalice that might shatter at any moment. Instead, she walked along, carrying his hat and wondering what the Reverend Whittley would say to that — a million years old! And how could it be?

The wedding was lovely. Everyone said so. The

Methodist Church looked festive, with banks of spring flowers on either side of the altar. Miss Ella made a beautiful bride in white silk satin, with a string of small pearls entwined in her pale gold curls. The Fellowship Room was usually piled with stacks of tracts, tired looking chairs and chalkboards. But it was dressed for the reception with potted ferns and flowers. Mama's crystal punch bowl sparkled with a poisonous-pink, non-alcoholic concoction. Neighbor ladies presided over several tables of homemade delicacies.

Professor Robert was immaculate in dove gray tails and a gray bowler. On his feet, over new, laced-up boots, he wore gray buttoned spats. The first ever seen in Santa Catarina.

"Pretty fancy, huh?" muttered his best man who taught mathematics at the high school and who was dressed in his usual school garb, a dark suit, the only suit he owned.

"They're spats — the latest thing back East. I had to send to San Francisco to get them. Nothing like that here, of course. I had a miserable time getting them buttoned. New and stiff," Professor Pudley confided.

The Reverend Spencer Whittaker presided at the ceremony, adding several of his own long-winded homilies to the traditional service. Miss Ella promised to love, honor and obey for better or worse, they were pronounced man and wife. She was Mrs. Robert Pudley. An accomplished fact. Amid all the congratulations and embraces from friends and neighbors, Miss Ella hardly remembered her dislike of her new married name.

After the reception, Miss Ella went home briefly to change from her wedding finery into a going-away suit of navy blue serge. Mama was there to help her with the hooks and eyes while Professor Robert waited downstairs in the parlor.

Mama had one last word of advice: "Now, Ella, you are a married woman. Don't be frightened tonight. Everything will work out all right. You may not think so at first, but it will."

Miss Ella hardly heard her. She was concentrating on buttoning her travel shoes. They were brand new, ankle-high, shiny black leather with a row of buttons up one side. The leather was stiff and the buttonholes seemed almost too small for the buttons.

"They'll ease up after you've worn them a few times," her mother said.

Finally, with the help of a buttonhook, the last shoebutton was put through the last buttonhole in the stiff leather. Miss Ella put a cape over her suit, kissed her mother goodbye, and was off on her honeymoon with Professor Robert. They walked together the short distance to the lower plaza. He carried her carpetbag and his own suitcase. There they waited a short time for the stagecoach, which drew up, dusty from the north coast run, with old Billy Bell handling the reins.

Several passengers got out. The Professor gave his bride a helping hand into the coach and said gallantly, "I wish it was Cinderella's pumpkin coach, my dear."

Miss Ella was thrilled. Marriage to this wonderful man was going to be everything she had hoped for and more... romantic, exciting, full of pleasant little surprises.

The stagecoach ride to Alviso took five hours of jolting and bumping over rough roads, past isolated farmhouses where Billy Bell made numerous stops to deliver mail and grocery orders. But to Ella it was a great romantic adventure. She could have been riding on clouds instead of a worn leather seat from which loose springs nipped at one's posterior when the coach hit bumps. There were a lot of bumps. But San Francisco would be different. She was sure of that. She had heard so much about it, although she had never been there. In fact she had never been out of Santa Catarina in all her nineteen years.

By the time they arrived at Alviso it was evening and they got some dismal news. The boat to San Francisco had left. They had missed it by half an hour and there would not be another until morning.

Miss Ella looked around the drab little settlement in

the mud flats at the edge of San Francisco Bay and realized there was no choice of places to spend the night. There was one run-down-looking rooming house. That was all.

They went in to get a room and she looked with distaste at the grubby tables where meals were served and at the untidy looking girl waiting on them. A group of workmen were eating there.

"I'm really not hungry," she said faintly, wondering if the plan to honeymoon in San Francisco was so wise, after all.

"My dear, you are weary, of course," the Professor said. "I'll have tea and biscuits sent up to our room."

"Thank you, Robert. You are so thoughtful."

It took a few minutes to get their room and order the tea, and in those minutes word got around that the Pudleys were newlyweds. Old Billy Bell couldn't hold the news. He let it out when the stable boy came to unhitch the horses. The stable boy mentioned it to the waitress and she spread it to everyone else. The men who were eating stared at Professor Robert and Miss Ella and one of them remarked loudly "Heerd you was just married — sure got yerself a pretty one."

Miss Ella blushed, the Professor muttered something under his breath, tipped his bowler politely and led his bride upstairs, aware that every eye in the place was following them. Imaginations and knowing grins, too.

Their room was not much better than the grubby dining room. There was a cane rocker and Miss Ella sank down into it and wished she could remove her new shoes. They were pinching her feet. The Professor lit the kerosene lamp on the small table beside the bed, then closed the door and came toward her. He looked so large, like he almost filled the room, and the lamplight cast his shadow like a giant cloud moving along the walls. For one brief moment Ella wondered what she was doing in this awful place with this man who almost seemed a stranger to her, and she wished she was back in Santa Catarina. Almost.

"This isn't what I had in mind for our first night

together, Ella," Professor Robert said. "But I'll make it up to you in San Francisco."

She nodded wearily. "It's all right. I understand. If we hadn't missed the boat ...."

"I'll help you off with your cape," be said, "and perhaps you would care to lie down and rest."

She looked at the bed which obviously had been slept in and not changed. "I believe I will rest here in the chair for awhile."

"As you wish, my dear."

The words reassured her. It was going to be all right after all. He was a kind, reasonable man. He surely would not make any unreasonable demands on her, under the circumstances. Why, the walls of this room were like cardboard, she thought. There was no privacy.

The tea came, delivered by the downstairs girl who grinned knowingly as she set it down.

"Heard you was bride and groom," she said. "The privy's out back behind the barn and there's a water faucet and a wash basin down the hall. Last door. Well, have a good night." She smirked again and left.

They drank the tea in silence and the Professor ate one of the biscuits. He cleared his throat: "Now, my dear, I believe I will go — um — outside. Perhaps you wish to — to go outside?"

"No, no. I'm all right," she said quickly. She had noticed a chamber pot under the bed.

He left, and she pulled the chamber pot out, hitched up her skirt and petticoats, and untied the drawstring in her drawers. She sat down on the pot carefully but quickly, mindful that the Professor might come back and she didn't want him to find her doing that. Then she slid the chamber pot back under the bed and straightened her clothes.

What to do next? Disrobe and get into her nightgown? That pink and white muslin gown with ribbon bows and lace trim. A honeymoon nightgown it was, meant for moonlight and roses instead of a place like this. She looked at the bed. The quilts were slightly grimy along the top edges where whiskered chins had rubbed. Oh well, San Francisco would be different.

Slowly, she began to undress, laying aside the smart little tailored suit, then the starched petticoats, unhooking the corset and bodice, and stepping out of the lace-edged drawers. For a moment she stood there in her shoes and stockings, almost naked. She looked down at her body and she was seeing herself differently for the first time. The full white breasts and the mound of golden hair below. What would it be like to belong to someone else?

She shivered a little. The bridal nightgown smelled faintly of lavender when she pulled it over her head. She adjusted the ribbon ties at the neck, then sat down to remove her shoes. The buttonhook. Where was it? She rummaged through her suitcase. It had to be there. She went through the case again, hastily. No buttonhook. She must have forgotten to put it in.

She knelt and struggled with the shoe buttons with trembling fingers. There were eight on each shoe. She got three unbuttoned on one shoe but the others refused to give. She tried the other foot and managed to unbutton two, breaking a fingernail in the process. She couldn't get the shoes off. For a moment she was close to tears. So much had gone wrong since leaving Santa Catarina. The coach's late arrival, missing the boat, this awful place, and now her new shoes. Then the absurdity of it struck her. She gave up the struggle with the stiff leather and she almost laughed as she climbed into the grimy bed with her shoes and stockings on.

Professor Robert knocked softly before he entered the room. He would always be polite — a gentleman, she thought, even under the worst of circumstances. She closed her eyes and waited. Then she opened them. She might as well get used to it. She watched as he removed his pearl gray coat and hung it carefully on the rocking chair. Then his stiff white collar, his vest and shirt, then he unbuttoned his trousers and let them fall to the floor. He stood there for a moment in his long-sleeved, long-legged union suit underwear, looking toward the bed, and she shut her eyes quickly, but not before she had noticed a conspicuous bulge. She waited while he knelt to remove his spats and boots, then opened her eyes a crack to see what he was doing. He was taking a long time at it, she thought. He seemed to be struggling. He was panting and his face was red in the lamplight. Then he was rummaging through his bag and she beard a faint word that sounded like "dammit".

Finally she spoke softly. "Robert, what are you doing?" She thought she knew and she was trying not to laugh.

"Ella my dear, I have done a very careless thing," he said solemnly. I forgot to pack my buttonhook and I can't get these dammed — pardon me dear — spats off. 1 can't even cut them off. I don't have my penknife with me. I feel so — so stupid."

Miss Ella did laugh then, just a little. Life with Professor Robert was going to be interesting.

"Come to bed, dear," she said. "I have a little surprise for you."

THE BIRD ON NELLIE'S HAT

Ladies' hats were important in Santa Catarina in the 1880s. The pioneer days were over for ladies in sun bonnets. Hired girls and women still wore them, but ladies didn't. There was a difference. Women and hired girls were the creatures who did housework and assorted domestic tasks for ladies. Ladies were the creatures who hired girls and women, and ladies wore hats. Proper hats. Big hats. Creations of straw, silk and felt decorated with stuffed birds, ostrich plumes, bluebirds' wings, bunches of fake cherries and a variety of silk flowers. Those hats were constructions. They had to be anchored firmly with several hatpins six or eight inches long, sharp at one end and jeweled at the other. Formidable weapons if needed, but ladies in Santa Catarina never seemed to need weapons in that day and age.

Ladies lived in big houses on the most desirable streets and they had their porcelain complexions to consider. They never ventured out without hats and pale kidskin gloves. Not even on the warmest days. In other words, ladies existed in a world very different from that of hired girls and ordinary women.

Since they had the hired help to cook, housekeep and tend their children, ladies had a lot of time on their lily white hands. They embroidered, painted china and carried on a rigorous social rite they referred to as "at home" and "calling."

One day a week was designated "at home" day. Other ladies donned their finery (plus hats and gloves) and came calling. In every Victorian entrance hall there was a marble-topped table, with a silver tray on it. The ladies who were paying the call, dropped their engraved calling cards into the tray. While making the call, they sat primly on horsehair sofas or settees in the parlor, sipped tea, nibbled a cookie or two, and partook of polite conversation. The ladies all took turns. They "called" on each other on certain days and they "received" during their "at homes" on other days.

But this is the story of hats and a girl who made them. Kate Paddon always wore the look of a woman whose heart was weighted with care. And concealed under her high-buttoned, tailored navy blue dress she wore a gold chain from which was suspended a curious piece of metal. Her customers never saw it. If they had caught a glimpse, they might have thought it was a religious medal. Kate never missed Sunday Mass.

Kate was a quiet-voiced woman with a hint of sadness in her eyes. She never married. After learning the millinery business during an apprenticeship in San Francisco, she came home to Santa Catarina to open her own shop and care for her aging mother. Her shop prospered and her skills as a milliner spread to neighboring towns.

But what the young Kate had really wanted — had her heart set on — was not making hats. Kate wanted a job at the newspaper, the Santa Catarina Weekly Wave. She wanted to discover and write about things that were happening, see her story in print, maybe with her name on it. She loved to write. The clanking linotype machine in the back-shop fascinated her. It put metal words together into sentences. She dreamed of running one herself. A far cry from sewing "the bird on Nellie's Hat" as the popular song went.

However there were several insurmountable obstacles to Kate's dream of a newspaper career. Her widowed mother raised the biggest barrier: "Nice girls don't work in newspaper shops," she stated sternly.

Kate tried: "Oh Mother, you just think that because of what Sister Mary George says about it."

Sister Mary George was Kate's teacher at the Santa Catarina Catholic High School. It was because of the nun leading her class on a field trip to the newspaper plant that Kate had got the idea at all. When Kate stepped into the busy newsroom she was fascinated. Editor McDevitt and two reporters sat at desks typing. In one corner a linotype machine clanked and coughed. The smell of hot lead assaulted her nostrils as she stepped closer. An ancient press took up the rest of the room. Typewriters clacked. Everyone was busy. The reporters looked up briefly, then went on with their work. The shop men — there were two of them — were busy with the press which wasn't running at the time.

Editor McDevitt came over and began explaining the process of turning out a weekly newspaper to the class. Kate's interest grew with every word. Finally, when the Editor mentioned school news — the possibility of getting it weekly, Kate could be silent no longer.

"I could get our school news and write it and bring it down," she offered.

McDevitt smiled and said, "Fine! Bring it down on Wednesday and we'll see how it goes. Remember your 'who, what, where and when.' That's the important thing."

Sister Mary George looked startled at first, then doubtful, then a bit pleased. After all, she could read everything Kate wrote and make sure it was all right. And school news — good news — was important. Kate was her top student in English and Composition.

Kate was delighted. She bought a new notebook for a nickel and two pencils — two cents each — and she was ready to report the school news. Notebook in hand, she prowled the four high school classrooms to collect tidbits: Sarah Morton was down with measles but would be back soon... Elsie Schmitt won the spelling bee... a sewing class was starting for ninth grade girls and they would be making tea towels and aprons.

Kate wrote it all and by the following Wednesday she had three pages full. After school, instead of going directly home, she walked the three blocks down to the shabby building where the newspaper was put together. She was so thrilled that she was writing for the newspaper that she went past the one reporter who was at work at his desk and straight to Editor McDevitt. He looked up. He looked puzzled. Obviously he didn't remember the eager young girl in the navy blue uniform who stood before him.

Kate wasn't fazed. "I'm Kate Paddon — the student from Santa Catarina Catholic High School and I brought the news you told me I could last week — remember?" she said in one breath.

McDevitt smiled. "Let's see what you have there."

That was the beginning of Kate's love affair with the Santa Catarina newspaper. All week she scurried around the school before classes started, during lunch time and after hours, collecting her news items. The High School was in the news every week and best of all, from Kate's view point, she had her own byline: "By Kate Paddon."

She began spending more time at the newspaper plant during her weekly visits. McDevitt took a liking to the girl with the wide, questioning eyes, who was so eager to learn about everything. On her third weekly visit he turned her over to one of the reporters who took her on educational tours of the plant, according to what was being done at the moment. At the linotype machine she met Samuel Henryson. He was nineteen, a roving back-shop worker with an itchy foot for travel who had already gone from town to town in California for the past two years, working at newspapers. She was soon calling him Sam and marveling at his expertise. He was smart. He knew how to run the linotype, he could set type right and operate the printing press with the best of them.

He let Kate sit at the linotype machine and showed her how it worked, how she could press the keys of the keyboard to create letters cast from hot lead, and how the letters formed words in "slugs".

"Then the slugs slide into that tray — it's called a galley," he explained. "The slugs are what's used to print the paper. Go ahead — print your name. It'll come out on a metal slug and you'll see how it works."

Kate was intrigued. She printed her name and when the metal cooled, Sam handed the slug to her. "A present," he said with a smile.

"Oh I wish I could work here!" Kate said.

"Well, talk to McDevitt. Maybe you can. How much more school do you have?"

"The rest of this year."

Sam frowned. "You'd better finish. Then come in and talk to McDevitt. He might hire you. I don't know if he would. Most papers won't have women. They say they're a nuisance, always getting hurt or sick or gettin' married and then leavin'. But you could try." He smiled again. "A paper I worked on up in Frisco had a woman writer — called her a 'newshen'. That's the only one I ever run across and I've worked papers from up there down to L.A."

"L.A.?" Kate was puzzled.

"Short for Los Angeles."

In the months that followed, Kate's weekly visits to the paper turned into a learning experience that she fell in love with. The smells of hot lead and printer's ink were perfume to her nose. When he wasn't too busy, Sam let her set a bit of the type for her own school stories.

"It's so interesting, Mama," she bubbled later at home.

Mrs. Paddon frowned. "Don't set your heart on it, Kate. It's no place for a woman to work. That's man's work."

"But you don't know, Mama. It isn't hard work at all when you like it. And Sam shows me all about it."

Mrs. Paddon didn't say any more but she did some thinking and she had a serious talk with Sister Mary George. They decided to let Kate continue with the newspaper reports for the rest of the school year. There were just four months left until graduation and summer vacation.

"And then — well, we'll just have to see," Mrs. Paddon said. "I do have a sister in San Francisco who is a dressmaker and milliner. Maybe I could send Kate up there to learn the trade. That would get her mind off this newspaper idea. And away from that young fellow down at the plant," she added. "I'm afraid he's encouraging her."

"Indeed," Sister Mary George said.

"Yes. Entirely too much. I don't like it. It's foolish for a young girl to think she could work there alone with those men and that machinery. It's no place for a woman!"

That was when Mrs. Paddon wrote to her sister in San Francisco and had a favorable reply the following week. She put the letter away after answering it and said nothing to Kate.

As for Kate, she was living in a dream world and forming a close friendship with Sam. When he appeared at their door one evening and asked Kate to go walking with him, Mrs. Paddon let her go but her disapproval was plain to see.

"Your ma doesn't like me," Sam observed as they strolled along the street.

"It's more the newspaper than you," Kate said. "She doesn't think girls belong down there."

"What's she going to say when you ask McDevitt for a job?"

"Oh, she'll fuss a lot at first but when she sees it isn't as bad as she thinks — besides I don't know if I'll get a job. Maybe Editor McDevitt won't want a girl working there. Remember what you told me about women in the newsroom."

"Yes, but he likes you and you are pretty good at it."

"Well, I hope so. I'd love to work there."

They were walking toward the cliffs that overlooked the Pacific Ocean and they came to a bench. Without a word they sat down.

"That's funny," she said.

"What's funny?"

"We both decided to sit down without saying a word about it."

"That's not so funny," he said quietly. "We get along real well, you and me."

"I do thank you, Sam, for being such a good teacher and showing me about the linotype and all — and for being a good friend.

"Kate —." He hesitated, then said "Kate, I would like to be more than just a good friend." He put his arm around her shoulders and drew her close. "A fellow could settle down in one place — a place like Santa Catarina, if he had a wife like you."

"Sam dear — oh I don't know what to say. I can't say anything now. I'm not even through school yet for another month." But she was smiling at him as she said it, and he leaned over and kissed her.

They walked back hand in hand, an intimate gesture that did not go unnoticed by Mrs. Paddon who was waiting behind the lace curtains in the parlor. The next day she had a serious talk with Sister Mary George.

"It's much worse than I thought," she said, explaining the walk and hand holding.

Sister's answer was reassuring. "In a few days it will end. School will be out and you can send her to San Francisco. She'll be safe and sound up there, learning a trade and she'll forget all about this boy."

The following week, with graduation so close, Kate got up her nerve and spoke with Editor McDevitt. He wasn't exactly surprised when she asked him about a job.

"So, you want to be a newshen, huh?" he said with a smile. He liked this girl who, he believed, had the makings of a good newspaper writer. "We could use a society writer. Club news, parties, women's interests, recipes, things like those," he said. "The men don't like to do it — we've never had a woman but we could try you out."

"Oh yes! I could do it! I am sure," Kate burst out.

"Well, we'll see what we can arrange," McDevitt said. "Won't be much pay at first. Part time work."

She nodded. Later she related the conversation to Sam with great excitement.

Kate, that's wonderful," he said. "We'll be working together." He put his hand on hers. "I'm thinking of settling here. Buying a house. And Kate, I'm thinking about asking you a question — when you're ready."

Kate blushed.

"You look so pretty when your face gets all pink like that. I'd like to kiss you but better not — might get fired." He laughed. "Everybody on this paper knows how I feel about you. I can't hide it."

The remaining school days went by fast, with rehearsals for the graduation program and fittings for the dress Mrs. Paddon was making for Kate. A dainty cloud of fine white cotton with lace trim at neck and sleeves.

"Oh Mama, it's beautiful," Kate said. Privately she was thinking it would make a perfect wedding dress.

The week of graduation was busy, with Kate gathering the stories of honor students, of which she was one, and summer vacation plans. It was the most ambitious job of reporting she had yet turned in and McDevitt was pleased. "You've done a good job," he said. "Come in week after next and we'll set up a schedule. Part-time at first."

Kate was ecstatic when she told Sam about it.

"Swell!" he said. "By the way, I'm coming to your graduation."

"I hoped you would."

And he was there, watching as she tripped across the stage in the church fellowship hall to receive her diploma from Father Hugh Moran. Afterward, he walked home with Kate and her mother who was coolly civil. They said goodnight at the door with Mrs. Paddon remarking how late it was.

Once inside, Kate decided to tell her mother about the newspaper job.

"Mama, I've got a wonderful surprise."

"Yes"

"I'm going to work part-time on the newspaper. Editor McDevitt asked me to come in week after next. Isn't that wonderful?"

Kate knew she was in trouble when her mother didn't answer right away.

Mrs. Paddon finally said "Oh Kate — you can't. It just isn't the place for a young girl."

Kate faltered. "I'd like to try it for the summer — at least. Then if it doesn't work out — I can do something else. Maybe get my teacher's certificate. But I do want to try it!"

Mrs. Paddon sighed. "It's impossible, Kate. Put it out of your mind. Besides, there's something else. Your Aunt Bertha in San Francisco wants you to come up and live with her and learn the dressmaking and millinery trade. I told her you'd try — it's a generous offer on her part. You can live with her and earn a little money while you're learning."

Kate was shocked. She looked at her mother for a moment, then said bitterly "You have it all arranged? Without even asking me? I have no say about it at all? I don't want to go!"

"Kate — Kate, it's for the best." Mrs. Paddon was crying. "I'm going to miss you — you'll only be gone six months — then you can come home and have your own business. You don't know what I've gone through all these years to raise you — your father killed in that logging accident — I can't sit by and see you ruin your life. You'd be jumping into something — you're too young to know — to see ahead. Believe me. Now I'm going to bed. I am very upset by all this. It's for your own good, Kate."

Kate sat with bowed head for a long time before she went to bed. She had no defense against her mother's tears and words.

Saturday and Sunday were gloomy days at the Paddon home. Kate was barely speaking to her mother. The newspaper office was closed on weekends so she couldn't contact anyone. She didn't even know where Sam lived. He had a room someplace. She wrote notes to both Editor

McDevitt and Sam, explaining that she was leaving town Monday morning on the train, going to San Francisco to work.

At the Depot on Monday morning, Mrs. Paddon bought the ticket and handed it to her with two dollars. "Here's a little extra in case you need it. Bertha will take good care of you. Oh Kate — I'll miss you!"

Kate was cool. "Yes, Mama." She took the ticket and the money, kissed her mother's cheek dutifully, climbed aboard the train and didn't look back. Once seated, she opened her purse and took out a small piece of metal and held it in her hand. The newspaper slug with her name on it. A tear fell on it before she put it back into her purse.

A DIP IN THE BRINY

He stood there at the edge of the cliff, high above the waves that crashed on the rocks below. Looking down through the darkness, he could see splashes of white foam on the wet rocks. Back toward Santa Catarina he could see gas street lamps shining and house windows aglow with evening lamplight. He sighed and turned for one more look at the beach where a square white building rose like a ghost to haunt him.

For a moment he remembered the pain. Then he thought of Adelia back home in Santa Catarinaand wondered if she was sitting by the table in her favorite chair. A familiar picture. A dear picture. He wished he could have left her a note. He put that thought out of his mind and looked down at the rocks again.

Would she miss him? At least she would be able to keep the house and live comfortably. He was sure of that and it made him feel better.

He looked up once at the sky sparkling with stars. It was a clear night. The fog hadn't come in yet. Then he took a deep breath. And stepped off the edge of the cliff. Seconds later Brad Thurston was a crumpled broken body on the rocks below.

The next evening, Thursday, October 4, 1884, the Santa Catarina Wave, which had grown by then from a weekly to a daily, came out with a front page story: LOCAL

BUSINESSMAN DIES IN FALL FROM CLIFF.

"Bradley Thurston, well-known member of one of Santa Catarina's prominent families and leader in the local business world for more than twenty years, died in a fall from North Cliff Road last night.

"Mr. Thurston, who has been a patient at Santa Catarina Hospital for the past two days, was taking an evening walk when the accident occurred. The Hospital is located on North Cliff Road. After notifying the hospital staff that he was going for a short stroll, Mr. Thurston failed to appear for dinner. He was due to return to his home today after several tests were concluded, according to staff members. He is survived by his wife, Adelia Thurston who is in seclusion. He will be sorely missed in the local business world, according to his longtime friend and partner, Morton Grace...."

Bradley Thurston grew up with a dream. A childhood dream that, as he grew older, be was determined to bring into reality. Some day. He would build a saltwater swim tank down on the beach near the ocean. Brad had always loved to swim. From the time he was old enough to go alone or with friends, he was at the beach, even in winter.

"Takes to it like a duck to water," his father observed.

Brad was an only child, heir to the Thurston business which was a thriving lumber mill in the redwood forests near Santa Catarina. But Brad wasn't interested in lumber. He had that persistent dream and it grew stronger over the years. Every time he went to swim at the beach he would look at the stretch of pale sand and imagine an indoor swim tank there, with salt water pumped from the ocean just a few feet away.

He drew plans for it during high school classes when he was supposed to be doing something else. He mentioned it a few times to his father who brushed it aside as a foolish idea.

"Who would swim in it?" he scoffed.

Brad was serious. "All the people and kids who are

afraid of the waves."

"It's not practical, my boy. Not practical at all.'

So Brad grew up, graduated from Santa Catarina High School and, after a few years working in the mill, married Adelia Moore. Adelia, a delicate looking girl, was in frail health, but Brad had loved her since high school days.

He worked at the mill under his father's direction until the old man died of a heart attack. Then, free for the first time in his life, he dared to dream again of a swim tank on the beach. It was a dream he had cherished secretly while supervising wagonloads of logs and whining saws.

"A heated tank would be suitable for all ages," he explained to Adelia. "Even for older people who don't care for the cold surf. And salt water from the ocean is healthful, my dear. It might even help your condition." Adelia had begun to suffer from what her doctor called rheumatism.

"But where would you build it?" she asked. "We don't own any land down on the beach."

He looked at her fondly. "Now don't you worry yourself about it, my dear. I've already talked to Morton Grace. He owns that strip of beach beyond the wharf and he's willing to dicker."

"But where will you get the money? It will cost a lot, won't it? And you just had to replace those saws at the mill. I remember you saying how expensive they were."

"I can work things out with Morton. We went to school together. I've known him all my life. I can trust him."

"Well, if you're sure...."

"Yes, I'm sure. It's something I've wanted to do all my life. And that tank will be the talk of the town. Vacationers will want to swim in it. It will be a paying proposition. I'm sure." He leaned down to kiss her cheek.

Adelia sighed and stretched out her hands with their swollen arthritic fingers. "I hope so, dear. Help me up, please. My legs are so stiff today. They ache, too."

He lifted her from the chair and took her arm to steady her. When he wasn't there to help her, she called the hired girl from the kitchen. He worried constantly about Adelia's health. But there was another thought that nagged him. *What if I die before she does?* And one day he talked to Attorney Lewis McLaren.

"There's no one to help her except me and the hired help," he said. "Our parents are gone — we have no children."

McLaren took a puff on his cigar. "How about your investments? The mill — your plan to build the salt water tank down by the beach? I heard about that from Morton, the other day. Word gets around fast."

Brad shook his head. He had just made a deal with Morton Grace. "I had to borrow for the tank," he said. "It's going to be more than I thought at first. I put the mill up."

McLaren frowned. "Well then, I would suggest that you take out some life insurance for Adelia."

That was the answer. Bradley took out a policy for Adelia the next day. If anything happened to him, she would get ten thousand dollars. "Enough to live on," he said to himself. The house was clear.

Then, with his mind at rest more or less, he went ahead with the salt water tank. He hired an Italian workman who was recommended by Morton Grace, to direct the job.

"He's a good man. Knows the building business in and out," Grace said. "If anybody can build a tank on that sand, he can."

The excavation proved a problem. "It keeps caving in," Bradley told Adelia. "But finally that Italian fellow figured a way to stop it." He didn't tell her how much it was beginning to cost. Didn't want to worry her.

The redwood timbers for the foundation came from Brad's mill. The cement for the tank itself came from Elias Purvis's lime kilns a few miles away. Iron pipes to carry sea water in and out, came from the foundry down near the Santa Catarina River. Six workmen were on the job for ten months and it wasn't finished yet.

Bradley also ran into a problem he had not considered.

When the pipes were laid they ran from the tank out into the ocean. They were buried of course, but they had to cross a strip of beach that belonged to someone else.

The workmen were busy digging the trench and laying the pipe one day when Bradley had a visit from Elvin Hall, Santa Catarina's first millionaire. The Halls had made their fortune from lumber and property and Elvin owned a good portion of the beach front.

Elvin came right to the point. "I don't want to be unreasonable, Bradley," he said. "But you're running your water pipes through my property. I own that stretch of beach."

Bradley looked unhappy. "It's my understanding that the beach is public property — I checked the records down at the Courthouse."

Elvin shook his head. "Only according to the tide line. I bought that strip of land about a year ago — plan to develop a vacation business there — put in a float and a rope going out to it — maybe a boardwalk. We're getting more and more folks today who like to come to the beach for vacations for a dip in the briny. Thought I'd put in some cabins and a camp back near the hill — away from the waterline. Folks can have it both ways. Now about your pipes...."

Bradley ended the discussion by promising to have the workmen dig up the pipes already buried, dig a deeper trench, and re-bury them. He also agreed to pay Elvin Hall a yearly rental for the water pipes crossing Elvin's land.

When he sat down that evening to figure it all out, be knew he was in too deep and he had to go to Morton Grace for more money. The mortgage on the mill was re-figured and Grace advanced Bradley the money he thought he needed.

"That ought to do it," Bradley said. "I still have to arrange for a platform and a pump out beyond the tide line — it will be like a short wharf almost. The pipes will bring the water in from there to fill the tank. And when it needs replacing with fresh water, the pipes will carry the old water out into the ocean."

He also went ahead with a building that enclosed the swim tank and included dressing rooms and a glass roof.

"Pretty fancy, huh?" he said to Aaelia. "Nothing else like it on the coast — that I've heard of."

The swim tank, complete with salt water pipes, pump, and water heater fired by gas, was finally enclosed in a square white building during the winter of 1886, two years after the first shovelful of sand was removed.

It was slow to gain the popularity that Bradley had predicted.

"Winter time, he said. "Bound to be slow. Just wait until summer comes.'

The natives of Santa Catarina were curious, but they also were cautious.

"It's a new idea, Bradley said to Adelia. "Might take some time to get going."

Adelia went down every day to sit in the shallow end of the tank.

"I do think the salt water helps," she said. "My legs feel better."

Bradley smiled. "If it helps you — that's the most important thing I want."

With summer, the swim tank business picked up a bit for about three months. Summer tourists came to Santa Catarina from the hot interior valleys for a cool "dip in the briny" as one advertisement in the Daily Wave described it. They were curious about the swim tank too. But the town's white sand beaches and rolling surf remained the most popular. The ocean was free, wasn't it. Why pay two bits to swim in a tank when you could do the same outdoors for free?

With the fall months and the departure of the tourists, business dropped off to almost nothing. Bradley knew he was in deep trouble when Morton came to him about the mortgage.

"It's been slow to get going, Morton, but I think if we can give it another year — another vacation time...."

Morton nodded. "I know. I understand. A new idea

always takes time. You've only had one summer with it. Tell you what. I'll wait. Give it another summer. It ought to get going good by then."

When summer came to Santa Catarina in early June with the first vacationers, Brad's hopes were high. He put advertisements in The Wave and had a large sign installed on top of the swim tank building. But June was a quiet month for the business.

"July will be better," he said hopefully to Morton.

Morton looked doubtful. "It is taking longer than I planned for that short-term loan."

The tourist season of July, August and September passed with no better results. Brad began to pore over his account books, spending longer hours and sleepless nights. By January of 1887 he was suffering continuing headaches.

Adelia was worried about him. "Brad you aren't eating and you stay up at all hours working on your books. It's telling on you. You don't look good." Finally she persuaded him to see their doctor.

"The doctor wants me to go to the hospital for several tests — it will be just a couple of days," he said to her. "Nothing too serious, my dear."

Adelia looked up at him from her chair. "I'm glad you finally went. I worried about you. You won't be away long, will you?"

"No, just a few tests." He didn't tell her that Morton Grace had foreclosed on the mill. The mill and its surrounding acres of forested land that had been in Bradley's family for two generations no longer belonged to him. It had been the final crushing blow.

"You will be fine, dear, with Elsie to take care of you."

"Yes, she's the best hired girl we've ever had. But I will miss you," Adelia said.

The hospital was located behind the cliffs at the edge of town, on a winding coastal drive. At the entrance Brad paused to look back. He could see it all from there. Santa Catarina, the main street leading from the waterfront back to the foothills. Back to the redwood forests. His redwood forest. The buildings and buggies and wagons on the street, a horsecar plodding along half-way up.

Closer, down nearer the ocean, the clusters of summer cottages, the curving pale sand beach and the one larger white building. His. His dream. His downfall.

A nurse opened the door. "Doctor is waiting, Mr. Thurston."

The next afternoon, after a series of tests, Brad had the news. It wasn't good. A problem with his heart. There were pills. But he would have to lead a very quiet life. And the doctor wanted him to stay one more day so they could adjust his medication.

Brad took it calmly. Then he returned to his room, got dressed, and left, telling the nurse at the front desk that he would be back in time for dinner. On the way out he paused. There was a young boy sitting on a hall bench. He looked forlorn. His hand was bandaged. Brad felt in his coat pocket, found several coins. His last.

"Here," he said.

The boy grinned. "Gee Mister, thanks."

A few minutes later Brad was standing at the edge of the cliff walk looking down at the water and rocks. He remembered how Adelia had looked up at him. That last conversation. Her trusting eyes. Loving eyes. And he was thinking of that when he stepped off the cliff.

MONKEY BUSINESS

Professor Robert Pudley, principal and science teacher at Santa Catarina High School, had no idea how easy it was to get into trouble in that small, provincial, California coastal town. He didn't even know he was in trouble at first. He was quite content to teach and run the school which had about two hundred students and a staff of nine teachers by the year 1886.

He also was happily married to Miss Ella Elizabeth Worthington, they had purchased an impressive home on Riverview Avenue and intended to fill it with four children.

"Three's a nice round number," Ella suggested.

"So is four," he said, smiling at her. They were still in the honeymoon stage after only nine months of marriage.

"We'll take what we get and love all of them," she said. She was expecting their first child in about four months.

Professor Pudley's life was perfect as far as he was concerned. So was his professional life. But that was where he was, unaware, treading on thin ice.

It began with a field trip for the senior class. Former teachers had always conducted field trips to the beaches to explore the marvels of the tide pools and collect shells. Few girls took the course; it was mainly the boys, who rolled up their pant legs and waded, splashed each other, picked up a few shells, learned little about ocean sciences, but had a great time.

That was the usual agenda. But Professor Pudley was serious. He took things a step or two further. He made it clear from the time of their arrival on the beach that there would be no time for horseplay.

"These are fossilized marine creatures," he explained as the class surveyed an eroding beach cliff. He dug one out with the slender, pointed trowel he carried. "See here. You can make out the part that was the shell — oh, perhaps two or three million years ago."

The students clustered around to look. "Two or three million years ago! Gee!" one of them said.

"Millions? Do you really think so?" another asked.

"Oh yes,"' Professor Pudley said. "There's a lot of research going on and we're learning more about the age of the earth and its creatures, all the time."

"How could things last that long?" someone wanted to know.

Professor Pudley went on to explain at some length that an ancient ocean had covered much of California in ages past, then disappeared gradually, leaving sea animals preserved in layers of earth, thus creating fossils.

"We'll go inland some miles for our later field trips," he promised.

"We'll dig up fossilized sharks' teeth. I have located a promising spot — I even found a couple of teeth on top of the ground where they had been washed out of the earth."

The class expressed great interest, all except one boy, Lewis Jedediah Wallace, who looked puzzled, then spoke up. "How old do you think the sharks' teeth are?"

"Oh, somewhere in the millions," Professor Pudley said. He was busy directing another student who had located and was digging out a fossil. "It's not easy to tell, exactly," Professor Pudley went on. "But we'll take these back to the school laboratory and work on them. Then we'll do the same with the teeth."

Professor Pudley went home that evening with a great sense of accomplishment. He was educating his students, opening their eyes and their minds to the wonders of the earth. Many of them came from uneducated families in this provincial town. He would strive to change that, at least for the next generation. He thought back to the more sophisticated schools he had left behind on the East coast and he felt a missionary zeal for the task ahead in this California coastal town.

"Who knows?" There may be a future biologist or anthropologist in one of my classes," he remarked to his wife that evening.

The following week, the class dug up sharks' teeth, some stained brown, others almost their original white depending on the composition of the earth in which they had been buried for — "Perhaps a million or more years," Professor Pudley explained. "These were prehistoric sharks. You might say they were the ancestors of the sharks we have today, swimming around out there." He gestured toward the ocean.

Most of the class was excited, busy digging, interested in the search. But one student raised a question. "How do you know they're that old?" It was Lewis Jedediah Wallace again.

Professor Pudley paused barely long enough to answer. "I have books that will explain the Theory of Evolution. We'll get into some of it next week."

That evening he went home with plans for a school fossil collection.

"No one's ever done it before — just imagine! With the wealth of materials in this area — fossils all over the place! I can order a glass case — it will fit in the hallway, right inside the main door. There's room for it there. And classes can add to it as we make more discoveries. I must send for Henry Osborne's book on ancient reptiles — we will study those also," he told his wife.

"Who is Henry Osborne?" Ella Pudley wanted to know. She hoped she would not have to study reptiles — even ancient ones. Learning about poetry had been enough. Robert had educated her about poetry during their courtship and they still sat together in the evenings reading from his collection of poetry books.

"Mr. Osborne is an instructor at Princeton. I was fortunate in being able to meet him before I came west, and I have a copy of one of his studies on warm blooded mammals, Professor Pudley said. "A most remarkable man, my dear. He's considered the foremost authority on vertebrate fossils in the country."

"Vertebrate?" Ella said, half question.

"Bones, my dear. Bones," Professor Pudley said half jokingly. "I correspond with him regularly and I have told him of the fossil cliffs here in Santa Catarina. He is working on a new book at present."

"I don't understand it all, Robert. But I trust that you do," she said, privately marveling at this brilliant man she had married.

The following week, Professor Pudley took several of his own precious books to the class. Among them, Darwin's *The Origin of Species* and *The Descent of Man.* He also took Osborne's study on vertebrate fossils.

In the classroom he announced "We'll make large charts as a class project. We can stretch them along one wall of the chalkboard. Then it will be much easier to study the progression of life on earth."

He divided the students into teams and set them to work with rolls of paper he had acquired at the office of the Weekly Wave, Santa Catarina's newspaper. Under his direction they referred to the books and began to divide the wall chart into eras, beginning with the Paleozoic.

"That's about five-hundred million years ago," he explained. "As we study and learn more, we may be able to put approximate dates on our fossil finds — I hope," he added.

"Where will man go on this chart?" someone asked.

"Oh, roughly, about a million years ago," Professor Pudley said. "You can look it up in more detail in Darwin's book. We'll get around to studying it, too."

"A million years!" one student exclaimed, and whistled.

Some grinned. Others looked amazed. A few shook their heads. But one boy stood up defiantly. It was Lewis Jedediah Wallace again.

"I am leaving this class," he announced. "My father says none of it is true." And he walked out.

Then, Professor Pudley had a premonition of trouble ahead.

Later, at home, he said "I never thought I'd run into that, my dear, although perhaps I should have known. A small town — uneducated people, many of them. A strong church town. My enthusiasm carried me away, I'm afraid. I never thought to be cautious about such things. Back East —" he shook his head. "The worst of it, that boy is Lewis Jedediah Wallace, the son of Reverend Wallace of the Santa Catarina Western Gospel Temple."

Ella Pudley looked worried. "Oh dear. What do you think will happen now?"

"We'll just have to wait and see," he said. "It may all blow over. I hope it does. And I will have to be more careful in future. That is going to be difficult for me."

But it didn't blow over.

Two evenings later, the Rev. Wallace and six members of his Gospel Temple came to the Pudley home. Ella Pudley was in the kitchen with the hired girl. Professor Pudley heard the bell and opened the front door. The Reverend Wallace's face was grave. He didn't smile or extend his hand. None of the others did.

"May we come in?" The words had an ominous sound.

Professor Pudley felt a sinking sensation in his middle but he recovered enough to say "Oh yes, indeed! Please do."

The committee filed into the parlor and took seats on the horsehair sofa and chairs, all except Reverend Wallace who remained standing.

"We have come, Professor Pudley, as a result of some upsetting information that has come to our attention," he said. "We have heard" — here he paused for effect — "that your science class is teaching our young ones blasphemy."

"Blasphemy, Sir?" Professor Pudley echoed weakly.

"Yes! Blasphemy!" The Reverend paused to clear his throat, then continued. "This committee feels that the idea that mankind came from monkeys is entirely contrary to Biblical teaching, sir!"

Several of the committee members were on the Board of Education and for one horrible moment, Professor Pudley had visions of his job vanishing at the end of the year, or possibly even sooner.

He had another speechless moment or two before he recovered. "Reverend Wallace, sir, I am sure there's been a misunderstanding. Won't you sit down, sir, and we'll endeavor to get this straightened out." He thought of Ella out in the kitchen, pregnant with their first child. He thought of the payments on this house, their first home. And he thought of his job. He loved teaching.

The Reverend sat down. Professor Pudley started for the kitchen door. "Just one moment — I'll get Mrs. Pudley to bring us some coffee."

The committee sat in stony silence. The ice melted a bit when Ella and the hired girl arrived with trays of coffee cups and fresh-baked cookies.

After serving everyone, Ella excused herself gracefully and went back to the kitchen while Professor Pudley sat down to one of the most difficult interviews of his life.

He discovered that Reverend Wallace's son, Lewis, had reported faithfully to his father every detail of the field trips, the class sessions, the fossils, Darwin's books, Osborne's study and various remarks regarding them by Professor Pudley. The Reverend Wallace recounted them all with suppressed anger and a great deal of sarcasm.

"We can't have this — this balderdash in our school, Pudley. We can't allow our young people to be misled by this this ungodly stuff. Now the Good Book — you're a church-going man, Pudley. I don't have to tell you what the Bible says!

"The Creation Theory — ah yes," Professor Pudley said thoughtfully. "Now the next part of my lessons will concern a comparison between the two theories, evolution and creation. Perhaps you hadn't heard about that?" He went on quickly. "The young people are going to hear about evolution sooner or later, Reverend Wallace, and I feel they should be prepared to understand both theories so they can make the right choice." He paused. "Im sorry if there's been a misunderstanding."

The Reverend Wallace sipped his coffee thoughtfully and frowned. "As far as I'm concerned, they don't need that monkey stuff at all."

"Oh, but they're bound to hear about it," Professor Pudley said. "News of the latest discoveries is becoming widely known in the academic world and eventually it will sift down to..." he wanted to say to small, ignorant communities like Santa Catarina, "to even the remote areas of our country," he finished.

The Reverend rubbed his nose thoughtfully, "And how do you explain those — those dead creatures, as you call them, in the rocks? Telling the younguns they are millions of years old — the very idea! Ridiculous!"

Professor Pudley swallowed. "That's part of the Theory of Evolution," he said smoothly. "Of course there's no way I can prove the age — no one can — yet. And perhaps never will."

"And they never will! the Reverend stated emphatically. "It's all balderdash. Rubbish!"

Ella Fludley came in again with another plate. "Do have one of these cookies, Reverend Wallace."

There was much bombastic discussion, with Professor Pudley giving answers that weren't exactly answers. Later he told Ella it was not a discussion at all — but a one-sided proclamation and condemnation by a few narrow-minded bigots.

The committee and the Reverend finally departed, leaving behind a clutter of coffee cups and a thoroughly crushed Professor Pudley. Ella came in and put her arm around his shoulders. "Don't worry so, Robert. They'll get over it, now they've had their say. It will blow over."

Professor Pudley was desolate. "Ella, tonight I have

done something almost criminal," he said. "I have denied everything I believe in. I have agreed to remove my books and never take them into the classroom again. I have been told I can't have the students collecting fossils. I can't discuss evolution. In other words, I have been told I cannot tell the truth to those young people."

"Robert, we can leave Santa Catarina if you think it best," she said.

"No. We can't. Our home is here. Our child will be born here. I refuse to run away."

"But how can you teach?"

"I'll do it, somehow, he said. "We'll collect butterflies and press flowers, instead of collecting fossils. At least I didn't get fired." His words were bitter.

She was horrified. "Oh — they wouldn't do that!"

His face was haggard. "They were ready to do that when they came here. It was close, Ella."

The next day he removed his books on evolution and he made a little speech to the class, noting that the next project would be a study of plants. As he spoke, he noticed a sly little grin on the face of Lewis Jedediah Wallace, who had turned up for class that morning after two days' absence.

Several evenings later, Professor Pudley was sitting in his study, musing on the unfortunate twists and turns life can take, when the doorbell rang. Almost afraid that it might be the Reverend Wallace and his committee again, he opened the door. A priest stood there. Professor Pudley was speechless for a second. The Franciscan priests kept to themselves in Santa Catarina. They taught in their own school, up near the Catholic Church, ran their own charity projects for the poorer families and seldom mingled with the Protestants. Professor Pudley finally recognized the priest as Father Peter O'Malley; he had seen him a few times, out working in the garden that surrounded the Catholic Church.

"May I come in?" Father O'Malley asked. "I would like to talk to you."

"Of course! Of course! Excuse my — my surprise. I don't believe we have met but I have seen you up at the church — out in the garden."

"Yes. I am Father O'Malley." He sat down at Professor Pudley's motion toward a chair. "I may not stay long. You see, I would like to talk to you about your science program at the public school."

Professor Pudley's welcoming smile faded. "That program has caused me great anguish. I'm sorry if it has touched your students also."

Father O'Malley interrupted. "Oh no! I'm not here to complain. I thought it was a wonderful program."

Professor Pudley just looked at him. "What did you say?"

"I said I thought it was a wonderful science program."

"You did?"

"Yes, I did. I got regular reports on your class from several of your students who are sons of my parishioners."

"I had no idea," Professor Pudley said weakly.

"I was sure you didn't," the priest said. He smiled again. "Actually, I have come to ask a favor. May I borrow one of your books? Darwin's *Descent of Man?* Now if you don't care to lend it, I will understand. One becomes attached to one's books. Especially when they are precious — and costly."

Relief flooded through Professor Pudley. "Of course you may borrow it. I am delighted. Have you read his *Origin of Species?*

I got hold of it when I was in Seminary back east. We weren't supposed to — but I read it. I would like to go through it again, after I finish the *Descent.* That is, if you don't mind lending it also.

"I don't mind a bit. In fact I am amazed. I always thought — the Catholic Church —," Professor Pudley stopped, embarrassed at his own words.

"I understand," Father O'Malley said. I was educated by Jesuits. They are scholars — sometimes at odds with the hierarchy because they study a wide range of subjects.

Too wide, sometimes!" He laughed.

Professor Pudley went into his study and came back with Darwin's book. Father OMalley took the book and ran his fingers over the fine leather binding, the gold lettering.

"I can't afford a book like this," he said. "A wonderful book, it is. Just think what Darwin went through when he published it — it was eighteen seventy-one, I believe. He died a few years later, still the center of a storm of debate, I understand."

"He's still the center of storms of debate," Professor Pudley said wryly. "Right here in Santa Catarina, as you know. But you are welcome to borrow any book I have. Our public library is — ahem — limited to say the least. A few old books on several shelves at the high school. I have a number of scientific books here, in my home."

"I appreciate that. Yes, I will borrow, thank you."

"It surprises me to find a man of the cloth — pardon the expression — interested in science — something that my own pastor feels is blasphemous," Professor Pudley said.

The priest looked at him keenly. "I have learned that an open, inquiring mind cannot be smothered, Professor Pudley."

"So you carry on two intellectual lives, sir? Your religious life on one hand, and your private mental life on the other?"

"More or less, yes. I can never abandon my Church's teachings, you understand. But I can investigate and read and study other views."

"Remarkable," mused the Professor. "Have you read Osborne on fossils? You know, Santa Catarina is a veritable treasure trove of fossils."

The priest shook his head. "My library is limited, sadly, by finances."

"I have his preliminary study here. You may borrow it too, if you wish."

Father OMalley got up to go. Darwin's *Descent* was tucked securely under his arm. "I feel I've made a friend here," he said. "A kindred spirit — intellectually. No matter how many closed minds there are in the world, thank God there are always a few open minds. Even though it can be a problem at times." He shook hands with the Professor. At the door, he stopped. "You know what really got me started on all this? Years ago when I was a student, I learned that the Church — my Church — the Church I loved and hoped to serve, to spend my life with, had set the Inquisition on Galileo. A most remarkable man, a great scientist. Mainly because he said that the earth moves around the sun! And he dared to publish his beliefs. Of course he made several great discoveries. But that statement — that earth is subject to the sun — was what ruined him. The Church forced him to deny everything. Then he was put under house arrest until he died. A blind and broken man. But you probably know the story. Anyhow, that's what got me started." He smiled again. "I won't keep you, Professor. I'll be on my way." He paused. "I'll return the book in a week or so, if that's all right."

"That's fine," Professor Pudley said. "We'll discuss it when you come back. I hope you will be able to stay awhile and have a cup of coffee with me. We can discuss the finer points of the theory."

"Thank you! I'll do that," Father OMalley said. It was the start of a close friendship that lasted thirty years.

Professor Pudley was thinking about the whole mess as he walked home from school the next evening. He was late. He had corrected papers after class hours. He strolled along, feeling better about things, thankful he still had his job. He liked Santa Catarina. The fog was rolling in off the Bay, the air smelled fresh, an ocean smell, a smell he liked. He had his job and he had found a friend he could talk to. His books were safely put away. True, he might not live long enough to see the Theory of Evolution discussed in a Santa Catarina high school classroom, but some day... some day....

He opened the door, thinking he would soon be a father, and was met by Ella Elizabeth's mother. She was upset.

"The baby — it's coming! She's upstairs and the doctor's here."

Professor Pudley bounded up the stairs. In the hall he stopped at the sound of a baby's squall. He was a father! Ella Elizabeth smiled at him weakly from the bed and his fears vanished.

Several weeks later, he was leaning over the crib admiring his new daughter. He offered a finger and she curled her rosebud hand around it. Then he offered another finger which she clung to with her other tiny hand. Then he slowly lifted his hands with the baby clinging to his fingers.

"Look Ella!" he said. "Look — see how wonderful this is. I heard that newborn babies would do this and I found it hard to believe. But it's true!"

He lifted the baby gently, so gently several inches from her bed, marveling at her instinctive ability to hang onto his fingers. He lowered her back down and a thought struck him. Just like a baby monkey clinging to its mother, he thought. But he didn't say so.

DING! DING! DING!

There was a certain musical, carefree lilt to the sound of the bells on the Santa Catarina streetcars. All the cars had them. The bells were operated with a foot pedal the conductor tromped on when the need arose — a horse and buggy on the tracks perhaps, or a kid on a bicycle.

The conductors also ding-dinged at the more important street corners and at turns in the line whether there were blind curves or not, more for the fun of it than for safety warnings. In Santa Catarina, commonly referred to as Santa Cat by the natives, streetcar lines tootled and rattled up and down Main Street and Wave Avenue downtown and out to the beaches and through the fanciest residential area. The lines all ran late during the summer tourist season when the seashore was the main attraction.

It was during the busy summer months when Mrs. Staples noticed something curious about the streetcar that ran regularly past her house. Seaview Avenue was one of the town's more prosperous streets, lined with stately Victorian homes and extensive Victorian gardens. Being a widow with little to do but observe the limited world of Santa Catarina from her lace-curtained windows, she noticed that it was always the same streetcar — Number 801 — and same driver, carefree young Harley Malone of the flaming red hair, with a hint of Irish brogue on his tongue and an eye for the ladies. But the curious part of it was about the

bell. Harley Malone rang it only in the late afternoon or evening, usually during the final seven-thirty run and...

"He rings it on the straight stretch," Mrs. Staples observed to a neighbor. "No corner, no turn or anything. Just a straight shoot. And he always rings it three times. Right out in front here. Sort of odd, isn't it?"

"Maybe just for fun," the neighbor said.

Mrs. Staples wondered. "What fun is there in that? No one out there to hear it or see it — everybody's inside getting supper or eating it. He does it all the time — like maybe it's a kind of signal or something."

"Oh you're just imagining things," the neighbor lady said impatiently. "Making mountains out of molehills. He's most likely tooting just for the fun of it — near the end of his working day. He's thinking about supper and bed after a long day."

She was right about part of it. Harley Malone was thinking about bed. And Mrs. Staples was right about the bell being a signal. Ding-ding-ding! A trolley bell message of lust right under the two ladies' noses. In fact it was going on just two doors down Seaview Avenue in one of the largest Victorian mansions on the street, set back in an acre of formal gardens.

Flora Lee Tillman lived in the mansion with her pedantic and rather stodgy husband, Wilbur, who was eighteen years older than she was. Flora Lee was twenty, the possessor of a curvy figure that even her corsets couldn't flatten, a winsome smile and a head of brown curls that was empty of the more mundane facts of life. She didn't have to worry about anything. Wilbur, who had been a confirmed bachelor until he met Flora Lee, had inherited his family's lumber mill as well as the Victorian mansion on Seaview Avenue.

At first it had seemed a marriage made in heaven to Flora Lee: the San Francisco honeymoon with a room at the Palace Hotel... the Opera, where she wore the small fur cape Wilbur bought for her... dinners in French restaurants, and the shopping! Stores that exceeded her wildest dreams.

Flora Lee, who had never been out of Santa Catarina before, spent her honeymoon in an entirely different world, a world she felt she could adjust to very well. But the honeymoon ended and Wilbur and Flora returned to reality. Santa Catarina. A small town, a summer resort town with honky tonk amusements at its famous beach, occasional traveling actors who put on a show in the barn converted to a theater, and Mrs. Borman's Sunday dinners in her boarding house.

"Now my dear," Wilbur had said on their return, "I expect you to take your rightful place here as matron of Tillman Manor." That was what his late parents had labeled the home. There was even a hand-carved redwood sign proclaiming that title at the entrance to the drive which half-circled through the grounds past life-sized iron deer statues and camellia bushes, to the front entrance which was double doors, set with etched glass plates depicting the lumber mill.

After several weeks of arranging fresh flowers in the mansion's numerous vases almost daily, serving afternoon tea to the sedate matrons of the town and trying on her fur cape — no place to wear it except church and that looked too ostentatious, Wilbur said — Flora Lee Was bored out of her empty head.

"But what will I do with myself?" she asked Wilbur. "I can't do housework or cook — the hired girls do all that."

Wilbur, who was out of town all day at the lumber mill, cleared his throat and said "I'm sure you'll find something, my dear." He had hopes for a child — an heir. That would take care of everything. But Wilbur was usually weary when he returned from work late in the day. The mill was four miles from town. He drove back and forth in a buggy. It was a long day and then there was the horse to hitch and unhitch and feed.

"Wilbur you really should hire a groom," Flora Lee suggested once. "You are so tired at the end of the day. A groom could drive you and take care of the horse."

"What? And sit out there at the mill twiddling his thumbs, doing nothing and wait for me all day?" he said.

"No sireee! It would be money wasted."

Flora Lee soon learned that Wilbur's word was law and his world was the lumber mill. He brought work home and spent hours at his desk in the library, poring over ledgers while she sat nearby, leafing through Godey's Ladies' Book or doing a bit of embroidery. What had begun in a San Francisco hotel room as an exciting intimacy was losing its luster because Wilbur was tired most of the time and his mind was always preoccupied.

"Is the mill — running all right?" she asked one evening. She bad seen it once from a safe distance, but she knew nothing about it. A jumble of smoke stacks, piles of boards and a lot of noisy machinery. Nothing she was interested in.

"What? Oh yes, my dear. Better than ever. Market for redwood is booming — a lot of building going on in San Francisco these days. Now don't you bother your pretty head about business."

She yawned that evening, rather obviously, and patted her lips with her lace handkerchief. "I believe I will retire, Wilbur. Will you be working late on your accounts?"

"Hmmm. What? Oh yes. These orders — yes, I'll be here for awhile."

Flora Lee climbed the stairs to the lonely double bed. A massive bed. With a headboard design carved out of mahogany. She was beginning to hate that bed and she had thought it so elegant at first.

The next day she went to visit her mother in the modest cottage at the other end of town.

"Mama," she said, She blushed and hesitated, not knowing quite how to proceed. "I — I wanted to ask you something."

Her mother jumped to conclusions. "You are in the family way?" she said with a smile. "Don't be shy, child. It happens."

"No Mama. It — it isn't that." She got brave and burst out with "I'm afraid I might never get that way. Wilbur is so busy at the mill and so tired all the time."

Her mother's smile faded. "I see. Well, I don't know what to tell you." She thought for a moment, then said "There is a tonic — it's said that it will help — invigorate — a person."

And that was what Flora Lee decided to try. She bought a bottle of Dr. Bush's Elixer — guaranteed to perform miracles of rejuvenation — and she persuaded Wilbur that he needed the tonic — "so you won't be so tired all the time, dear, and your work won't suffer." Work wasn't exactly what she had in mind, however.

Flora Lee gave up. She decided it was hopeless. She was trapped in a marriage that had turned to ashes as far as she was concerned. Married in June, bored to death six months later. And that was when she began riding the streetcar. Just riding at first, out of sheer boredom with her existence. She would get on at the corner down the street from the Tillman mansion, ride out to the beach, get off and sit on a bench for an hour or two, watching the waves and the seagulls. There was something fascinating about the ocean. Winter storms thrilled her. There was a little roof over the bench, built originally as a shelter from the sun for waiting streetcar customers. Now it sheltered her from the storms.

After dropping her off, the streetcar would rattle off down the street to make its regular loop trip and return in about an hour. Sometimes it made two loop trips before Flora Lee decided to get on and go home. There were few passengers in winter in the middle of the day and often she was the only one.

After a week or two the driver's curiosity got the best of him and he started a conversation. The driver was Harley Malone of the red hair and the touch of blarney in his speech, and he was curious about the shapely young matron who looked so sad, who sometimes wore a fur cape over her gowns, and who rode his car to the beach three of four times a week. Just to sit and stare at the water. She was obviously a member of the upper strata of Santa Catarina society and he wasn't. So he proceeded with caution one day to break the silence when he let her off.

"Will ye be stayin' at the beach long, today, ma'm?" he asked respectfully as he offered his arm at the steps.

Flora Lee looked at him and really saw him for the first time, red hair blazing in the sun, rugged jaw, conductor's cap in hand and a look of curious sympathy in his eyes. She smiled a little.

"I don't rightly know," she said as she stepped down and opened her umbrella.

"Well, I'll be back. Now don't you worry none about gettin' home, ma'm." He put his hat on, tipped it to her, climbed in and kicked the streetcar bell a couple of times with his foot, then grinned at her. And that was how it started.

Flora Lee thought about his Irish grin while she was lying in her lonely bed that evening. Wilbur was downstairs at his desk. When he came up to bed he asked what she had done that day.

"Oh, I rode the trolley out to the beach," she said. "The waves were grand. Big and crashing."

Wilbur grunted as he pulled off his boots. "I don't see anything unusual about that in winter time. But I really think, my dear, that you should have some of your friends in for tea more often. I would appreciate it if you would invite Judge Mills' wife — it's important to me. A business matter." He climbed ponderously into the bed.

"Of course, Wilbur," she murmured as she turned away from him. He was soon snoring.

The next day she planned the tea and sent handwritten invitations. She also took a streetcar ride to the beach, and the Irish smile was just as she had remembered it. Warm, with a hint of mischief. But respectful too. He never forgot his place.

He tipped his cap as she got in and dropped her coin in the glass box at his elbow. "To the beach, ma'm?"

She nodded. "I suppose so. It doesn't really make much difference."

"Can I say somethin' ma'm?"

"Of course."

"Did you ever ride clean to the end of the line — past the beach and out to the cliffs? I turn the car around there — it's a grand view of the water for sure."

That day she rode to the end of the line where he turned the car around. They carried on a more or less conversation about the weather, the seals riding the waves and lying on the rocks, the size of the waves, and finally she asked him what his name was. Then she told him hers. He was young, he was friendly, he was someone to talk to, and he smiled at her.

The ride to the end of the line became Flora Lee's regular route. Sometimes she stayed on and made the loop twice and she began taking the seat directly behind him so they could talk. When passengers got on they maintained silence. Before long she was calling him 'Harley' and he was addressing her as 'Miss Flora'.

She learned that he lived with his mother who was an invalid. He knew that Flora was married but she never discussed her life and he didn't ask. He didn't have to. The rides continued into the spring, their friendship grew, and then one warm day in July it happened. She was stepping out of the empty car at the end of the line, intending to wait outside while he turned the car around — it was on the turntable at the end of the line and he pushed it around by hand so it was heading back to town. He had opened the folding door for her and was standing at the foot of the steps waiting to give her a hand down, when she lost her footing and half-stepped, half-fell into his arms.

"Oh dear! I think I have twisted my ankle," she said.

His arms tightened around her. "Dear Flora," he said tenderly. She looked up at him and her hat fell to the ground. Suddenly she saw him again. Clearly. Differently. He was concerned.

"Dear Harley," she whispered.

His fingers ran gently through her brown curls. Then his arms dropped to his sides and he stepped back. I — I beg pardon, ma'm," he said. "I forgot myself."

She looked up at him. "I don't care, Harley...."

He leaned down and kissed her fiercely, passionately. And that was how her months of lonely streetcar rides developed into a love affair with clandestine meetings signaled by the trolley bell.

Ding-ding-ding! That was the signal for Flora Lee to slip out of the house after Wilbur had fallen asleep. The servants had gone home, the house was empty and Wilbur wouldn't awaken until morning. His snoring almost seemed to rattle the windows.

The bell signal preceded Harley's final stop for the night at the Car Barn downtown where he left the streetcar, then walked swiftly through the darkness up to Seaview Avenue. There his pace slowed as he surveyed the street to make sure no one watching as he entered the landscaped grounds of Tillman Manor. Once through the gates, he slipped quietly down a brick path that wound through camellia bushes and past the iron deer statues to the rose pergola at the side of the house. There, waiting for him, was Flora Lee. Not much conversation took place. When they spoke it was in whispers.

"We shouldn't be here, meeting this way," he said.

She put her finger to his lips. "I told you I don't care," she said. "You don't know what it's like — living in that — that house."

"But your — your husband ...."

"He doesn't give a snap of his fingers about me," she said. "All he cares about is his business."

Flora Lee was discovering passion. She pulled his head down until their lips met and she twined her arms around his neck. Harley's initial reluctance melted. His hands were busy with the fastenings of her robe which fell open, then off, revealing a thin cotton nightgown. He drew her down gently to the wood bench in the pergola. She lay back on the boards and hardly felt them.

"Wait," he whispered. He folded his uniform coat, then his trousers, and placed them under her for padding.

The next hour passed all too quickly for Flora Lee,

who was experiencing carnal delights far beyond her wildest dreams.

Finally Harley extricated himself. "I must go," he said. "My Mother will be worryin'."

"I wish you didn't have to," she said.

"But what about your husband?"

"Oh he's sound asleep. Snoring. Dead to the world. Dead to me." There was an edge of bitterness to her words.

"Look, little flower," he said. Flora Lee had told him that her name meant flower. "When I can make it, I'll ring three times. That way, you'll always know."

He dressed hastily and after one more passionate embrace, slipped off through the garden. Flora Lee was soon back in bed listening to Wilbur's snores.

For the next two months they met two or three times a week. August and September, mild months in Santa Catarina. Flora Lee bloomed. There was no need for her to take the trolley rides now, and even Wilbur commented on how cheerful and contented she seemed.

The lovers had a couple of narrow escapes. One night the hired girls stayed late at a kitchen task and when Flora crept downstairs they heard the front door open. One of the girls came out to see and caught Flora just stepping off the porch to greet Harley who was standing by the iron deer statues.

"Oh, Mrs. Tillman!" the girl said. I heard the door and I wondered who — at this time of night — I didn't know —." The girl was flustered.

Harley stepped quickly behind the larger of the deer — fortunately the shadows hid him — and Flora Lee recovered from the shock enough to say "Oh, I have a headache and sometimes fresh air helps." She seated herself on one of the porch chairs and added "You may go home now." The girls left shortly afterward and Flora Lee scurried out to the pergola.

That night she and Harley decided that he should enter the grounds from the alley which ran behind Tillman Manor and the adjoining homes.

"Them deer are right handy, little flower," he said with a laugh. "That girl almost saw me."

And then one night Wilbur awoke with a gas attack, noticed her absence and began calling for her. They heard him. Flora Lee straightened her nightgown, slipped on her robe and was back inside the house before Wilbur came down to the kitchen for baking soda.

"Where were you?" he wanted to know.

"I had a headache. I came down for a glass of water."

Wilbur was so involved with his own troubles that he didn't stop to wonder why she hadn't gone to the upstairs bathroom where there was a cup and several faucets.

The next day after this aborted meeting, Flora Lee decided to take a streetcar ride, something she hadn't done for awhile. Waiting at the regular stop down at the corner from Tillman Manor, she was surprised to see a new sign in the front window of the approaching car. In bold black letters on white cardboard it said FLOWER.

"Like it?".. Harley was grinning at her.

"Oh Harley," she breathed. They had to be careful. An old man was sitting in the rear of the car.

"I have to take it down when I go into the car barn," Harley said. "But during the day it reminds me of you, little flower."

October brought cooler days and evenings to Santa Catarina, and a special problem to the lovers. It was cold in the pergola. The trysts were considerably shorter and caused Harley to wear his overcoat and Flora Lee to put a coat over her robe. Not exactly the most romantic climate conducive to passionate embraces. After two such chilly meetings Flora Lee had an inspiration.

"We can go into the carriage house," she suggested with chattering teeth.

"Right-O," Harley agreed. "We've got to do something, pet, or we'll freeze solid."

So they began meeting in the carriage house and Flora Lee was even able to smuggle a quilt from the house to make their straw bed warmer. But it was the alley-carriage house approach that almost brought disaster to the lovers.

One cold moonlit night when Harley was making his way carefully up the alley, Mrs. Staples happened to look out her bedroom window and saw him. She didn't know who it was, but the sight of the dark figure slipping through the shadows alarmed her and she watched until he turned into the Tillman estate. The following morning she paid an early call to Wilbur before he left for work.

"I saw him enter the carriage house drive," she reported. "Mr. Tillman, I felt it my duty to warn you — there may have been a robbery committed in your carriage house or there may be some dreadful person — a tramp perhaps — staying there."

Wilbur, who was eating breakfast, promised to look into it and she finally left. Flora Lee had come downstairs in time to hear most of it.

Terror raced through her veins but she took a deep breath and remained calm.

"She's a scarey old woman," she said. "It's probably nothing."

Wilbur finished his coffee. "I'll take a look before I go."

While he was getting his overcoat and business papers together, Flora Lee slipped out to the carriage house to conceal the quilt beneath the loose hay. When Wilbur entered, she was standing outside as if waiting for him. After a cursory look upstairs in the loft, he grumbled a bit about old ladies seeing things, then led the horse out, harnessed it and took off in the buggy. Flora Lee could breathe easily again. Almost.

That afternoon she waited at the streetcar stop for Harley. The car was empty when it rumbled up to the stop and Harley got out to help her up the steps. She was crying.

"Harley dear — it's all over." And she proceeded to tell him.

They both knew it would be folly to continue their trysts. Discovery was inevitable.

"Ay — I knew it was too good to be true," he said. He hesitated. "Ye wouldn't consider — ah no, ye wouldn't. Ye couldn't."

"You mean leave Wilbur? — and...."

"Ay. I was thinkin'of it. But there's me mom as well. No, it wouldn't do." He looked back at Tillman Manor sitting elegant and austere behind the camellia bushes and lawn. "Ye can't leave all that," he said.

It was a quiet ride that day, once around the car's regular route. A few passengers got on and off but Flora Lee was oblivious to them. She sat staring out the window, in her usual seat behind Harley.

The last time, she thought. This is the last time I'll see him. She wanted to memorize the back of his head, the way the fringe of red hair bordered the back of his cap, the width of his shoulders in the dark blue uniform coat. That coat she had used as a pillow. Those shoulders she had clung to.

So she sat in quiet desperation, knowing that she wouldn't ride the streetcar again; it would be too painful. Better to cut everything off now.

And then, as the streetcar turned away from the shoreline and started back toward the residential streets, there was Mrs. Staples waiting on a corner. She climbed aboard.

"Mrs. Tillman! What a lovely surprise," she said. She plumped herself down next to Flora Lee and proceeded to relate in dramatic detail her sighting of the furtive figure in the alley. "And you know," she paused for effect, "I am just sure that he entered your carriage house — as I told Mr. Tillman."

Flora Lee tried to look polite and interested but failed miserably. She murmured something about a headache and by the time the car reached Seaview Avenue she was sure she had one coming on.

"Oh dear! Here we are," trilled Mrs. Staples.

Harley brought the car to a stop, worked the lever that opened the folding door, and got up to offer a helping hand as Mrs. Staples stepped down.

"Oh thank you!" she bubbled. "Such a polite young man." Suddenly she stopped and looked at him. "You haven't rung the bell," she said. "You know — the three rings. Almost always three. I am so used to hearing that bell. I always wondered why you rang it on the straight stretch — the middle of the block. Habit I guess. Well, goodbye."

Flora Lee got up slowly and stepped down carefully. Harley offered his arm but she didn't take it. She felt that if she did, she would be powerless to let go of it — the arm that had swept her off her feet so many times into a passionate embrace.

She looked up at him just once, as if to etch on her memory forever every rugged plane of his face, then she turned away.

"Habit," she said softly. Then "Goodbye."

She sighed and entered the gates of Tillman Manor without looking back.

Life changed on Seaview Avenue after that last streetcar ride. Harley no longer rang the bell in the middle of the block and Mrs. Staples felt a pang of guilt, wondering if what she had said made the difference. She had kind of enjoyed hearing it, she confided to her neighbor.

Flora Lee went on serving her teas and arranging flowers for about eight months when her first child — a son and heir — was born. Wilbur Lemuel Tillman the Second. He was a handsome baby, he yelled a lot and kept his mother busy. And his mother fancied that when she held him in the sunlight, she could detect a faint hint of red in his hair.

GROWING UP

Dr. Matthew Davis was uncomfortable. Not puzzled exactly, but bothered by feelings he couldn't quite identify. Feelings of doubt. Uncertainty. And through his years of medical practice in Santa Catarina, he had learned to pay attention to what he called his 'hunches'.

He had just finished examining Dale Stanton. Beautiful girl. Age sixteen. Daughter of D. J. Stanton II, who was a pillar of the small California coastal town of Santa Catarina.

The girl was pregnant, and entirely ignorant of that fact. She was sixteen.

What had gone on here, Dr. Davis wondered as be washed his hands carefully in a disinfectant soap while the girl got dressed.

He wiped his hands on a towel and went out to the waiting room to tell her father who had brought her there.

D. J. Stanton sat in one of the stiff chairs, the picture of solid civic leader and prominent businessman. He looked up at Dr. Davis. "Well?"

The doctor didn't believe in softening blows. "Mr. Stanton, your daughter is pregnant. About two months along, I would judge."

If Stanton was surprised, he didn't show it. "You're sure? Then get rid of it," he growled.

"Yes, I am sure. And she is not aware of it."

"Don't tell her," Stanton ordered. "No need to upset her or her mother. I rely on your professional discretion." Then he said angrily, "That damned young whelp! I ought to fire him!"

"Bring her back tomorrow morning. Eight o'clock," the doctor said.

Dale, dressed and looking pale, came into the waiting room. "Well?" she inquired.

Dr. Davis cleared his throat. "A slight problem. Minor surgery tomorrow morning."

Dale looked worriedly from the doctor to her father.

"Don't worry, girl," Stanton said. "Dr. Davis knows his business." He took her arm and they left.

Dr. Davis sat down at his desk, wondering why he felt so uncomfortable about this whole thing. Abortions were not against the law in California in 1890.

God knows I'm not worried about the surgery, he thought. *I've done enough abortions to know what I'm doing. And I'll get Eleanor to assist.* Eleanor was his wife; he could depend on her not to talk.

But why did he feel so puzzled about this entire case? The chauffeur? That young fellow? Of course it was logical. But there was something about the whole thing that troubled him. For one thing, he felt that Dale was not the kind of girl who would allow intimacies on a casual basis. He was sure of that, having known her from birth and through numerous childhood diseases. Measles. Chickenpox. Mumps. Sore throats and colds. He had seen a lot of her during her growing up years and she had always impressed him as shy, withdrawn. The kind of girl who always bad her nose in a book. Who got good grades at school. Too immature to be interested in boys. Too timid to even look at a boy.

Dale and her father rode home in silence in the Autobat, the family's electric automobile, driven by Jeff Hunter, chauffeur and handyman. Once she started to speak but her father cut her off: "Nothing serious, my dear," he said. "And we must not worry Mother with it."

Dale was an only child. Beautiful already, although she was only fifteen years old. She had everything a girl could wish for in 1892. Frilly gowns, a fur coat, and access to her father's auto with a chauffeur to drive her.

Jeff Hunter was in his late twenties, a sturdy young man in a well-pressed uniform. He kept the Autobat polished and running, re-charging the batteries regularly after every forty-five miles or so. And he was the only young man in Santa Catarina who had got to know Dale Stanton. She seldom laughed but sometimes he could make her smile when they were alone. But even then, he noticed an underlying sadness about her and he felt sorry for the lonely girl whose eyes never smiled.

To Santa Catarina she was Dale Stanton, the shy, quiet young girl who was named for her father who had always wanted a son but got a daughter instead. The daughter of a mother who was a semi-invalid, unable to have another child. The daughter of a father who dealt in properties and made a lot of money; a fullblooded, middle-aged man of hearty appetites whose wife had retreated into her own private bedroom world from which she seldom appeared. A world of dinner trays with servants waiting on her, bathing her and dressing her, on the top floor of the Stanton mansion.

Dale had invited schoolmates home once or twice.

"Your Mother isn't well — she can't stand the noise and goings-on," the housekeeper, Myrtle Jones, warned.

And when Stanton came home that evening he heard about it. "Those youngsters make too much noise," he said sternly. "They run up and down the stairs and through the halls — no upbringing — no manners — more work for Mrs. Jones and too much noise for your Mother. Dale, we simply cannot have it. You see them at school. That should be enough."

The twelve tall-ceilinged rooms with their damask drapes and heavy walnut furniture were lonely caverns where Dale lost herself in books. Her dutiful visits to her mother were brief, restrained. Mrs. Stanton was never allowed to forget that she had produced a daughter instead of a son.

By the time Dale was fifteen she had began to mature. Her child's shape was filling out, rosebud breasts were blossoming, her matchstick figure was softening. She was in bed reading, one evening, when her father came into her room. He didn't knock. He just opened the door, stepped inside and closed it.

Surprised, she looked up. "Yes, Father?"

He pulled his silk dressing gown closer around his body and sat down on the edge of her bed. "I — I wanted to talk to you, Dale," he said heavily. He rarely called her Dale. Usually it was 'Girl'. Unless something was wrong.

Worried thoughts flew through her brain. Was it something she had done? She couldn't think of anything. Was her mother worse? She waited for him to speak.

"Girl, you are growing up," he said. "Becoming a young lady." He paused.

"There are certain things...."

She felt herself blushing. She put her book down. "Yes, I know, Father. Mother had Mrs. Jones speak to me about — about it. I understand. You don't have to...."

He reached over to stroke her hair. She was surprised. He had never done that before.

"Perhaps I haven't shown you the affection I could have," he said. His hand, still moving, went from her hair to her cheek, then to her shoulder. A flood of warmth went through Dale. He did love her, after all. She had never believed he cared about her.

His hand lingered on her shoulder, stroking gently, then moved down to her breast.

She drew a sharp breath.

"Don't be afraid," he said. "It's part of your growing up, girl."

His hand slid beneath the neckline of her thin nightgown. She shrank back.

"Father...."

"Don't say anything." His mouth was on her neck. She smelled the lotion he used when he shaved. Bay rum, he called it.

He was breathing heavily. She felt bewitched, bewildered, yet grateful for his affection. He did love her, after all.

He reached up and turned off the light. Then he drew the bed covers down into a bunch below her feet. Without a word he lifted her nightgown. "Take it off." A command.

Wondering, half terrified, yet longing for his attention, she struggled to obey. When she lay there, naked in the moonlight, confused, yet afraid not to please him, he began to play with her body. His hands. His fingers. His mouth. Once she gasped "Father!"

He silenced her with a finger on her lips. "Part of growing up," he said. "Part of your growing up."

He didn't rape her, that first time. And when he had finished with her, he said sternly, "This is something we don't talk about — not to anyone, girl. Remember that. Not to anyone. It's a private part of your growing up. Do you understand?"

She couldn't speak. She nodded her head.

When he had gone, she turned on the light and looked at herself in the long mirror on the marble-topped dresser. There were red welts on her chest and abdomen where his whiskers had rubbed. Her breasts were sore. An unfamiliar moisture between her legs where his fingers — she pushed the thought away. Growing up? Was that what this was? She slipped quietly into her bathroom, feeling the need to wash herself, wash all of it away. Hours later, she finally fell asleep.

Dale cried the first time he raped her. "It hurts," she sobbed.

"Hush girl. The hurt will go away." And it did.

She got used to him coming to her room every few nights. She got used to the caresses, the bruises, and his thrusting body on hers. When she thought about it, which was not too often, for she usually pushed the thoughts away, she wondered why this secret ritual had to be part of growing up. Yet it was the first time one of her parents had paid any special attention to her. She was tempted to discuss it with her friend, Melanie Harris, but she was afraid to. He — the powerful father figure — always warned her not to talk about it. So she endured in the ignorance of a young girl of the 1890s. And he was her father; he called her his dear girl, and she was starved for the affection he showed her.

A year passed. Dale was sixteen and she had become more of a recluse than ever. Her friendship with Melanie Harris had withered into nothing more than a casual hello in passing. Dale attended classes, completed the lessons and moved through her days automatically. At night she had troubled thoughts, disturbing dreams, wakeful hours. Deep inside she instinctively felt guilt, revulsion. She felt trapped and helpless.

Someone else was troubled about Dale. The live-in housekeeper, Mrs. Myrtle Jones, had observed the girl's withdrawal into solitude and seclusion. She felt sorry for the girl, yet she hesitated to say anything. She had a good job and she wanted to keep it. Finally, she took it upon herself to mention it delicately to her employer. She learned immediately, not to her surprise, that her concern was unwelcome.

"Mrs. Jones, you are employed to over-see my house, not my family," he stated sternly. She retreated to the kitchen.

But then, after several months, something happened. As part of her duties, Mrs. Jones also supervised the girl who came weekly to do the family laundry. She noticed the absence of certain soft, folded cloths used by Dale during her monthly periods. But Mrs. Jones was afraid to question it. Perhaps Dale was disposing of them instead of having them laundered? It was possible. Besides, it was really none of her business. She was the housekeeper. She must mind her own business or lose her job. So she said nothing.

A month passed. Then one morning Dale, who was

eating breakfast alone as usual, almost immediately vomited it up. Instead of going to school that day she went back to bed, complaining of nausea and headache. When her father came home from his office and learned that she was ill, he went directly up to her room.

"What's the matter?" he asked, although he already had a premonition. "How do you feel?"

Dale was touched by his concern and she had no idea what was ailing her. She tried to make light of it. "Probably a touch of dyspepsia, Father."

"Stay home tomorrow," he ordered. "I'll take you to see Dr. Davis."

She dared to question him: "I'll probably be better by tomorrow, Father. Do I have to see the doctor?"

"Yes," he said firmly.

During the visit to the doctor's office Stanton sat alone in the waiting room and he seemed not too surprised by the news that Dale was pregnant. He took it calmly but his brain was going ninety miles an hour. Suddenly he burst out with "That damned young cur! I ought to shoot him!"

The doctor looked puzzled. He had questioned Dale carefully while examining her, and he had his own ideas.

"The chauffeur, of course," Stanton said quickly. "We will have to get rid of it. The pregnancy, I mean. How soon can you —?"

Dr. Davis nodded. This wasn't the first 'catch colt' he had aborted in Santa Catarina.

"Tomorrow. The sooner the better Mr. Stanton. Does Mrs. Stanton...."

"No, of course not! It would be too upsetting — might kill her. I don't intend to tell her. And I might say that I rely on your...."

Dr. Davis nodded. "Yes, of course."

The day following the physical examination, Dale went back to Dr. Davis for 'treatment', then she was taken home for bed rest and recuperation. She accepted the information that she had something with a long Latin name, something that would keep her in bed for a few days. Two weeks later, she was declared well enough to return to school.

The most surprising thing to her was that her father ceased his nighttime visits. At first, she almost missed them. It had been a form of affection, something she had experienced seldom in her life.

When she started back to school, her father insisted that she should not walk the seven blocks to and from. "Jeff Hunter will drive you," he ordered. And that became the routine.

Jeff would tip his cap and offer his arm when she stepped up into the electric car. Their conversations, awkward at first, evolved into lengthy, friendly exchanges. One day she asked him about his parents.

"Both died in the diphtheria epidemic a few years back," he said briefly.

"Oh Jeff, how awful!" And she started calling him Jeff. "How old were you?" she asked.

"Fourteen."

"But how did you — manage?" she wanted to know. "Left all alone? Did you have grandparents? Or other relatives?"

"Nope. I'm alone. I did odd jobs — worked for old man Carter for my room and board. I made out. This job for your father is fine. I'm saving a little money every month."

Dale looked at him with new eyes. "Oh Jeff," she put her hand on his arm, "you deserve a lot of credit. It must have been very hard for you."

He looked at her. A long look. "You don't have it easy, yourself. Miss Stanton," he added properly.

She frowned. "No — call me Dale," she insisted.

That was the beginning of Dale's romance with Jeff Hunter, although it was a romance that neither of them had intended or even dreamed of. Two lonely people... Dale's excuses to run errands in the Autobat... her frequent visits to the Stanton kitchen when he was eating his meals. The 'errands' often took them the long way, out around the Beach Drive that bordered Santa Catarina.

"Stop here," she would command. When he parked, if no one was around, she would slip out of the back seat and into the seat beside him. She trembled with longing the first time he kissed her. Yet, she thought, it was different. Not like the forceful caresses of her father. Jeff was hesitant. Tender. Delicate with her.

"We shouldn't be here, doing this," he would say. "Your father...."

She murmured, "I don't care, Jeff. I want you to kiss me."

At first he hesitated, torn between desire and duty, but before long be hesitated no longer.

It went on that way all through the summer vacation. Mrs. Jones probably suspected although she was fearful to say anything.

Then, soon after a day when Dale burst into tears and told Jeff she couldn't stand it any longer, they drove off in the Autobat to Salinas where they found a Justice of the Peace who had never heard of D. J. Stanton II. He married them. They drove back to Santa Catarina and faced the music. Surprisingly, D. J. Stanton got over his anger sooner than they expected.

BIRDS FLY FREE

Santa Catarina in the mid-1890s was a town that was hard on girls. Boys, growing up, had all kinds of freedom. They could hang their clothes on a hickory limb and jump into the river naked on a hot day, or disappear for hours to play keepsies with their marbles without anyone worrying, or walk down to the wharf to watch the fishing boats unload. They experimented with cornhusk cigarettes behind somebody's barn, and had contests to see who could pee the longest distance. A group of boys even hid and watched the forbidden ceremony when old man Alvarez was hanged for horse stealing. They lost their dinners later but could brag that they had seen the hanging.

Girls in the small California coastal town could do none of those things, even had they wanted to. They were under constant guard while growing up, to be 'ladies'. They learned to cook, to sew, crochet doilies and keep house. Life was distinctly unfair to females, young and old; they missed a lot of the fun and got a lot of the drudgery.

The rare female who rebelled and managed to become a tom-boy, was generally looked upon with compressed lips, raised eyebrows, much shaking of heads and the observation that "Maybe marriage will settle her down."

That was why friends and neighbors of the O'Fallons were shocked when Kevin O'Fallon began taking his oldest child fishing with him along the Santa Catarina River. The oldest O'Fallon was a girl, Lily. So were the next three children. Lily was eleven years old.

"I guess he got tired of waiting for a boy to grow up," commented Mayor Marvin Farris who lived across Cliff Street from the O'Fallons. The O'Fallon boys were ages two, three and four, too young to be anything but nuisances on fishing trips.

Kevin's wife, Louise O'Fallon, wasn't happy about Lily going fishing with her father.

"People will talk," she insisted. "Kevin, it just isn't right for a girl to go off fishing — not even with her father! "

"Lily enjoys it," he said. "She caught some fish. There's nothin' wrong with that."

"But she's a girl," Louise insisted. "It isn't natural for a girl to be doing what boys and men do."

Kevin ignored the complaints. He even began to let Lily come down to his gun repair shop to watch him work. She was interested and she made herself useful in small ways.

"Guns! Kevin O'Fallon what crazy idea will you come up with next! I absolutely forbid it."

Louise raised such a storm that Kevin had to quit taking Lily to the shop but he still took her fishing, and she learned a lot about how to catch a trout in the river which ran through the town. They would pack a lunch, the two of them, and go off in the morning, always on Saturdays. Sundays were reserved for Mass at the Catholic Church followed by a big Sunday dinner cooked by Louise, and visits from relatives and friends.

Lily was a pretty little thing. She took after her father with his dark hair and striking blue eyes. Louise O'Fallon, after six children and two miscarriages, was sallow looking with sandy hair turning gray and faded eyes that always looked tired. Lily also had an active brain. She wanted to know how guns worked and on her few visits to the shop, before her mother put a stop to it, she even dreamed of working with her father.

"I could learn the business, Papa and help you. I could keep books and do things like that — sweep out, even."

Kevin looked at her fondly and smiled. Lily was his favorite, although he wouldn't ever admit it, not even to himself. When she was born, his first born, he had looked down at the tiny mite and lost his heart. Two more girls were born who survived, then the three boys, and he loved them all. But he loved Lily the best.

They had special times together on the fishing trips. Once, walking quietly, they went further up the river to a place where he showed her a water ouzel dipping and bobbing in a riffle. Lily watched the bird, enchanted. Suddenly it darted beneath the overhanging river bank.

"It's got a nest under there," her father said. They approached carefully and he lifted the ferns to show her a mossy nest with pale eggs. "We mustn't touch anything or frighten the bird," he said.

They sat for hours with their lines in the water, watching great gray herons wade in a pool a short distance away.

"Look Papa! He caught a fish!" she cried one day. "It's easy for him", she said with a smile. "He doesn't need a pole or anything."

The river pools where the largest trout lurked, the rippling song of the larks in the meadows near the river, a deer drinking warily at the river's edge, a raccoon waddling off into the bushes, all were part of Lily's growing-up education.

Once she sighed and said, "Papa, I wish I could be a naturalist. But I'm a girl. Maybe I could be a teacher and teach some kind of nature class. I would love to do that."

Kevin laughed, then grew serious. "Girls don't teach those things, Lily. You had better plan on marrying an outdoorsman."

She sighed. "An outdoorsman who goes fishing and hunting and camping in the hills. Maybe I will."

"I declare Kevin! You spoil that child," Louise would

say.

But the truth was, Lily was one of those rare children who cannot be spoiled. She seemed wise beyond her years, even when she was only four years old.

"Four going on forty," Kevin would say with a grin. There was a special bond between the two of them and Louise tried not to resent it but she did.

Kevin started taking Lily fishing when she was eight. He showed her the best holes where trout lurked, how to bait her hook with a grasshopper or a worm, and how to clean the fish she caught. She performed each task diligently, but her greatest interest was in the birds they watched as they fished.

One day while approaching the river bank they came across a bird's nest that had fallen from a branch. There were three baby birds in it. Lily put one finger down close to them and three hungry beaks opened simultaneously.

"Papa — can I take them home and feed them?" she asked excitedly.

Kevin looked around. "I'll tell you what — we'll wait awhile and see if the mother bird comes back. If she does, we'll put them up in the tree — they fell from that branch up there — see? That one has a fork in it."

They waited at a distance, watching carefully for the mother bird but she failed to return.

Kevin carried the nest and baby birds home in his hat and Lily skipped alongside, overjoyed. She dug worms in the garden and squashed them so the baby birds could eat them. When they got older, she borrowed a cage for them and when they could fly she let them go, one by one.

"Papa! Look at them fly! It's like they knew how to, all along."

"Maybe they do, Lily. It's* born in them I guess."

"Now they are free," she said. "Oh Papa — I wish I could fly!"

One day Louise approached Kevin. "She's almost twelve, Kevin," she said. "It's time she began acting like a girl."

"Oh now Louise, a little harmless fishing never hurt anyone," Kevin said. "Remember, I make our living from fishermen and hunters."

His shop catered to all the sportsmen in the area for miles around. He made a modest living but he loved what he did and was never more content than when he was repairing a shotgun or advising a fisherman what bait to use. But Louise was determined. She had a private talk with the nun principal of the Catholic school Lily attended. Lily was a bright child, her grades were good. Mother Mary of Assisi was slightly shocked to hear that Lily actually went fishing. That certainly was no proper activity for a young lady, she agreed. Arrangements were made for Lily to attend special religious classes on Saturdays.

Lily couldn't understand why she had to go to those classes. She went to Catholic school all week and to church on Sundays.

"Why Papa? Why!" She was almost in tears. He was going fishing without her.

Kevin sighed. "Maybe it's for the best, Lily. Mama wants you to grow up to be a lady and ladies don't crawl along river banks to catch trout." The fishing trips ended that year when Lily was twelve.

However, Louise wasn't satisfied yet. She dropped strong hints that Lily would make a fine nun and she mentioned that possibility at every opportunity, both to Lily and to the nuns and priests at the church.

At first, Lily was bewildered. "But Mama, I don't want to leave home," she would protest.

"Lily, you are too young to know what you want," was the answer. "You would be a very lucky girl indeed to be offered such an opportunity to serve God and the church."

Like drops of water on stone, Louise worked on the child for the next three years and Kevin was helpless to prevent it. He had long before given up any hope of Lily working with him in his shop.

And then one day Louise told him that Lily had been accepted by the Holy Sisters Order in Michigan. "Just think,

Kevin! One of our children serving the church. She's a lucky girl and you should be a proud man!"

"Does she want to go?" he asked after a long silence

Louise shrugged her thin shoulders. She had a way of answering difficult questions with another question. "Does any fifteen year old girl know what she wants?

Kevin's shoulders drooped. Then he tried again. "Louise, she's such a help to you with the younguns. I don't think she should leave home yet. She's only fifteen — she's never been away from us — never been out of Santa Catarina. She could be awfully homesick back there, so far away."

"We can't deny the church," Louise said. "They'll be good to her. She can come back home if she doesn't take to it. She won't make her final vows for years — there's plenty of time for her to decide back there."

Lily appeared in the doorway while they were talking. "Do I have to go?" she asked, almost crying.

Kevin couldn't speak over the lump in his throat but Louise answered. "No one *has* to do anything," she said quickly. "But you should be honored to be offered such a chance — to serve the church. You're a lucky girl, Lily."

Lily nodded.

Kevin spoke up: "If it isn't right for you — God forgive me for the thought," he added with a quick glance at Louise " — you can come back home, darling." It was the first time he had ever called one of his daughters darling.

Lily looked at him. Her eyes were pleading. "Are you sure, Papa? 1 can come home if I don't like it?"

"You have my word," he said. "We'll come get you."

"But you must give it a try — remember that! You can't get back there and turn right around and come home," Louise said.

"No Mama."

"Mother Mary has made all the arrangements for you to leave next week on the train. One of the nuns will go with you, Lily."

Lily's face was white. "So soon?" she cried.

"My God, Louise, you sure are pushing it fast," Kevin said angrily.

It was all arranged. There was nothing he could do. Louise had engineered the whole thing. In spite of Kevin's reverence and respect for the church, a wave a bitterness swept over him. He knew what would happen. They would get Lily back there and they would play on her conscience; she would never come home again. Her dark curls would be cut off, down to her scalp. Her developing young body would be encased in layers of heavy wool, shutting out sunlight, shutting out life itself. He wasn't sure he could ever forgive Louise for doing this to Lily. Ever. He would have to go to confession soon. There was a bitter taste of brass in his mouth as he left the house to go to his shop.

The next days passed slowly, sadly, with Lily telling her teachers and school friends goodbye. It was a time for goodbyes, because school was letting out for the summer. Lily's last year of high school would be taken back in Michigan behind high gray stone walls, inside buildings constructed of the same stone, with a class of girls like herself, postulants.

While Lily was saying her goodbyes that week, Louise O'Fallon was proudly spreading the word: "Yes, our girl has decided to answer the call — she'll leave Friday — Sister Josephine is traveling with her on the train."

Kevin spent a bitter week in silence. Confession didn't help. The priest tried to comfort him and he heard the same phrases Louise had used: "proud father"... "noble calling"... "honor to serve the church".... But every time Kevin looked at Lily that week he could feel his heart breaking. She was so young, so innocent, and she was trying to be cheerful, to make the best of it. He began to blame himself. *I should have stood up to Louise before it was too late*, he thought. But it had started years before with the fishing trips. Damn the fishing trips!

Friday arrived. The Friday that Kevin had wished would never come. The train left early, eight o'clock, from the Santa Catarina Depot, for San Francisco. A buggy, driven by one of the priest's assistants, arrived with Sister Josephine, to pick up Lily and her parents. There wasn't room for all the children, Lily kissed them goodbye and climbed in, to sit between her father and mother. A little straw hat covered her dark curls and she was wearing a cape that Louise had cut down from one of her own. She looked back once at her brothers and sisters standing in the doorway, and a tear slid down her cheek.

At the Depot, a grim and silent Kevin helped her down from the buggy. He pressed a gold coin into her hand "If you need anything...," he said.

Louise hugged her and wiped her own eyes, seeming to realize for the first time that her child was really leaving.

The conductor yelled "All aboard!" Kevin placed Lily's small suitcase at the top of the steps and turned to Lily who was clinging to his hand. Sister Josephine had already climbed the steps. She was anxious to get on board, to avoid last minute demonstrations of sorrow.

Lily stood there, holding her father's hand. She looked up at him. "Papa, won't I ever see you again?" Then the train whistled, she went up the steps without looking back, and went inside.

The O"Fallons rode home in the buggy in silence so thick that it smothered any thought of conversation. Louise and Kevin entered their home and were immediately surrounded by the younger children who clamored for information. Was it a big train? Did it have a whistle? Did it have a conductor? Where did Lily sit in it? And so on.

Louise answered them but Kevin went out again, slamming the door. Louise moved quickly to open it and call after him "Where are you going?"

He turned to face her. "Down to the shop. I've got to get away from here."

Louise looked at him, the thin set of his mouth, his rigid shoulders, his eyes cold as ice.

"You should be a very proud man today, Kevin O'Fallon," she said.

"I'm not," he said shortly. "God forgive me, woman.

I'm trying not to hate you."

Lily never came home again. Kevin and Louise's marriage survived in name only. He slept on a couch in the dining room until the day be died. Louise became more and more devout as she grew older. Mass every morning. And to anyone who would listen, she would tell them proudly: "My oldest daughter is a nun. Her name is Sister Francis."

Kevin and Louise died, their other children moved away one by one, and eventually there were only a few oldtimers who remembered the gunsmith who took his daughter fishing.

In the late 1930s a small item appeared in the Santa Catarina newspaper. Three paragraphs on a page with the obituaries:

"Sister Francis, the eldest daughter of the late Mr. and Mrs. Kevin O'Fallon, died on September 12 of this year in the Sacred Mother Convent in Wisconsin.

"Sister Francis was born in Santa Catarina and attended school here before entering the Order which was based in Michigan at that time. She is survived by a number of nieces and nephews.

"When she made her perpetual vows, she chose the name Francis in honor of St. Francis of Assissi. She was known for her interest in wild birds and she established a feeding station at the Convent which was located on a well-known bird migratory route. The station was known to bird researchers nationwide."

A RIVER STORY

When they climbed off the wagon in Santa Catarina, Mo Dutton looked down at his wife and smiled.

"It's not a big town Amelia, but maybe you'll like it better than the city."

She smiled up at him. He was tall, she was short. "As long as you can get a job and Tyler can go to school next fall."

Tyler, their four-year-old son, was clinging to her hand.

"If they won't let Tyler in, we'll leave." Mo promised.

Mo was black. All black except for teeth that gleamed white when he smiled. Amelia was white, blonde, and Tyler was an in-between color, tan.

The wagon ride to Santa Catarina cost them two dollars, almost all the money they had. They came down the California coast from The City. For the first fifty miles, Mo trundled their bedding, cooking utensils and clothing in a wheelbarrow and they walked, camping along the way. When a farmer with an empty wagon offered a ride for two bucks, they took it gratefully.

At first, the town went into shock when it saw them. It was 1890 and there were no blacks in Santa Cat, as the natives called their town. There were a few Orientals — they built the railroad and worked as servants for the wealthy families. There were Italians — they farmed and raised fruit, made wine and some were in the bootleg business. But there were no blacks. And the idea of a black and white combination was unthinkable.

"It's not natural!" exclaimed old Mrs. Potter when she caught a glimpse of them. That was several weeks after they arrived, because at first they camped outside the town limits while Mo hunted for a job. Finally, he was hired by the school principal as janitor. And that set off fireworks in the principal's home.

"She's white! And how could she marry that —, that —, and why did they have to come to Santa Catarina?" demanded Mrs. Preston, wife of the school principal. The Principal was calm. He had a budget; he had hired a man, cheap, to do all the dirty work.

"Who knows, my dear," he answered. "Maybe for a job. He's going to be the janitor at the school. Old man Smith died, you know, and the school's in terrible shape. We need someone."

Mrs. Preston looked at him in horror. "You mean to say you hired him? You — oh I can't believe it!" She shook her head. "I don't think it's right to have a black man around our children, not even in a janitor job."

"Well, no one else wanted the job and we had to get someone. The school is in bad shape — Old Smith got so he couldn't do much the last year or so. It needs a complete going over. Steps are sagging, paint peeling off — that and more. He won't have anything to do with the children, Martha."

"Well, I don't think it's a good idea at all! None of the women in town will want to have anything to do with her. I sure won't ! And where are they going to live? Not near me!"

Indeed, living was a problem for the Duttons. Word got around fast because Santa Cat was still a small town. They were camping out while they looked for a place and Mo walked miles. Finally he found one. Surprisingly, it was near where they camped, on Farmer Shelby's chicken farm, at the edge of the river.

"It's a rough old cabin but I can fix it up," Mo told

Amelia. "A few boards missing, three rooms, no water — you'll have to carry it from the river but maybe I can put in a pipe. And there are fish in the river — we won't go hungry."

There was a cookstove standing on bricks, a rusted tin roof and an outhouse behind the cabin. Amelia looked, then said "I don't care, if you can make it liveable," and Mo got to work.

When his neighbors complained, Farmer Shelby shrugged his shoulders. "Never thought I'd rent that place out. Not even to a black man. Who'd want it? It's falling apart. I was gonna tear it down for the firewood in it but might as well get a few dollars every month. He's got a job up at school. "Black -money's as good as white, I reckon."

Mo spent some of the last of his money on nails to fix the cabin, and on seeds for Amelia's vegetable garden, and he worked every weekend on the cabin. Weekdays he was up at the school.

To get to the school he had to cross the river on the rickety wooden bridge which served foot traffic as well as horses, buggies and wagons. Then he went a short distance down the main street, past the grocery and the hardware store, then up a steep hill and out to the schoolhouse, which was located on about four acres of playgrounds. The school was a tall, two-storey building with classrooms on each floor and a basement room for supplies. So part of the town got to see Mo every morning and evening.

"I don't know why we gotta have a n..., a black man walking our main street every day," complained Grocer Swift.

"Mo don't do no harm. He works at the school — janitor job," commented Hardware Merchant Biggler.

"Why couldn't they hire a white man?"

"Reckon no one wanted the job. Only pays forty bucks a month, and they say the school's real run-down. A lot of work to be done."

And that was true. Floors were dirty, windows were streaked and finger-printed, woodwork was grimy, steps were sagging, railings were coming loose and that wasn't all. "Facilities" as they were called by the teachers, were unspeakable. Toilets were located out behind the main school building in a small hut with doors on opposite sides, one for boys, one for girls, which opened into separate cubicles. Flush toilets were still a rarity in Santa Cat. The whole small outhouse "stunk" as Mo put it bluntly.

He got busy with mops, soap, brooms, and scrub brushes, and after a day or two the "facilities" were respectable, as Principal Shelby said.

Mo's job went on peacefully for about two weeks when all hell broke loose. He got to school one morning to find his basement storeroom a disaster. Mop and broom handles were broken, buckets were smashed, rags thrown around, soap and cleaning stuff all over everything. A crude sign pasted to the wall said "WE DON'T LIKE N------ !" Mo took one look and went to Principal Shelby.

The Principal visited every classroom trying to find the guilty parties. The students squirmed in their seats, eyes downcast, no one would talk.

An extra lock was bought for the storeroom door, Mo cleaned up the mess, got new broom and mop handles, and that was that.

News of the incident spread through town with nods, grins and chuckles. Mo didn't tell Amelia about it and there was no way she could hear about it because the town's women refused to speak to her. She spent her days working in her vegetable garden and tending Tyler.

Tyler had no playmates but he wasn't lonely. He helped Amelia in the garden and they took walks along the river bank.

"Next year you'll be in school," she promised him. "You will learn to read and write."

"Up where father works?" he wanted to know.

"Yes, he'll be there."

Tyler smiled. "Good."

"We'll get you a lunch bucket your very own, You'll carry it every day. I'll put your lunch in it every morning. You'll see — it's going to be fine, You'll like school, Tyler."

Tyler looked up at her, then said "Will the other kids

play with me?"

Pain came into Amelia's eyes, remembering. But she said cheerfully "I think so, Tyler."

It was through her outdoor work in her garden that Amelia finally got to know one of the town's women who would talk to her. The Widow Pezzoli's house was above the river flat, higher than Farmer Shelby's house, set back in trees, but she could look down and see Amelia working in her garden. The widow had her own hard time in Santa Cat: her late husband had been the garbage man. One day she walked down for a closer look at Amelia's garden.

"Puttin' in tomatoes, I see."

Amelia looked up. "Yes — we like 'em. I'll put some up, too, if they do well here."

That was the start of sporadic visits by the widow. She never mentioned Amelia's black husband, but one day she did remark, "What a fine boy Tyler is to help his mother in the garden."

When Mo came home from his job he worked on the cabin or explored along the river for trees and branches for firewood and once in awhile he went fishing for the trout that lived in the river. In the evenings he sometimes sat by the stove and played a flute while Amelia cooked dinner. It was an old wooden flute he found at school — someone had discarded it, thrown it into the garbage bin. He picked it up and experimented with it until he could play several simple tunes.

"Where did you learn about music?" Amelia asked him one evening.

Mo shrugged. "Never learned. Just figgered it out. I'm no good at readin' and writin' but I can blow a tune I guess."

Amelia laughed and did a little dance. "I like it."

Mo smiled. "I like you to be happy, little mother hen."

Life in the river cabin settled into a quiet routine. The townspeople became accustomed to seeing Mo going to work, and Amelia going to the grocery store periodically for flour, sugar, salt and coffee. She got milk and eggs from Farmer

Shelby, and churned butter in an old churn she bought from the junk man for two bits.

At school the students got used to the black janitor, whom they ignored. One day at work, Mo came upon a boy sitting outside his supply room. He stopped and looked at the boy. Classes were in session. Why was he here?

"Boy, whatta you doin' here? You oughtta be in class."

The boy shook his head. "I got sent out."

"Sent out? What for?"

"I was chewin' gum. The teacher caught me. She was mad — she said to get out. Oh gosh, my father's goin' to whip me." The boy started to cry.

Mo went closer and put his hand on the boy's shoulder. "Son, you lissen to me. Wipe your eyes. Now you go in and tell the teacher you're sorry. Tell her you won't do that again. Things'll straighten out. You'll see."

The boy looked up at him. "I'll try." And he was gone, back up the steps to his classroom.

Several months passed, fall turned into winter, and Amelia kept the wood stove going most of the time. Then the rainy season arrived, light sprinkles at first, followed by heavier storms. The river got swollen with muddy waters that threatened to flood out over its banks.

"Does it always do this?" Amelia asked Mrs. Pezzoli.

"Depends on how much rain we git in them mountains up there," the old lady said. "Sometimes more than we want. But the river stays put. Nothin' to worry about."

But Mrs. Pezzoli was wrong that year. Santa Cat, which lay directly below the high mountain range, was in line for flood waters from what became the worst storm in fifty years.

Amelia and Mo watched the river for several days, worrying.

"What'll we do if it comes over the banks?" Amelia asked.

"Take Tyler and git out — go up the hill."

"And you have to cross that old bridge down there to get to work. What if it falls?"

"Don't you fret none about me, little worry hen, you just take care of Tyler if I ain't here. Tyler and you." Mo looked down at her and smiled. "That's all that matters."

It was raining and blowing when Mo left for work the next day, but he was cheerful. "Likely won't last long," he said to Amelia. When he crossed the bridge he noticed that the water was so high it almost reached the bottom supports.

At school he got busy with his usual tasks and worked until twelve-thirty when he sat down to eat the lunch Amelia had prepared for him. Principal Preston came into the storage room; he looked very upset.

"Mo, we've got a real problem. The river is flooding the town down below and our roof — the east side — is leaking so bad that we had to move the students out. Everything in there is getting ruined — books — everything. When you're finished eating your lunch will you come there right away?" It was more an order than a request.

But it was the Principal's first words that hit Mo like a brick. "The town is flooding."

He looked at the Principal. "I can't do the roof now. I gotta go home. My wife — my son — they're down there."

Principal Preston just looked at him, then said, "We need you here. But if you go — don't bother to come back."

"But you're all safe up here...." Mo began to speak but the Principal had slammed the door and gone.

Mo hurried into his jacket and rain hat, left the school and headed down the hill. The rain and wind almost blinded him but he could see the river waters swirling through the streets below. He went down the steep slope in leaps and bounds, sliding, almost falling. When he got down to the town he was waist deep in water. Store keepers were desperately trying to keep the water out of their buildings. Mo headed for the bridge. He almost fell when a wave of dirty water caught him off balance, then he grabbed a floating fence post and used it as a cane.

"Amelia... Tyler...," he groaned, thinking of the cabin under water, as he struggled toward the bridge. He could finally see the bridge up ahead. Or parts of it. Only the highest wooden structure was visible above the muddy waters.

As he approached, soaked through, panting for breath, he heard a shout: "Hey — you can't go there! It's going down." A policeman was shouting at him from a nearby doorway.

"I gotta go! My wife — my boy —" Mo plunged into the deeper water and grabbed a bridge rail. Cold, dirty water washed over him. He fought for breath and pulled himself further along the rail. "If it holds..." he thought. "If it holds I can make it."

Tree branches, tree trunks, weeds, tin cans, rags, fence posts, a dead cat, and once, a woman's shoe, floated past him on the surging current. "Oh God," he said when he saw the shoe.

His hat blew off although he had tied it on and he was blinded by the spray and wind. He was almost at the other side of the heaving bridge when it broke loose, sections of it floated away or sank. He pulled himself to shore on a remaining timber and tried to see the cabin but it was invisible in the storm. He was on higher ground now and the flood waters were only waist deep. He slogged past Farmer Shelby's barn and stopped on the hill to look down at the cabin. There was nothing standing. Just a jumble of collapsed boards and pieces of tin roof, most of it floating in the flood.

"Oh God no!" He ran down the hill, his face wet with rain and tears. Then he stopped. The water swirling over the cabin wreckage was deeper. It was harder to get there. He struggled and made it.

He found Tyler first. The boy's arms were still wrapped around a table leg. He had drowned. Amelia lay near him, her head crushed by a falling wall.

Stricken, unbelieving, yet faced with the awful truth, Mo almost collapsed. Then, after a few minutes he began the work of removing their bodies. He took them up, one by one, into Farmer Shelby's barn, and placed them on a pile of hay bales, above the water. He sat there grieving, until

Farmer Shelby found him the next day. Mo stayed in Santa Catarina until Amelia and Tyler were buried three days later in the town cemetery. The Methodist Church offered to hold the burial service and donated sheets to wrap the bodies. The coroner found a wooden coffin. Tyler was buried with his mother. There was a simple service with only Mo, the coroner and the Methodist minister in attendance.

Someone asked Mo what he planned to do. He shook his head. "I'm leavin'."

Someone else asked "Where to?"

Mo answered in a low, sad voice. "Don't know. It don't matter none, now."

THE ROCKING CHAIR

Herbert Clarke's wife hadn't been in her grave long, when several maiden ladies in Santa Catarina had their eye on him. Herbert lived out of town about eight miles but he was a prosperous rancher and a member of a family well known in the town. Leona's death had been a lingering one from consumption, as tuberculosis was called in the 1890s. She left Herbert a daughter, Joyce, who was eight, and two sons, Herbie, six, and Billy, five.

The funeral was a somber ceremony held on the ranch, with a few neighbors standing around the box at the edge of the hole, and the Reverend Lawlor reading from the Bible. He had come out from town on horseback. Leona was put to rest in the ranch cemetery alongside Herbert's parents and several destitute ranch workers who had no families and nowhere else to go when they died.

The children stood by tearfully, watching as the men lowered the wooden casket. Especially Joyce. She stood there in her best gingham dress with the ruffles she loved, a dress her mother had made for her. As the shovelfuls of dirt fell on the coffin, Joyce thought her heart would break, her chest and throat hurt so bad.

Mama I will never forget you, she vowed silently, with tears running down her face.

Among the neighboring ranchers at the funeral were

Mamie Colbus and her mother, Annie Colbus, and Julia Becker. Mamie was past the first flush of youth and she was rapidly and helplessly turning into the kind of old maid who stays home to make a career of caring for her aging parents. Mamie had all but given up hopes of ever finding a husband. She was bone-thin, she dressed in plain cotton housedresses and she wore her hair pulled back into a severe knot on the back of her head.

"It's less trouble that way," she would say. "And why should I dress fancy? I'm not going nowhere."

Julia Becker was younger than Mamie, more flighty. She probably would have caught a man if she had lived in Santa Catarina, but out on her family's mountain apple ranch her chances were few. Julia was small, with wispy blonde hair that flew in careless straggles around her face most of the time. The Beckers were considered haphazard farmers by their neighbors. They didn't always get the pruning done on time and the weeds were usually ahead of them.

Herbert Clarke's ranch was on the county road, acres of pasture grassland for his cattle, groves of redwood for his small sawmill, and the house he had built for Leona. A comfortable house. To the east of his place was the Becker orchard and home; on the west was the Colbus family. Herbert was flanked on two sides by women who were figuring the time to a decent interval after the funeral, but who definitely had their eye on him as husband material. They had grown up knowing him, going to school together. But when Leona came to visit another neighbor, Herbert fell in love with her and married her. The children came soon after. Joyce first, then Herbie and Billy. Leona got thinner and thinner with each birth, and started to cough. A little at first, then more. She lingered on, in her rocking chair by the kitchen window where she could watch what went on outside in the barnyard, or in bed on what she called the 'bad days'. She still sewed Joyce's dresses by hand, as sick as she was. There was one half-done when she died.

For a few days after the burial, a stream of cakes and pies made their way to Herbert's house from neighbors and friends. Conspicuous among the donors was Mamie, who appeared with a custard. It had taken a degree of courage for her to do that. Mainly, the courage to make the custard, with her mother watching, knowing what she was up to.

"Humph. Going over to Herbert's, are you?" the old lady said. "Ef I was you I would sure think twice before I took on a passel of younguns, somebody else's younguns."

What Annie Colbus was really worried about was losing Mamie. It was mighty handy to have a daughter at home to do the cooking and housework.

Mamie said "I'm going, Mama. I made up my mind."

Annie waggled a finger at her. "You'll find out it ain't so easy takin' on a ready-made family, even if the man likes his bed warm."

Mamie's pale face got pink and she didn't answer. When the custard was done, she slipped a knife into it to make sure, then she got her gray cape and set out with the custard in a pie basket. She knew her mother was watching from the window but she didn't care.

"He's going to marry somebody and it might as well be me," she said to herself. "I'm tired of being an old maid." She walked through the dusk and when she knocked at Herbert's door her hand holding the basket trembled a little. But it was too late to change her mind even if she had wanted to. She didn't want to. The thought of Mama back there in the window — Mamie squared her shoulders and tried to smile at Herbert when he opened the door.

"I know how hard it must be for you, Herbert," she said breathlessly. "Losing Leona and all. You have my heartfelt sympathy. If there's anything I can do — I brought this for you and the children. I hope they like custard. It's good for them." She said it all in a flat voice almost like she was reciting. That was because she had gone over and over what she was going to say as she walked to his house.

Herbert nodded. "I appreciate that, Mamie. Mighty kind of you to think of us." He put his hand on her shoulder and Mamie's heart began to beat faster.

"Herbert — I — I want you to know I'll do anything I can to help you and the children." Her voice faltered.

He took his hand away. "Thanks, Mamie. I'm not so good at cooking. The custard will go good with the kids too."

She hesitated. "If there's anything I can do — cooking — housework — just let me know, Herbert."

She turned then, and left, feeling that at least Herbert knew she was alive now.

Mamie hadn't been gone an hour when Julia arrived at the door with a pie. Apple. Warm. Just out of the oven. She was a little out of breath because she had hurried. She opened Herbert's door and yelled "Yoohoo" a couple of times. Then she went in. "Herbie,'" she said, using the old familiar schoolday name. She put the pie on the table and went over to where he was sitting. Her eyes were bright with unshed tears. "This pie's for you and the kids." She put her arms around his shoulders and hugged him. "Poor Herbie. I'll be back." Then she left.

Julia's pie was delicious. So was Mamie's custard, and the handouts kept coming every day or two.

Mamie felt encouraged when Herbert smiled at her. She kept reminding him that she was available, ready and willing to do anything that needed doing.

"That sideboard needs dusting, Herbert. I'll do it before I leave." Not only the sideboard but other odd jobs caught her eye. She spent several hours working and even got the children to do their homework. "Your Mama would want you to keep up your schooling."

Joyce looked at Mamie from under rebellious brows and said nothing, but Herbie said "Yes Ma'm" and got to work.

"There now," Mamie said before she left. "The house is fairly clean again and the children have done their homework for tomorrow. Everything's in order, Herbert, just the way it should be."

It was different when Julia came. She usually breezed

in with a pie, she never noticed the dust on the furniture and sometimes, if the kids were home from school, she took them for a walk or played catch with them.

The weeks went on into months and Herbert was hard pressed to choose between them. He knew he was going to choose eventually, but he wanted to wait a decent time. Folks would talk. They'd talk anyway, but it would be worse if he remarried too soon. That's the way it was in Santa Catarina. Everybody knew everybody's business. Besides, Herbert's ranching was suffering. He wasn't free to spend the hours needed on horseback to mend fences, keep water pipes running into stock tanks and count cattle to make sure they were all there. To say nothing of new-born calves arriving. Summer was coming on.

Leona had been gone six months. Herbert and the kids had got through the holidays with the ever-present help of Mamie and Julia and the Sunday School. But they had been hard months. Lonely months. He needed a wife.

Mamie thought he might pop the question any day now, and so did old lady Colbus who lived in fear of that day.

"Seems to me that snip of a Julia spends a lot of time at Herbert's place," she said to Mamie. "Maybe he'll marry her."

Mamie felt a little clutch of fear. "What makes you think so, Mama?"

"She's younger'n you are, Mamie. Men like spring chicken. I'm just tellin' you. Don't go and get upset."

"I'm not upset, Mama." But that afternoon Mamie baked a batch of sugar cookies, changed to her best dress and went over to Herbert's.

When she knocked, Joyce answered the door. Mamie tried to hide her disappointment. Herbert wasn't home, Joyce told her politely. "Papa's out on his horse, looking for newborn calves, Ma'm."

Mamie went past the child into the kitchen which, she observed grimly, was a mess. Toys scattered. Dirt tracked in on the wood floor. Dishes left from breakfast. Dirty clothes piled in one comer. Herbert took them into Santa Catarina to the Chinaman, but they got ahead of him. Then Mamie looked out the back window and saw the boys making mud pies in the barnyard near the pump. She compressed her lips into a thin line and decided it was time to get to work.

"Come children!" she said. "We're going to clean up this place!"

She started with a fury of energy, although she was sorry she had worn her good dress. She'd have to be careful.

"Joyce, you can sweep. Herbie, you take a shovel and clean up that mess you and Billy made out by the pump. Billy, you can pick up those toys and put them away where they belong. Next we'll make the beds and do the dishes."

She went through the house like a whirlwind and there wasn't too much rebellion or grumbling until she started rearranging the parlor furniture.

She moved a rocking chair away from the window so the seat cushion wouldn't fade from the sun. Joyce confronted her.

"That's my Mother's chair and she always kept it there by the window. Always." Joyce said firmly but politely.

"Well, you don't want the cushion to fade, do you?" Mamie moved the chair.

In Joyce's bedroom Mamie looked around with a degree of satisfaction.

"I'm glad to see you are a neat child," she said.

"Mama taught me," Joyce said.

"You even made your bed and that's good. But what's that I see under your pillow? What on earth —?" Mamie pulled out the pink and white piece of cloth and held it up at arms length. "What is this?"

Joyce looked at the floor. "It's a dress Mama was making for me. I — I like to sleep with it."

"Sleep with it? For heaven's sake, child! You've wrinkled it up so that I couldn't tell what it was. Well. I'll just take it home with me and wash it and sew it up —

finish it."

"No," Joyce said. "I want it the way it is."

Mamie looked at her. "Now now, Joyce. You've got to learn to grow up. You're not a baby anymore. You're a big girl now."

Joyce snatched the dress from Mamie's hand and without thinking, Mamie slapped her. It was a reflex action that even startled Mamie herself.

"I don't want you here!" Joyce yelled at her. "I don't like you!"

Mamie was shaken to her roots. She went back to the kitchen where the boys were sitting, looking sad. "Would you like a cookie?" she asked.

They shook their heads.

Mamie felt terrible. Where had everything gone wrong? What had she done? Or what hadn't she done? She didn't know. She put the broom and dust mop away and got her jacket and said "I guess I'll go home now."

"Goodbye," the boys said. No emotion. No words like "Please stay" or "Don't go."

Mamie paused in the yard to look back. To think. Those children were out of hand already, she decided. They were badly in need of a firm hand. She turned around and started to go back to the house when Joyce darted around the corner of the house. She had a wad of mud in her hand and she threw it. It spattered on Mamie's skirt.

"Oh! Oh! Oh!" Mamie shrieked. She couldn't believe her eyes.

"Go home!" Joyce yelled. "We don't want you here!"

And Mamie left. She walked fast. Anger and humiliation boiled in her.

At home her mother wanted to know what had happened to her dress.

"Oh — I had an accident. I think it will wash out all right. I've got to tend to it right away, before it sets the stain." She hurried into her room to take off the dress and suddenly there were tears running down her cheeks.

"How is Herbert?" the old lady called, not without a

touch of malice.

"He wasn't there but the children were home," Mamie said, mopping up her tears quickly.

"Remember what I told you — moving into a ready-made family is no picnic — you never know what you're getting into."

"Yes, Mama, I remember." She knew she was beaten. Beaten by three small children. And what had she done to them? Only tried to be kind. To straighten out their lives a bit. To bring some order into confusion.

She sat on her bed and cried for awhile, then when she felt better, she went over to the pitcher of water on the commode and held a wet washcloth to her eyes. She wondered what Herbert's reaction would be when he came home. What would the children tell him? Or would they tell him anything? She would wait and see. That would be best. And now — there was that ugly stain on her dress.

Shortly after Mamie left the Clarke home, the children had another caller. Julia Becker. When no one answered the front door, she went around to the back and found the boys making mud pies. Joyce was there too.

"Well — it looks like you are busy," she said. "Where's your Pa?"

"Out looking for calves in the east pasture," Herbie said.

"Oh. I guess I'll walk out to meet him." She lifted the latch on the pasture gate.

"Can we come too?" Joyce asked.

"Sure. Come along." Julia noticed Joyce's eyes; she had been crying.

They walked along through the tall pasture grass, golden in the summer sun. Julia first, with her bright cotton skirt swishing with every step, Joyce beside her, and the boys following.

Julia stopped. "Look! There's a meadow lark — we scared him up out of the grass."

"What do meadow larks do?" Herbie wanted to know.

"Well, I'll tell you," Julia said. "They have just about the best song I've ever heard. Real pretty — so sweet and full of trills — and when you hear it, you feel like you could almost fly, yourself."

"What are trills"" Billy asked.

Julia held up one hand. "Let's stop and listen. Maybe he'll sing to us. He's over there — not too far away."

They were standing there listening to the lark's song when Herbert came over the hill on his horse. "Hey — what's this?" he called.

"We saw a bird," little Billy said.

"A meadow lark," Joyce added.

"And we heard it sing," Herbie added.

Herbert got down from the saddle and looped the reins over the horse's neck. "Guess I'll walk back with you," he said. Then "How'd you kids get so dirty?"

"We were making mud pies," Billy said.

"Out by the pump," Joyce said.

"It's nothing a little soap and water won't cure," Julia said with a laugh. "Did you find the calves?"

"Yep. They're all in the little corral out there now. Safe and sound. Just have to keep an eye on them for awhile." He turned to Joyce. "You been crying, young lady?

Joyce stammered. "I fell down."

"No she didn't," Billy said.

"Miss Colbus came and brought some cookies," Herbie said.

They walked back to the house, Julia beside Herbert and the horse, with the children running along ahead.

"It's lonesome for them," he said to Julia. "They miss their Ma and now school's out they don't know what to do with themselves. Especially Joyce."

Julia said "I know."

Herbert put his hand on her arm and stopped. "Julia...."

"Yes?"

"Julia, I know it's too soon and it's asking an awful lot of you — but well, I've been thinking about it and I...."

He stopped. "I don't know how to put it. Asking you to marry me and take over my three young'uns. It's not fair to you," he said. "You might want a real wedding in the church with all the trimmings. What I had in mind is a quiet one in the Judge's chambers. Oh shucks, Julia. I'm no good at this."

Julia had to look up at him because her head didn't quite come up to his shoulder. "The answer is yes," she said softly. "The Judge's chambers will do just fine."

Herbert kissed her. "I hope you will come to love me and the children," he said.

"I do already," she answered as she smiled up at him.

He put his horse in the barn and gave it some hay. Julia waited for him, then they went into the house together. The boys had washed their hands and were sitting at the kitchen table.

"Where's Joyce?" Julia asked.

Herbie spoke up. "She's in there —" and motioned toward the parlor. "She likes to go in there and sit in Mama's rocking chair and look out the window just like Mama used to do."

"I'll call her," Herbert said.

Julia put one finger up to his mouth. "No. Leave her. She'll come when she's ready."

A RUDE AWAKENING

The great California earthquake of 1906 shook up a lot more than just brick buildings and chimneys in Santa Catarina. For years afterward, when a group of longtime residents gathered to reminisce and gossip, someone was sure to ask "Wasn't there a doctor who got caught...." The tongues would wag as the memories flowed and everybody would have a good laugh.

Medically speaking, Santa Catarina was without a resident doctor during the early 1800s, but by 1895 several real doctors had arrived. "Real" meaning a physician who had actually had some training, either in medical school or as apprentice to an older, established doctor.

Gone were the days when the only recourse was old wives' remedies which ranged from spider webs, blood-letting, calomel, sarsaparilla, horse manure and a whole panoply of plants both tame and wild. Sometimes the home remedies helped, sometimes they didn't. The main attitude of the early pioneers was that when you got sick, you either got well again or got worse and died.

For years, Granny Henkle swore by a concoction of honey and kerosene for all kinds of ailments. Señora Lorenzo mixed potions of liverwort and newt's eyes for stomach ailments, and old lady Gittels rolled pills of horse dung, and molasses. Good for anything from toothache to aching joints, so she claimed. When Doctor Lem Crawford came to set up practice in Santa Catarina in 1898, Granny Henkle was dead, Mrs. Gittels was in her dotage and couldn't get out to scoop up the horse manure, and Señora Lorenzo had moved to Merced.

Doctor Crawford found a little competition. Mechanical medicine had arrived in Santa Cat several years before. Doctor Willard Wooster specialized in electrical treatments via an iron cage to which he fastened batteries, a new-fangled idea which was slow to catch on because most prospective patients were afraid of being electrocuted. He even lowered his rates. Three treatments for five dollars. All the patient had to do was crawl into the iron cage, and lie still for half an hour. But Doctor Wooster didn't get many patients and Doctor Crawford didn't look at him as much competition.

Then there was Doctor Professor William Whittle. He preferred the double title. He had an office on Pacific Ocean Street where he specialized in salt water enemas to "purify the system" and "cleanse the blood". He also rolled his own brand of pills and made tonics from sea water which he collected from a particularly accessible spot on Cliff Drive where the town's sewer emptied into the Pacific Ocean. No one told him about that, but patients who knew where the sewer emptied, told other patients and pretty soon the Doctor was wondering why his tonics didn't sell.

When Doctor Lem Crawford set up shop on Pacific Ocean Street, he chose three rooms over Oliver Pearson's Pharmacy. He was pleased with the location. The red brick building had a solid, professional look about it and the drugstore was handy below. He hung his sign over the entrance to the stairs and waited for patients, living in one of the three rooms and reserving the other two for business.

People were stand-offish at first. They wondered what his specialty was going to be. They all knew that a new doctor had arrived in town. The population of eight thousand wasn't so great that newcomers weren't noticed. And everyone knew what the other two doctors' specialties were because every week they ran startlingly graphic advertisements in the Santa Catarina Wave. Doctor Wooster's ads showed a drawing of his iron cage which promised "Immediate relief from fever, coughs, consumption, biliousness, weakness, lack of vigor (aimed at men), stomach pains, bad backs, rheumatism and failing eyesight."

Doctor Whittle's ad showed an enormous enema bag with a long tube hanging from it and big black letters that shouted "HIGH COLONICS — THE ONLY WAY TO PURIFY YOUR BLOOD AND GET RID OF THOSE ACHES AND PAINS." Below it was a pill bottle and Doctor Whittle's head smiling at you, but the drawing didn't much resemble Doctor Whittle.

So everyone wondered what kind of ad Doctor Lem Crawford would put into the weekly newspaper. No one expected it to have anything to do with childbirth or cuts and bruises or broken arms. Childbirth took place at home, of course, in bed, with Granny Somebody-or-other pulling the baby out. Cuts and bruises called for kitchen medicine at home too, and the same mid-wives who delivered babies knew how to line up the broken bones and wrap the arms — and legs — in torn-up sheets. For anything really serious, those who could afford it went to San Jose or San Francisco where there were real doctors who had gone to medical school.

The town gave Doctor Crawford time to settle in, all the while observing him closely. The way be dressed, always formally in a black suit with a vest, was very professional, they all agreed. His gold watch chain was prominently displayed and he tipped his hat at local businessmen as they passed on the street. True, he lived in the one room behind his offices. He hadn't bought a house and really settled in, but that would no doubt come as his practice grew.

In the small room at the rear of his two medical rooms, Doctor Crawford had a bed, a bureau, a chair and half a dozen hooks for hanging his clothes. He furnished his waiting room with a bench, two chairs, a desk and a small wood stove. There happened to be a chimney hole in that room. The third room was his operating room. In it he had installed a high examination table covered with a sheet, a cupboard for medicine, some shelves for his books, a cabinet for his medical tools, a hanging kerosene light and several large, colorful charts showing various body parts. There was a corner sink with running water. Cold.

Everybody knew what he had, because he bought it all at Jesse Hayes' Mercantile Store and paid cash. At least he wasn't going to be one of those fly-by-nights, Hayes told his friends. The hanging lamp had to be ordered from San Francisco and it took two weeks to arrive. It had special mirrors attached to it which focused the light when adjusted.

"Sounds like he intends to stay," Hayes said. "Looks like he'll cook his meals on the stove or go to Mrs. Pitts' boarding house."

In the meantime, everybody waited to see what his ad would say, and watched him as he walked about the town, a handsome figure in his black swallowtail coat. He was tall, dark-haired with a hint of gray at the temples, and cleanshaven which was unusual in a day of beards.

"Kind of aristocratic looking," the wife of Judge William Mills told her friends. "He minds his own business and he looks like a real doctor."

In looks, Doctor Lem had it all over his competitors. Doctor Whittle was short and heavy with a big puffy mole on one eyelid. Doctor Wooster had faded red hair and a sour, down-turned mouth that seldom smiled.

Even more impressive was Doctor Lem Crawford's advertisement in the Wave. It took up half a page and it showed a pill bottle. That was nothing new, but the message was: "GEENO" — Miracle Pill of the Century." The smaller print went on to ask: "Tired? Head ache? Nerves on edge? Joints ache? Do You Often Feel Faint? Ladies and Gentlemen of Santa Catarina, Doctor Lemuel Crawford, fresh from New York, has the answer for these and more. He has brought the miracle pill of the ages to Santa Catarina."

People read the ad and wondered, but their timidity was short-lived. Doctor Crawford began attending church regularly and dropped hints that he was interested in joining the Bible Study Class. Obviously he was a God-fearing man who could be trusted.

First to brave a visit to his office was Mrs. Judge Mills (she liked to refer to herself that way, borrowing her husband's courtesy title. He was not a real judge.) Mrs. Mills suffered from what she called 'sick headaches'. They came on usually about the time the Judge began thinking romantic thoughts which was seldom as he grew older. Nothing had helped her headaches, not even Doctor Whittle's colonics — administered by his ancient nurse. Mrs. Mills had even crawled into Doctor Wooster's electric cage (fully clothed) without any helpful results. One day she said "I'm going to try this new doctor's medicine. Swallowing a pill is nothing when I think of all I've gone through — that iron cage and those enemas!" So she prepared herself for the visit by washing, then rubbing baking soda under each armpit and into other strategic areas, then climbing into clean drawers. All this, even though she was reasonably sure there wouldn't be any disrobing required for pill taking.

She was right. There wasn't. Doctor Crawford shone a bright light into her eyes, said "Hmmm" several times and took her pulse, timing it with the gold watch he wore on the chain across his vest. He peered into her throat, holding down her tongue with a spoon, then he placed a stethoscope on her back and chest and listened to her heart through four layers of clothing that included a whalebone corset. He said "Hmmm" again a few times, questioned her at length about her headaches, and made notes in a small black book.

Finally, when she had recited every detail she could think of, except the Judge's sexual habits, he closed the book and said, "My dear Mrs. Mills I believe I can help you relieve your suffering. It is clear to me that you have been undergoing severe pain. Now I am going to prepare a prescription of pills for you. A special formula. They will be ready tomorrow. I want you to take one every morning, upon rising, and one every evening before retiring." He went on at length to explain the wonderful qualities of the new drug

he had acquired. His manner was so reassuring and so —
so professional, Mrs. Mills later told her lady friends, that
she was just sure he was a fine doctor who knew what he
was talking about. She could hardly wait to try the pills.
The next day she sent her niece, Alice Mills, who lived with
her and the Judge, down to Doctor Crawford's office to get
them. Alice was the daughter of Judge Mills' never-do-well
brother who had the bad luck to get hit over the head with
a wine bottle and killed, in a San Francisco saloon brawl.
Alice had been working with a midwife, learning the
business, when she was orphaned. She had no one to go to
except Judge and Mrs. Mills. Her mother was dead. The
Mills took her in with some reluctance on Mrs. Mills part
when the shapely seventeen-year old 'child' appeared.

"We were never blessed with children of our own,"
the Judge said. "And we're kind of old to start having a
family, but the Lord's will be done. We'll do our best for the
girl."

Alice, on the other hand, was not pleased to be coming
to Santa Catarina. She took one look down the main street
and sniffed, "How am I going to get on with anything here
in this one-horse town?"

"Maybe you can be a school teacher," Mrs. Mills offered
hopefully.

But Alice shook her dark curls vigorously.

"I don't understand how you can be so attached to
working with a midwife, my dear," Mrs. Mills said. "Those
duties are not always very pleasant ones." She was thinking
of the slop pans that had to be emptied and the naked bodies
that had to be washed and wiped.

"Oh I didn't do any of that," Alice said, understanding
her Aunt perfectly. I kept the office books and records and
I wrote down the patients' ailments. Kept track of everything
for the head nurse."

Alice went for the pills. Mrs. Mills began taking them
regularly and her headaches did seem to decrease in
severity. Word got around that the new doctor was
competent, if not a down-right miracle man. Women began

going to his office; women who had never suffered a headache in their lives, or back aches, or any of the mysterious ailments and weaknesses that many women complained of. They were eager to try the new miracle pills anyway. And in a remarkably short time, Doctor Lem Crawford began building up a thriving practice.

This was not without notice by Doctors Whittle and Wooster. Hardly anyone was going to them for high colonics or iron cage treatments. The two doctors consoled themselves with the hope that Doctor Crawford's miracle pills wouldn't work, he would get tired of scraping by, eventually, and would leave Santa Catarina.

"He hasn't got a wife," Doctor Whittle observed.

Both he and Doctor Wooster had wives. Wives were a big help in the medical business. They made cakes and pies for church socials, they went to prayer meetings, they could be called upon to help with more difficult patients and they were practically a guarantee that the doctor was an upright, married medical man whose mind would not stray to impure thoughts while he was working on women patients.

Alice went regularly to get her Aunt's weekly supply of pills and one day she was ecstatic when she returned.

"Doctor Crawford needs an office nurse," she said. "I can work for him! I will continue my education and he'll pay me — not much at first."

Mrs. Mills was pleased. She had been wondering what to do with the girl. Now it was settled. Alice could work and earn a little money until she found a suitable husband.

Mrs. Mills escorted Alice to the first session with Doctor Crawford to satisfy herself that there would be no unclothed bodies to tend.

"After all, Doctor, she's a young, innocent girl," she reminded him. Later, to the Judge, Mrs. Mills said, I certainly don't want her taking care of — of men who are not properly dressed. I don't want that on my conscience, even if she is your brother's child and he died in that awful barroom fight."

The Judge winced a little; he didn't like to be reminded

of Jack, his drunken brother.

Doctor Crawford presented Alice with a large ledger in which to keep the accounts, and said, "Of course you will be assisting me in the examining room, for women and children patients." As he spoke he noticed bow her dark lashes flickered over her eyes — were they blue? Or green? After another look he decided they were certainly green. "Do you know how to take a pulse?" he asked. His own pulse was pounding away slightly faster than usual, as he asked.

Alice began working regular eight hour days, six days a week, and was paid eight dollars a week. She felt rich.

"Why, it's easy!" she told her Aunt. I take down the patient's name, age, address and then I take their pulse and write that down too. Oh, Auntie, I am so happy with my job. And I am saving money too."

Mrs. Mills was pleased. Sensible girl after all. She would amount to something some day for sure, even with such a terrible upbringing. No mother to guide her and such a terrible father. Mrs. Mills original reluctance to take Jack's child under her roof, began to fade.

The practice thrived. Patients, hearing about Doctor Crawford's magic pills, began coming to him from surrounding towns. Some, who worked long hours, began coming in the early morning or late evening. Doctor Crawford obligingly opened his office early and late.

"How can I say no to them?" he explained to Alice. I can't turn them away. I took a very serious oath as part of my profession, you know." Then his voice softened. "Dear girl, I don't like to ask it of you, but could you extend your hours? There'll be more pay, of course."

"Oh yes," Alice breathed, thinking how noble of him it was to give so much of his life to helping the sick.

At first, Mrs. Mills complained and worried about Alice's erratic hours. But she calmed considerably when Alice told her about the extra pay. The hours became even more irregular, with Alice coming and going quietly so she wouldn't disturb her aunt and uncle. She had started work in October and soon it was Christmas with a five dollar bonus, then a cold January with New Year's Eve welcoming the year 1906, followed by a wet February.

February. The month of hearts, Valentines and rain. They had worked later than usual one night, and when the last patient left, Alice put her head down on her desk to rest for a moment. She was tired. Doctor Crawford came in and found her that way, sound asleep. He put his hand gently on her dark curls. She opened her eyes and looked up at him.

"Dear girl," he said tenderly.

"Dear Lemuel," she answered. The first time she had called him by his first name. He lifted her to her feet and held her close. She clung to him. They kissed. A long, passionate kiss. It was inevitable. He said so. They were meant for each other. He led her back to the room where he lived and began to unbutton her shirtwaist. It fell to the floor. Then he unhooked her wool skirt, her cotton chemise and her petticoat. She said not a word and finally stood there in a puddle of clothing with only her drawers on.

"Alice, you are beautiful," he said, leaning down to touch the rosy tip of one white breast with his tongue.

She gasped once, when he untied the drawstring on her drawers. He peeled down her long cotton stockings and she stood still as a statue carved from pale marble while his hands went over her body, stroking, caressing, teasing, playing with her.

"Get on the bed," he said.

She obeyed blindly. He undressed quickly and lay down beside her. His hands were busy again with her body, his mouth on her breasts. When he parted her legs there was a sharp stab of pain that made her gasp again. And again. And again. Then again, finally, and not from pain.

That was the beginning. It went on regularly all during February and March with Alice creeping in and out of the Mills home at odd hours. Pharmacist Oliver Pearson, in his shop below, began to suspect that something non-medical was going on. When be blew out his lamp and locked up shop most nights the Doctor's lights up above were still on and he hadn't seen a patient climb the stairs for two or three hours.

The Judge's neighbors began to wonder. They had accepted Mrs. Mills proud announcement that Alice was working with the new doctor, but the work hours seemed to be most peculiar, they told each other. Not only the neighbors were wondering, so were Doctor's Wooster and Whittle. There were few secrets in Santa Catarina in 1906. But just the way Alice and Doctor Crawford looked at each other in church was enough to cause speculation. Only Judge and Mrs. Mills never seemed to notice. Of course they were getting old; their eyesight was not the best. There was no talk of marriage between Doctor Crawford and Alice. In fact there was very little talk at all except for sentences like "Get on the bed" or "Take off your shirtwaist" although he usually took pleasure in doing that himself. Words weren't needed between them. Only a furtive, urgent, hot sexual contact which he dominated with a growing passion and to which she gave herself completely. Once — only once — she mentioned marriage. He hushed her words with his finger on her lips. "Dear girl, don't spoil this precious thing we have."

April brought more rain. The patient load had lessened through the winter months, but the work hours remained the same for Alice. She was needed. Wanted. And loved, for the first time in her life. She also had fallen in love, with sex as well as with Doctor Crawford.

The evening of April 17 was a quiet one. A single, late patient left about eight o'clock. As the door closed behind him, Doctor Crawford looked at Alice in the way he had that made the blood pound in her ears. She nodded and went through the office and back to his room. He locked the office door, turned off the lamps and followed her. In a few minutes they were on his bed locked in a feverish pursuit of each other's body. When it was over, he said "I wish you could stay the night instead of going home."

"But I can, tonight," she said, not bothering to explain

that the Mills were in San Francisco to attend the Enrico Caruso Concert. The great Italian opera star, also known as the 'world's greatest tenor', was performing there at the Opera House.

The very thought of a night — a whole night — of such intimate delights, inflamed the Doctor again and he was so urgent in his ministrations and demands that, to her surprise the whole process they had just finished, happened all over again.

"I didn't know you could — so soon again," she said delicately.

"Just wait — you'll see," he said.

"Why, Lemuel, that's wonderful!"

They didn't bother to eat dinner. They stayed in bed and at intervals made love again until finally, they both slept, worn out. He set the alarm clock so she could get up early and leave before dawn.

The clock ticked away the hours as they slept. Midnight passed. Then a new day, April 18. Four a.m. Then five, and the alarm was just about to go off when, at exactly five-fifteen, the earth beneath Santa Catarina began to heave and shake. The brick building in which they slept tossed and shook like an angry beast in a frenzy. Bricks loosened and fell. Stovepipes clattered down into the street, stairs buckled and collapsed, chimneys crumbled, whole walls gave way and crashed into the streets. All in less than two minutes. The quake rippled the earth in waves and ripped it apart in places.

"It's an earthquake!" Alice screamed as she fumbled in the dark for her dress and shoes. The room around her, the very bed she sat on, were doing crazy dances to the tune of creaking, groaning timbers and the crash of falling bricks. The rumble of the earthquake was terrifying.

"We've got to get out!" Doctor Crawford shouted above the din. He grabbed his trousers and struggled through the debris of the wrecked examining room and through the office where Alice's desk lay in a paper storm of scattered records and bricks. The outside door which led to the hall and down the stairs was jammed. The door frame was sprung and the wall was buckling, threatening to cave in on them. He threw his shoulder against the door but it wouldn't budge. He picked up the sturdy wood bench from the waiting room and hammered it against the door until the door finally splintered. They crawled out. The hall was a shambles and the stairs were hanging in shreds of wood, plaster and fallen bricks. Too dangerous to use. They took one look and shrank back against the only wall in the hall that was still half-way intact. The entire outside wall was gone, collapsed in a pile of bricks and dust that covered the wooden sidewalk and most of the street.

Lem Crawford took one look and turned to her, choking with the dust. "We'll have to wait for help," he said.

The rumbling of the earthquake faded, the exposed hallway was filled with a dust cloud from the shattered brick wall and the ruined stairway. An eerie silence fell over the town until the fire bell began ringing.

Alice was trembling from fright and shock. "I — I guess there's nothing else we can do," she said, half crying. "Unless you have a ladder — or a rope."

He shook his head. "This will be the end of my practice here," he muttered. "I shouldn't have asked you to stay."

"I'm not sorry," she said. "It was wonderful. I'll never forget it." Then she said "We could get married."

Doctor Crawford shook his head again. "I — I have a wife. She won't live with me and she won't divorce me. I'll just have to move on — go somewhere else — start over again." He looked at her. She was half naked, covered with brick dust, no shoes on her feet, her skirt gaping beneath the corset cover she had struggled into. "But what about you?" he asked. "You know how this town is. You won't be able to live here when the word gets around. Your aunt — your uncle ——." He shuddered.

Alice was surprisingly calm then. The worst had happened and they had lived through it. "I'll be moving on too," she said. "I can't stay here now. I know that. But I don't want to if you leave."

"You'll find someone and get married," he said.

"No, I won't." She sounded firm. "I've seen enough of marriage to last me the rest of my life. My father beat my mother when he was drinking. My aunt bosses my uncle around. Oh she is clever at it — but she doesn't fool me. No. I don't want to get married. Ever. Not unless I could marry you. And that can't be." She sounded sad for a moment.

Suddenly there were firemen and police in the street below. They had lanterns and ladders and someone was calling out "Doctor — are you up there? Are you all right?"

Doctor Crawford braced himself. "Up here!" he called and they came, placing the ladder carefully against one still standing wall. He. climbed down, his feet were bare and he hadn't buttoned his trousers. His shirt was lost somewhere in the rubble above. Alice followed him down. She was wearing only her shoes, the wool skirt and the corset cover. The firemen and policemen gaped and then one of them offered her his coat.

The pharmacist, who had come down to rescue what he could from his shop, saw them. They were seen by other citizens of Santa Catarina who were outside their homes from fear of another shock to come, or who were downtown to save what they could from their businesses. A good number of concerned town fathers got clear looks at Alice and the Doctor climbing down the ladder.

The big quake of 1906 was the talk of the town — of the State of California — for months afterward. San Francisco was badly damaged and what the quake didn't destroy, the resulting fire did.

Doctor Lemuel Crawford took his stock of pills — he managed to save quite a few the next day when he crawled up a ladder to his ruined office. He left town almost immediately for greener pastures; he didn't say where and no one asked. Doctors Whipple and Wooster privately congratulated each other and said things like "I suspected all along," and "Where there's smoke there's bound to be fire."

As for the Mills, when they returned from their harrowing stay in quake-ridden fire-flattened San Francisco, they found a note from Alice saying she had suffered a terrible shock to her entire system from the earthquake, and had decided to study nursing at a school in the Mid-west. Hopefully, a state where no earthquakes ever happened.

"She has relatives there — on her mother's side," Mrs. Mills announced. Privately she was relieved that the girl was gone. She never knew the whole story, or if she did, she didn't let on. Rumors reached the Judge's ears but he didn't want to hear them. No one was brave enough — or foolish enough — to press the point.

So Alice was gone when they arrived home two days after the quake. She had taken her savings, bought a stagecoach ticket south to Los Angeles and that was as far as she went. She found work right away in Madame Felice's House of Joy, a high class bordello which catered to the well-to-do male population. Occasionally she had fleeting dreams of the Doctor's showing up one day, but he never did, and she discovered clients with talents similar to his. After a few years she had saved enough money to start her own establishment — Madame Alicia's House of Many Pleasures.

Judge and Mrs. Mills wondered occasionally why they never heard from her.

"Not a word! Not even a postcard from that place in the mid-west," Mrs. Mills said. "That's gratitude for you!"

If they had seen her they wouldn't have recognized her. With prosperity Alice had put on some weight, she favored rouge on her cheeks, a golden dye on her hair and silks and satins for her clothing. All with handy, easily unhooked fastenings, of course.

THE SECRET

By 1909 Miss Stella Binkelmott had become the most feared teacher in Santa Catarina Grammar School. That was the year she personally marched Billy Lethington down to the City Jail for a close look at what happens to boys who steal.

She had caught Billy taking a couple of pencils from the supply on her desk when she was busy at the back of the room. They were well-used pencils, not new. But that didn't matter to Miss Binkelmott, who was widely known for her rigid standards of conduct. She immediately marched to the front of the room, to her desk. Miss Stella Binkelmott didn't walk, or glide, or stroll, or saunter. She marched, with the heels of her high-top laced leather shoes making solid thuds the length of the room.

She was a large, solid, gray-haired woman who had never married and who looked sixty instead of thirty-five. Her parents were dead. She was alone in the world. Teaching was her life. Teaching, and saving boys from sin.

At her desk, she faced the class. By then, Billy was back in his seat, feeling safe, with the pencils in his pocket. He didn't know she had seen him take them. But Miss Binkelmott had eyes like a ferret.

"Billy Lethington, come forward," she commanded.

For a second, Billy looked bewildered. Then, as the awful knowledge sank into his head that Miss Binkelmott must have seen him take the pencils, he sank down into his seat as if he hoped to melt and become invisible. Then he got up and came to the front of the class.

"Billy, are you familiar with the Ten Commandments?" Her voice was terrifying.

Thoroughly frightened, Billy gulped and nodded.

"And are you familiar with the Eighth Commandment?"

Billy nodded again.

"And pray tell me, can you recite it?"

Confused, Billy thought for a moment, then shook his head.

Miss Binkelmott looked triumphant. "Aha! I thought so! Billy, put those pencils you stole from my desk back, and you will write 'I will not steal' one hundred times on the chalk board."

Billy looked like he might burst into tears, but he didn't. Instead, he blurted "Miss Binkelmott, I wanted to take them home so I could draw. We don't have any pencils and I like to draw things."

"Drawing things!" She snorted. "A waste of time. And pray tell me what good will drawing pictures do if you turn into a thief!"

Miserable, Billy put the pencils back and went to the board to begin writing 'I WILL NOT STEAL' one hundred times.

When classes ended at three-thirty, Billy was still at his task. He finally finished and started for the door to escape. Miss Binkelmott, who was sitting at her desk correcting papers, called him back.

"Billy! You are not excused. Take your seat!"

He slunk back to his desk.

She got up, went to the cloak room where she got her wrap and her hat, and announced "All right, young man. You are coming with me!"

That was when the visit to the City Jail took place. Miss Binkelmott marched at a brisk pace down Santa Catarina's wood sidewalks with Billy almost trotting to keep up.

"I am going to show you what happens to boys who grow up to become thieves," she announced, stopping at the City Hall which also housed the jail. They entered the office and she spoke with authority to the policeman on duty: "This boy —" she pointed at the shrinking Billy — "is in danger of his mortal soul. He was tempted by Satan and he stole! I intend to show him what happens to thieves!"

She took Billy firmly by the arm and swept past the policeman who was not too surprised; he had had visits from her before.

Down the hall, past several closed doors, then there were four small cubicles with iron bars. More like cages than rooms.

Miss Binkelmott stopped. "Look here, Billy! You take a good look, boy. This is where you will end up if you continue to steal!"

Billy looked, and he shuddered. An unshaven, grinning head of uncombed hair looked back at him from behind the bars. A toothless grin. Ragged sleeves, dirty hands reaching out, a hoarse voice that said "Well, well, boy. You comin' in here with me?" and laughed.

Billy stood, petrified, and took it all in. A wood bench to sleep on. A chamber pot in one comer. Dirt everywhere. The floor was dirty. The walls had once been white but were now covered with handprints, scribbled foul words.

"Now you have seen it — you see what stealing leads to!" She let go of Billy's arm. "You're excused to go home."

And he went, as if the devil himself was chasing him.

The Lethington home was small, shabby, uncared for, with weeds growing in the yard under the long clotheslines. Billy's mother did laundry for several well-to-do families to make the money the Lethingtons lived on. Billy's father's job at the lumber mill had closed down months before.

When Billy turned in at the broken-down gate, he could see his friend and classmate sitting on the front stoop, waiting for him. Harry Parker held out two brand new pencils as Billy approached.

"Here. For you. I've got more. And if you need paper I've got some." He looked at Billy sympathetically. "Whew! Old Tinklepot sure took it out on you today. Where'd you go? Down to the jail I'll bet! She's a holy terror, isn't she! Even my Dad says so."

Billy had trouble holding back a tear or two when he took the pencils. "It was awful," he said. "I'm not a thief! What's a couple of old pencils, anyway. They were half used up."

Harry grinned. "You remember what she did to me? All I did was punch Charlie in the stomach and he threw up. She took me to the Poor Farm to show me where bums end up."

Billy shuddered. "What was it — was it as awful as the jail?"

"I'll bet it was worse," Harry said. "Old sick people — they pee in their clothes and do worse than that. No one cleans 'em up. Some of 'em are crazy — clean out of their heads. One old man grabbed my arm and he wouldn't let go. He thought I was somebody else. My Dad said it was a sickness old people get. He called it see-nile or something like that."

Harry's father was a doctor.

Billy stirred from where he sat. He began to feel better. "I gotta go in. Thanks for the pencils, Harry. See ya tomorrow."

The next morning before school, Billy handed Harry a torn piece of paper with a drawing on it. Harry looked at it. "Hey, that's real good, Billy. Gee, thanks."

Billy smiled. "It's not very good. But maybe you can tell it's your dog."

After the jail visit with Billy, Miss Stella Binkelmott went home with a great feeling of satisfaction. She had done her duty. She had taken the first important step in saving another boy from sin. From Satan. From almost certain disaster. A disaster she was all too familiar with. Hell-fire itself.

She removed her coat and hung it carefully, then she

took out the hatpins that anchored her hat. She sat down heavily, folded her hands beneath her chin and began to pray aloud. "Lord God Almighty," she intoned, "on this day I have endeavored to save a soul from the eternally burning fires of hades...." She always began her prayers the same way: Lord God Almighty. She could not possibly bring herself to address God as the Father. That was unthinkable.

Later, she built a small fire in the kitchen cookstove, heated a pot of stew, ate, and did the two dishes she had used. Then it was time for bed. A dreaded time in Miss Binkelmott's life. Would the nightmare come to haunt her again? She never knew when it would come. She wished with all her might that she could forget — put the whole haunting memory behind her forever. Never have the awful dream again... the dream that brought it all back in vivid detail.

Miss Stella Binkelmott sighed. She struck a match and lit a small kerosene lamp on the bedside table. She took her hairpins out and shook her head wearily. Thin wisps of gray fell below her shoulders. She removed her gray dress and hung it in the closet. Then the wool petticoat, the high-laced shoes, the heavy wool stockings, the corset, the chemise and the drawers. She felt uncomfortable, naked. She pulled a flannel nightgown down over her head as quickly as she could. Then a few swipes with a washcloth. Cold water. The chamberpot. And she was ready for bed. She blew out the lamp and settled in. Reluctantly, she closed her eyes. Then she prayed again. Out loud, as if God was in the room. She liked to think He was hovering above her bed, somewhere up by the ceiling, in the dark, watching over her. But if He was up there, why did He let the nightmares come? Finally she murmured "Thy Will Be Done," and drifted off to sleep....

It was always 1894. She knew the year because she was fifteen years old. That was the way the dream always started.... Winter, early evening and she was home in bed with a mustard plaster on her chest because she had a bad cold. Her mother was at a Ladies Section meeting at the church. Her father, who owned a hardware store on Santa Catarina's main street, was not home yet.

Stella had undone her braids and was out of bed, brushing her hair, when she heard the front door downstairs. Father, she thought. Or Mother, who was due home any minute. Stella got back into bed, then she heard the door open and close again. There was a low murmur of voices, her father and mother. Then she heard sobbing. Wild, uncontrolled sobs. Her mother. She had never heard her mother cry like that. And her father's voice trying to quiet her mother.

Stella crept out of bed to peer down through the carved staircase. Her mother was still sobbing, but quieter now. Her father was saying "Hush — hush — you'll wake Stella. She must not know. It's all over and done with now. In a few weeks we'll have the insurance money and maybe I can start over. No one will ever know."

"Oh, how could you? How could you? If anyone ever finds out —" Her mother moaned.

"No one will find out! I did it very carefully. Kerosene — tipped over — probably by the cat — spilled on rags. That could happen. Near the stove. It's all perfectly logical. Now dry your eyes — the firemen will be sending someone here any minute to tell me. You've got to act surprised. Wipe your eyes — quick!"

"All right," her mother said. "I just never thought you'd do it — and I wish to God you hadn't. We could get by, somehow."

Stella was in a state of shock as she went back to her room and crawled into bed. She felt numb. Her body seemed to weigh a ton. Thoughts that were unthinkable, whirled through her brain. But it was true. Her father had burned down his store. She had heard it in his own words. True, he had talked about problems this past year. A new hardware store had moved into town and it was taking some of his business. He was worried. But this was unbelievable. She settled down and tried to tell herself she hadn't heard it.

Then she could hear the town firebell; it hung on a high scaffolding above the fire house where the hose carts were kept. It was really happening. She lay there with tears squeezing out from under her closed eyelids and tried not to think. When her mother came to her bedroom door a few moments later, Stella pretended to be asleep. Her mother looked in and went away. Suddenly there was pounding on the front door below. A fireman was there. She beard her father's shout of "Oh no!" The door slammed as he left with the fireman and there was the sound of her mother's sobbing again.

Stella got up and went to the bedroom window. It was almost dark. She could see flames shooting high into the sky just two blocks away where her father's store was located. She stood watching for a moment, then threw on a coat, slipped her feet into shoes, pulled a shawl over her head and crept down the back stairs.

She went quickly through the gathering darkness to the corner where a small crowd of neighbors had collected to watch the spectacle. No one noticed Stella. They were all watching the flames and the firemen who were attempting to direct a hose stream of water.

"Where did it start?" someone asked.

"In old man Binkelmott's store," someone answered.

"Huh — do you think he set it?" another person asked. And laughed.

Stella turned and fled back to the house. She slipped back to her bedroom window in time to see one of Santa Catarina's volunteer hose teams race past, headed for the fire. As she watched, the flames in the distance seemed to grow and expand until the whole sky seemed to be afire.

Her mother came into her room. "Oh Stella, you're up."

"Yes. I — I heard the fire bell."

Her mother sat down in the rocker near the bed. "I have some bad news, my dear little girl. Your father's store is burning. A fireman came to tell us awhile ago. Your father has gone with him."

Stella was silent for a moment. She didn't know what to say. She couldn't — wouldn't — say what she knew. Finally she said "What happened?"

"We don't know," her mother said. "Something must have caught fire in the storeroom. You know, your father keeps kerosene in there. Perhaps the cat — we just don't know, my dear. We must wait and see. Your father will be back with the news soon. You mustn't worry, dear. Now get back into bed and I'll cover you. I don't want you to get chilled."

Her mother left and Stella lay in bed until she heard the front door slam. She got up and went to the head of the stairs again. Her father was moaning. Her mother was crying again. Her father sounded desperate.

"I never meant for that to happen, so help me God — the whole block is going. Oh God! There's nothing they can do — they can't stop it. Oh if I hadn't...." He choked off his words.

Stella crept back to bed. The whole block! That meant the hotel, the bank and other stores. She was shivering with terror when she pulled up the covers.

What would happen? If anyone found out, would her father go to jail? To prison? She began to cry. Finally, much later, she slept.

Two days later, after tortuous visits from concerned friends and neighbors, after living a lie of terror, Stella went down to view the wreckage. She wasn't allowed to get very close. There were barricades along the entire length of the block. Blackened timbers, collapsed brick walls, open sky where there had been roofs, broken glass and wisps of smoke still rising from the ruins. Stella looked and she felt sick.

Then there was school. She had always liked school and had done well in her studies. But now she dreaded going. Most of her classmates were sympathetic but there were several who weren't.

One boy looked at her slyly and said "My Pa says he'd bet a dollar that fire was set."

Another boy piped up: "The police and the firemen are trying to find out."

"Aw, they'll never find out," the first boy said. "My Pa says it was done real clever-like to make it look like an accident."

Stella couldn't stand to hear any more. She walked away, fighting back tears. She went through hell for weeks. Her own private hell.

The Santa Catarina Daily Wave came out with headlines and stories. The Bank had lost some records which would keep it closed for several months. The bakery next door was a total loss and not expected to open again, due to financial problems of the owner, who had no insurance. A shoe store would open eventually, after rebuilding was completed, and so on. One front-page story dealt with the cause of the fire which, it stated, was under an investigation which, it was expected, would yield nothing specific.

Stella hated to see neighbors approaching. She began to avoid people. And she began to suffer the nightmares which were to pursue her to the day she died....

It was night and she was in her nightgown with bare feet. The flames were shooting high, higher, until the whole world above and below her seemed to be on fire. When the flames reached for her, she awoke, ice cold and shaking. Stella lost weight. She grew pale and nervous, but her lips were sealed permanently over the horrible secret. She vowed to herself that she would never let it out. Never. Not if she lived to be a hundred. She also began to realize that she would never marry. How could she? And so she lived a lonely life of going to school, and later, teaching.

The most difficult times of those years for her were when her father showed his affection toward her. She had always loved and admired her father. And being an only child, her father had indulged her, he had shown her off to his friends and bragged about her to relatives, because she was a bright girl who did well in school.

Now, when he called her "My little Stella," and stroked

her fair hair, she pulled away with a shrinking feeling in her stomach. He didn't seem to notice and she was thankful for that because she pitied him in her own way. In just a few months he had changed from a distinguished looking, middle-aged man of substance, into an old, uncertain human being whose eyes were shadowed and who shuffled when he walked. The insurance money came, but her father never smiled, he always seemed worried about something and a cloud of sadness surrounded him.

Just two years after the fire, when Stella graduated from Santa Catarina High School at age seventeen, her father died. He had never started another business — said he'd lost heart in it. They had lived carefully on the insurance money and it was almost gone when he died. Stella immediately took the examinations to become a teacher. A college education was not necessary in 1896. She passed the oral and written tests and got a job in the grammar school the following fall. From that, she went on a few years later to teach at the high school she had once attended. Her mother died and Stella continued to live alone in the modest family home. She had few friends. Her students half admired her and half feared her in a way that students have, and behind her back they referred to her as 'Old Tinkelpot.' Not even fellow-teachers got close to Stella; she kept herself aloof from everyone and people sensed an invisible wall around her.

What they didn't know was that when she was fifteen, she had made that ironclad vow to herself, the vow she lived by. Her mission in life became to save her students from sin, as well as to educate them. She didn't live long after she retired from teaching at age forty-eight. Her eyesight was failing, her health was frail. Almost as if she couldn't bear to look at the world anymore. She once said "I can't stand the bright sun — it hurts my eyes."

About Billy Lethington, who toured the town jail: he graduated from Santa Catarina High, left for San Francisco to work his way through art school, and became a successful graphic artist.

Billy's friend, Harry Parker, went away to medical school, following in his father's footsteps. He came back to Santa Catarina and took over the practice.

Stella is buried in the Protestant cemetery just outside Santa Catarina, alongside her mother and father. Her tombstone is engraved with the motto "Faithful Unto the End." Yes, indeed. More faithful than the distant relative, who came to town to bury her, could know.

SHE HAD TAKING WAYS

Annette Bowles took to kleptomania in her old age like a duck to water. Not that she would have called it that. She might have thought of it as "borrowing" or a "hobby." She didn't know the word kleptomania although she reminded everyone — constantly — that she was an educated woman who sometimes wrote social pieces for the Santa Catarina weekly. Things like church socials, potlucks, meetings of the Daughters of the Great Grizzly and the Temperance Society. She didn't work fulltime for the newspaper. Just piece work — enough to make a dollar or two for an article, to stretch her limited income.

Annette's late husband, Morley Bowles, had worked for the Weekly Wave first as a reporter, then as an editor, before he died of a heart attack in 1910. Annette never let anyone forget that either, and every chance she got she referred to her late husband, "The Editor."

Annette and Morley had a son and a daughter, both grown, married and gone to greener pastures. "My son is an educated man," she liked to say. Education was important to her, perhaps because she herself had gone only through the sixth grade, a fact she never mentioned. "When Morley Bowles and I came to Santa Catarina thirty years ago, there were more people here who couldn't sign their own names than those who could," she'd say.

Annette was a packrat at heart, a quality that used to annoy her husband and children. She saved bits of string, tied them all together, thick or thin, long or short, for no real purpose at all.

"String is always useful," she'd say. "Waste not, want not." But she never used any of it. She saved newspapers — copies of The Wave, tied in bundles which collected in piles almost up to the roof out in the woodshed. "You never know, I might want to look something up some day," she said, but never did.

She saved pieces of cloth, all kinds, all colors. Pieces cut from wornout skirts and shirtwaists. Piles of the pieces began to fill bureau drawers and corners of closets. "I might want to make a quilt some day," she remarked but never did.

Editor Bowles used to get impatient. "My God Annette! We'll have to build more rooms on if you keep at it," he would growl.

She would look at him reproachfully. "I am sorry to hear you take the Lord's name in vain, Morley." But she went right on collecting.

Their son, Ralph Waldo Emerson Bowles (named for the American poet) secretly believed his mother was a bit daffy. Shelley, the daughter (named for the English poet), had a different theory.

"Mama was raised poor," she'd say privately. "It's because of that. And anyway, it's harmless. Kind of like a hobby."

"Hobby indeed!" muttered Emerson, whose bottom bureau drawer was being invaded. He had gone off to college and come home to find piles of 'quilt cloth' accumulating where he had always kept his shirts.

Editor Bowles solved the problem by dying. Emerson solved it by departing for a fine job in San Francisco, and Shelley married a hard working farmer and moved to Fresno. Annette was left alone in her old age, in reasonably good health, with a small pension. She lived simply, her cottage was paid for and she wrote occasional social bits and pieces for the Wave, to pay for extras. There were donations from Emerson for taxes and the heavier expenses. He came to see her a couple of times a year when his conscience bothered him. Shelley was so busy birthing and raising a brood of farm kids that she didn't have time to think about her conscience. She sent Christmas and birthday notes.

So Annette, who had always considered herself a cut above the ordinary Santa Catarina housewife, lived a lonely life. She lacked the money, the fine Victorian house and the fancy clothes to mingle with the town's social set.

She could be seen walking down, or up, one or both of the main streets every day. A tall, thin woman (she had beat Editor Bowles by a good four inches in height), wearing a long, gray wool coat and a gray turban style hat over her gray hair which she pulled back in a bun. The only color was in her face: her pink cheeks (rouge) and her blue eyes. In summer the gray coat was replaced with a gray dress, tailored with long sleeves, pockets and a row of gray buttons. Annette seemed to own nothing but drab gray garments in which she floated up and down the streets of Santa Catarina like a gray cloud.

The pockets were a necessity, both in the coat and dress, although they didn't start out that way. Originally they were intended to hold handkerchiefs and necessities like gloves. But they became critical in Annette's career as a kleptomaniac.

It began one day in Jensen's drugstore. Annette had awakened that morning with a slight headache, had gone to the bathroom cabinet for a pill and found the bottle empty. She looked at the bottle for a moment, shook it as if to make sure, then decided it might come in handy some day and that was the start of her bottle collection in the back porch. She figured she could move the empty fruit jars — maybe give them away. She wasn't putting up preserves any more. That would give her two long shelves for bottles. She leaned toward colored bottles and remembered happily that she already had a dark blue seltzer bottle — almost empty too.

But the headache still bothered her. So she dressed, drank a cup of coffee, ate a piece of toast and left for town which was a short walk from her house. By then it was ten o'clock. The drugstore was open. Annette knew where the pills were and as she entered she nodded to Olaf Jensen who was putting a display of enema paraphernalia in his front window. She went directly to the pill shelf and selected a bottle. Then she looked thoughtful for a moment before she took another bottle which she popped into her coat pocket. At the counter while she waited for Olaf to come, she noticed a box of breath mints handy and a packet of mints joined the extra bottle of pills in her coat pocket.

Olaf Jensen can afford it — he's rich as Croesus, she said to herself. Not that she knew who Croesus was, but she had heard Editor Bowles use the term and she thought it sounded elegant. Educated.

She paid Olaf Jensen for one bottle of pills and left with the other bottle and the mints in her pocket. And that was the start of Annette Bowles' secret life of crime, if it could be called that. At first she limited herself to small items she felt she needed, articles that she could conceal in her hand and slip quickly into a pocket. New tortoise shell combs and a hairbrush from the department store. A jar of cold cream from the drugstore. A package of hairpins, a box of face powder, a bottle of cough drops — because winter was coming and she might catch a cold. Last winter she had a terrible cough, she reflected in a moment of self-justification. And no money for a doctor's visit because the roof leaked and it cost dearly to get it fixed. It wouldn't hurt to have cough drops on hand.

She looked longingly at a pair of new lovely patent leather shoes in Gerby's Shoestore but she couldn't quite figure out how she could acquire them.

She began to visit Olaf Jensen's drugstore several times a week to pilfer small articles and penny candies, often smiling at him sweetly and saying she was "just looking, thank you." But Olaf was no fool. Soon he invested in new glass cases with sturdy sliding lids that were not easy to open.

Then Annette began to haunt the glove and ribbon counter at McLeavitt's Novelty Store. On her first visit she asked to see a fine pair of gray kidskin gloves, then after laboriously trying them on, forcing each finger into the right-handed glove (the right hand was always considered to be larger than the left), she complained that the glove was too tight. The harried clerk, a Miss Forbes, then got out several boxes of slightly larger sizes. Then Annette spent a busy half-hour going through gray kidskin gloves, managing to stash a well-fitting pair in her coat pocket when the clerk's back was turned, and leaving a pile of gloves with the fingers turned wrong side out for the confused Miss Forbes to straighten out. Annette spoke politely to the clerk as she left the store, explaining that none of them was exactly what she wanted, thank you, and she had decided to wait.

At the ribbon counter on another day she managed a similar scene of disaster although the ribbons were on small spools. Before she was done, the clerk had spools of many colors unwound on the counter top as Annette struggled to decide the exact lengths she needed. She left without making a purchase, saying she had to go home and make more measurements but she'd be back another day after she figured it out. When she walked out there was a spool of emerald green silk ribbon in her pocket.

She didn't need emerald green ribbon or, for that matter, any other color, but she put it into her top bureau drawer and told herself it would make a nice trim for a robe, if she ever wanted to make a robe.

When the department store had its annual sale of yard goods remnants, odd lengths left over from bolts of fabrics, Annette made a killing. She had both coat pockets stuffed and managed to conceal a length of silk in her skirt pocket as well. Enough pieces for a new nightgown, a cotton house dress and a silk blouse. But she tucked them away at home and never got around to making the garments.

Annette was so busy acquiring treasures that she

hadn't written any society notes for the Weekly Wave for some time. She also was running out of closet space and shelves and drawers and was considering making shelves from cardboard boxes on her back porch and in her garage where there were still a few empty spaces.

"Plenty of room out in the garage," she said to herself. The family had never owned a car. Once, when Emerson wanted one, Editor Bowles had snorted at the suggestion and reminded them of the expense of keeping up a car — especially when they lived a mere three blocks from the newspaper office and all the downtown stores.

One day when Annette was taking her usual walk downtown, she happened to pass the Santa Catarina Ladies Exchange. She had passed it often but with total lack of professional interest. It was a charitable project to which the wealthier ladies of the town donated clothing and objects of art they had tired of, to be sold with the proceeds going to an orphanage run by the Catholic nuns. Annette had never considered going inside. Lace and rose-trimmed hats and sealskin fur capes and Chinese vases didn't appeal to her. Neither did Persian rugs or crystal goblets. But on this particular day she happened to catch sight of an amethyst brooch in a tray of brooches, rings and bracelets in the window. Beautiful. She stopped to look. The brooch was star-shaped, paved with small and larger stones that winked purple and lavender at her, inviting her to possess it, or so it seemed to her.

"Amethysts. My birthstone," she said to herself. She went in.

Volunteer society women waited on customers at the Exchange, and behind the counter on that particular day was Mrs. George Ferris, wife of the managing editor of the Wave. Annette stopped in her tracks for a second and almost turned to leave, then gathered her courage.

"Good day, Mrs. Ferris," she said, hoping her words sounded pleasant.

"Why, Annette Bowles! How nice to see you. What can I help you with?" Mrs. Ferris, knowing Annette's financial status, hoped her words sounded cordial and not too surprised.

Annette hesitated. She didn't intend to mention the amethyst brooch which she felt should really belong to her. After all, her birthday was in February.

Finally she said "I am looking for a gift for my daughter — I thought perhaps a brooch or a bracelet. Something not too costly."

Mrs. Ferris went at once to the window jewelry display and returned with the velvet lined tray. It held more than twenty pieces.

"We have some lovely things here, " she said.

Annette made as if to pick one up, then hesitated. "May I?"

Mrs. Ferris said "Why, of course. Feel free to look at any of them. And make sure the clasps work — they are all supposed to, but sometimes — we can have them repaired, of course."

Annette picked up a garnet pin and looked at the price tag. "Lovely," she said, and placed it on the counter. Soon she had a half dozen there. "I don't know," she said. "I can't decide. Do you think garnets are suitable?"

Mrs. Ferris smiled. "The garnets are lovely. But wait a moment. We have several more garnet pieces in that glass case in the comer." She crossed the room to get them, giving Annette the perfect opportunity to slip the amethyst brooch — which she had not yet touched — into her pocket. Mrs. Ferris returned with a bracelet and another pin which Annette surveyed briefly.

"Mrs. Ferris, I really can't seem to decide today. I believe I will have to give it some thought for a few days."

Mrs. Ferris laid the garnet pieces on the counter. "Well, if you think that's best, certainly. We're always here, you know. And we do have these nice garnet pieces. You think it over and you can always come back."

Annette thanked her, trying not to sound in too much of a hurry, and left. Mrs. Ferris looked after her with a faint feeling of puzzlement and sorrow. Sorrow because she suspected the prices were beyond Annette's means and she liked Annette. Puzzled because — she didn't know why she felt puzzled. Oh well. She busied herself putting the pieces on the counter back into the tray. Such pretty things. She hummed softly as she fitted the brooches into the little velvet grooves. Then she stopped. The star amethyst brooch — the brooch she had herself donated to the Exchange — was gone.

"Oh my God!" she said softly as realization hit her.

Annette fingered the star brooch in her pocket as she walked home. She didn't take it out for fear of dropping it, but she could hardly wait until she was inside hanging up her coat. Then she put it on the kitchen table where she could look at it while she fixed herself a cup of tea. She counted the amethysts. There were twenty-two. Then she looked at the price tag. Fifteen dollars. She toyed with the idea of pinning it to her dress. But no. She couldn't do that. What if someone came to the door — the mailman or one of the women from the church. It would be the first thing they would notice. No, she couldn't take a chance on wearing it. It was too noticeable — too different — too unique — too beautiful. She sighed. She would pin it to her nightgown and wear it to bed, she decided. She just had to wear it somewhere.

She put the lovely pin away in her dresser with the gold-plated bracelet Editor Bowles had given her years ago and which she didn't wear because it caught on everything. Then she did some thinking. Not consciously, but her brain was busy as she sipped her tea. Jewelry. Small things. Pretty. Easy to get. To hide. And not so likely to be missed. She had never owned many pretty things and it would be nice to have a few — just a few to look at. Maybe to wear if she went to visit Emerson or Shelley. Away from Santa Catarina. She couldn't go back to the Ladies Exchange, but there were other places. The novelty store had trinkets. Not as expensive as the Exchange, but some were very pretty. Things made of abalone shell and redwood burl. And then there was McLeavitt's Department Store. There were cards of jeweled buttons — rhinestones — gold and silver colored filagree and some enameled ones. Maybe she could even replace some of the plain gray buttons on her dresses. How would that be? If she kept her coat on....

Kleptomania for Annette had become a way of life, a hedge against boredom, a challenge. She set about making plans for a collection of costume jewelry and buttons. And that was her undoing.

Over a period of several months she worked her way through a number of trinkets at the novelty store where they were displayed openly, and she acquired a collection of buttons from McLeavitt's where they were fastened to cards which hung from small metal racks on the counter. She even considered going back to the Ladies Exchange but thought better of it. Then everything changed. Suddenly. With a letter from Emerson.

"Mama, I want you to sell the house and come to live with us in San Francisco," he wrote. "I will come down in a week or two and start making arrangements. You have been alone too long and we worry about you...."

Annette shook her head as she read it. She couldn't believe it. Emerson and his wife had never paid much attention to her — she had met his wife only once, briefly. She sighed. She didn't want to leave Santa Catarina. But when Emerson made up his mind...; he was just like his father.

The letter was not prompted by Emerson's sudden concern for his mother. Actually it came about because of a meeting in Santa Catarina. Every year the merchants and the newspaper editor, George Ferris, got together for lunch and a discussion of the state of business in Santa Catarina. Olaf Jensen was there. So were Jerrold McLeavitt of the department store and Preston Draper of the novelty store. There were others: Irving Parks who owned the undertaking parlors, Joe Perry of the local butcher shop, Jesse Hayes, the proprietor of the hardware store and Matt Gerby who owned the shoestore. Annette had never 'collected' from these four.

When the luncheon conversation got around to profits and losses a number of the merchants agreed that 'pilfering' as they put it, was becoming a serious problem. Olaf sat back with a little smile and said nothing. Editor Ferris, who was recalling a surprising conversation with his wife, looked startled at first, then listened carefully as the merchants compared notes.

"I don't think it's the kids," one said. "Kids don't go for shell beads and such. They snitch penny candies or gum."

"It's not the kids," McLeavitt said firmly. "My ribbon clerk — she handles the gloves too — she has an idea who it is. At first I didn't believe it. But now.... I've lost buttons — whole cards of 'em — more than I care to count. And those kidskin gloves don't come cheap. They cost me a pretty penny."

"With me it's mostly odds and ends — shell jewelry, those little redwood novelties, things like that," said Preston Draper. "But it sure adds up."

"Hmmm. I haven't lost a thing," commented Matt Gerby. "Business's been pretty good this year."

"That's easy to figure," McLeavitt said testily. "How's somebody going to lift a pair of shoes? Pockets ain't big enough to hide 'em in — neither is a lady's purse."

Editor Ferris spoke up then. "Boys I think I know who it is. In fact I'm sure I know. Don't ask me how. But I do. And we have a problem. I can tell you that. It's a lady who is well-known in town, highly regarded, she's a widow — not much money, church member, mother of two, well-thought of — now what're you going to do? You can't send a woman like that to jail, can you?"

They looked at him with degrees of amazement, all except Olaf Jensen who continued to smile and now he was nodding his head too.

McLeavitt said "My God! All those buttons. What could she do with them?"

"Now I think I can handle this for all of us," Editor

Ferris said solemnly. "Without a lot of fuss — without hurting anyone."

"The hurt's already been done — those gloves ain't cheap," muttered McLeavitt.

"Give me a week or two to see what I can do," Editor Ferris suggested.

"You've got my vote," McLeavitt said.

"And mine," Draper said. "Go ahead, if you're sure you know who it is."

"We ain't stupid," McLeavitt said. "I think we all got a pretty good idee who it is. I won't mention any names."

"Mentioning names won't help," Editor Ferris said. "Olaf, you haven't said a word. How do you feel about this?"

"Don't need to say nothing." Olaf said. "I fix it my own way. Yes, I lose stuff too. Little things. Lots of them. Pills. Lots of pills. Face powder. Hairbrush. Combs. Cold cream. You name it, I lose it."

"But what did you do to stop it?" Draper wanted to know.

Olaf smiled. "I got me some of them glass cases. New ones with good lids that slide. Kind of heavy-like. They work fine."

They all laughed.

The meeting broke up with Editor Ferris's promise to take care of the problem. He knew Emerson Bowles well — in fact they exchanged news stories regularly, with Emerson sending him the more important stories from San Francisco.

About a week later Annette received that letter from Emerson.

"At your age, Mama, you should have family near by to watch over you," he wrote. "We'll sell the house and you will have plenty of money to live on. At your age you shouldn't be alone...."

At first Annette didn't want to leave Santa Catarina. But then she got to thinking. San Francisco. All those great big department stores. Lovely things they had. It might be interesting.

She decided to go.

A LOAF OF BREAD,
A JUG OF BOOZE, AND...

Those were the best nights, the safest nights, when the moon was blinded by fog and a signal from shore would bring a motorboat into Capper's Cove. Joseph Stavovich waited on the cliffs above the Cove, just three miles north of Santa Catarina. His flashlight was fire in the night, wide sweeping arcs that brought answering signals — sharp pin dots of light, from a large ship anchored out a mile or more.

Then there was the wait in the darkness while the waves churned below. Finally, the soft sound of a motor, muted voices and a boat grating on the sand. Another cargo of bottles coming ashore. Bottles filled with alcohol, bottles wrapped in straw. Illegal alcohol. Those were the days of Prohibition in 1921 when Joseph Stavovich and his pal Pete Donetti were going to make a fortune bootlegging. Rum running.

In the process, Joseph became adept at predicting the weather and its effect on moonlight.

"Them are the best nights — cloudy or foggy," he said to Pete. Pete ran the Little Italia Card Room in Santa Catarina. Formerly a saloon, until the Revenooers as he called them, shut down the liquor. Pete didn't give up easily and for a time, his bathtub gin was served to thirsty card players. He made it at home and kept a small supply locked in the storeroom behind his card room. That was before he and Joseph started their rum running business.

Pete managed to get away with his home tub operation, which went well until the Sheriff caught on and threatened to close down the card room and all, unless Pete stopped making bathtub booze. So he stopped.

Joseph Stavovich was a big, broad-shouldered hard-working man. Four days a week he drove his Model T Ford truck and delivered the loaves of bread his wife baked for residents of Santa Catarina and several nearby towns. It was good bread. On delivery days he loaded the wood trays of crusty loaves into the back of the truck and started off on the roads. On the other days he split wood for his wife's big black cookstove with the double ovens, hauled sacks of flour home from the grocery store and helped her with the dough. Sundays they went to church. Nettie Stavovich was a dedicated Methodist, although she had married Joseph who was a casual Catholic. He attended dutifully with her.

It was hard work but they made a decent living and owned their cottage and the Model T Ford 'free and clear' as Nettie liked to say. She was a good woman, satisfied with her lot in life. But Joseph wasn't above making a few more dollars. And the fact that it was bootlegging didn't bother him a whit. At first.

"The guvmint's got no business cutting out all a man's pleasures," he would say of Prohibition. He liked a horn once in a while. Nettie just frowned. Joseph and Pete got their idea for combining bread and booze one evening when he was at the card room for a game of poker.

"You got anything to drink, Pete? I'm dry tonight."

Pete shook his head. "Hell, I could sell gallons of whiskey if I could get it," he complained. "I had me a fellow with a still up Buzzard Canyon. Corn likker. He was bringin' it down here every week until the Sheriff got him. Now all I got is the gin I make. Not much of that. Can't take a chance keeping it here. That Sheriff is hell on wheels. He was here sniffing around again. Threatened to shut me down."

"There's gotta be someone else in the hills making likker," Joseph said.

"Not right now there ain't," Pete said. "Not with that fine they slap on you — that and jail too. Ferget the stills in the mountains. I know a feller owns a motorboat — he's got real connections. There's a ship delivers along the coast. Could be a hell of a good deal. But I can't do nothing about it. The Sheriff's watching me like a hawk ever since he caught the feller up the canyon. Guess be suspects he was selling to me."

"A boat?" Joseph was interested.

"Yep. The ship loads up down south, brings it up and has drops along the coast. Diego to Frisco. Regular."

"How does he know when to send the stuff ashore?"

"Light signals. They got a small boat that brings it in. All good stuff. Bottles wrapped in straw so they don't break easy. I had me one delivery but I can't keep an eye on the card room and do that too. The Sheriff would be right on my tail. So forget it!"

Joseph went home and thought about it. His evenings were free, or could be, after the bread dough was set. The whole idea intrigued him. The more he thought about it the more excited he got. Nettie would have a fit. She even wore a white ribbon pinned to her coat when they went to church, to show she favored Prohibition. He couldn't tell her, of course. But he had to tell her something when he went off at night. It was risky.

Pete provided the excuse. "Tell her you're helpin' me down at the card room," he suggested. "She won't come down here to find out."

That was how Joseph got into the booze delivery business.

He did some more thinking. He would have to put a deeper box on the back of the truck. Something he could hide the booze in and cover it with the bread. He got busy and built it in a couple of days, telling Nettie it was an improvement since their bread business was growing.

The box he constructed had a false bottom so he could carry two layers of bottles below and the usual trays of bread above.

"Now all we gotta do is get word to the right people," Pete said. "And I gotta put a flea in the ear of a certain deputy."

Joseph looked at him and whistled. "A deputy! But the Sheriff...."

"Nothin' to worry about there," Pete said. "Deputy Lewis is all right. He knows when to keep his mouth shut. He don't talk none."

Joseph quit worrying. It was going to be easier than he thought.

"But we gotta pay him off," Pete said.

"Pay him? How much?"

"We gotta dicker with him. He'll be here tonight for his regular poker game."

Joseph was worried again. "How do we know he won't talk? My God — if Nettie ever finds out —."

"Don't worry. Lewis had a close mouth. Nettie won't know nothing. But we got to make sure. Lewis gets his cut and his brother gets a piece too."

"His brother!"

"Whoa Joseph. You gotta know the ropes to keep outta trouble. His brother is that new judge over in Centerville. He gets an 'insurance cut' just so we're double protected."

"My God man, do the payoffs ever quit?" Joseph said.

Pete put his hand on Joseph's shoulder. "If this deal works out — and no reason why it can't if we do it right, Joseph, we can have us a regular run up to Whaler's Point and Salt Flats. Then down to Centerville. There's a lot of thirsty customers around these parts. Card rooms, lodges, eating places."

"I'll have to count on my bread days to make deliveries," Joseph said.

"Don't worry — I make the contacts, you deliver, and it'll pay. It'll pay!" Pete reassured him.

"It better pay," Joseph said. "With all those cuts

coming out of it."

Pete was pleased. "I been wantin' to set up a deal like this for months. Now we're partners and we'll both make plenty of cash. We keep track of how many bottles — write it down — you bring them here — we put them in my storeroom behind the card room. There's plenty money in it for us both."

"How do I know when to make the pick-ups?"

"Leave it to me. I let you know. Telephone. I call Lewis and let him know what nights to be on duty. It'll work, Joseph."

"Sounds all right, I guess. But I sure don't like all those cuts. We take all the chances and they get a free ride!"

"Gotta do it that way," Pete said. "No other way to keep in the clear with that Sheriff around. I know Lewis. He's all right and he'll square it with his brother. We got us a deal."

They shook hands. It was settled.

Joseph's nerves were jumping when he made the first pickup and he never got over feeling that way every time he waited on the cliffs in the dark. The first few times he used a lantern. But lighting it took time, especially if the wind was blowing So he bought a flashlight and carried an extra battery.

The routine was simple. Pete made the phone calls and set the schedule. Joseph cleared it with Nettie by telling her he had to help Pete at the card room that night. At first she objected.

"You work all day — then all night too," she said. "And down to that card room — that place...."

"There's no drinking, Nettie. It's all cards — no harm in a man playing cards. And it's extra money for us," he said. So she shut up.

The beaching point for the booze was north of Santa Catarina at Capper's Cove, a small indentation in the cliffs with a patch of sandy beach and a steep trail down to it.

Joseph waited until dark, then with a word to Nettie that he would be working at the card room, he took off. The coast road was a rough track used mainly by farmers and fishermen. Almost exactly three miles out of Santa Cat, he turned toward the cliffs on an almost invisible path that ran to the edge. He parked and waited. The fog was drifting in. The sickle moon danced in and out of the mists. The only sound was waves breaking on a small inlet stretch of sand below the cliff. One hour. Two hours.

Maybe they ain't comin' tonight, he thought.

Then, through the fog, a dark shape loomed out on the water. The boat. The big boat. A ship. A flash of light. Joseph counted. Five flashes. It was them. He raised his flashlight and pointed it at the dark shape, then he swept it in a wide are. Three times. There were three answering flashes from the ship and Joseph started down the trail to the beach.

Below on the sand, he waited. Soon there was the sound of a motor and he made out a small motorboat coming ashore. Two men in it. As soon as it touched the sand, they jumped out and began unloading boxes of bottles. They didn't talk, just worked fast. Then each man shouldered a box and carried it up the trail to the top of the cliff near the truck. They made a number of trips with the boxes which held a dozen bottles of booze each. It was schnapps, from Holland, as Joseph was to learn. He began loading the boxes into the back of his truck and soon it sagged under the load.

One of the men approached Joseph. "There's more down there. Your truck won't hold it. You'll have to make another trip tonight. We'll wait but we can't wait long. You gotta make a delivery and come back to get the rest. You better hurry."

Joseph drove back to Santa Catarina as fast as he dared over the rough coast road. He pulled up at the back of the card room where Pete was waiting. Together they unloaded the heavy boxes and stacked them in the storeroom behind some boards.

"God, they're heavy," Joseph groaned. "And I gotta go back for another load. Couldn't carry all of it."

"Good thing they wrap them in straw so's they won't break," Pete commented. Joseph nodded. "Maybe you oughtta get a bigger truck," Pete suggested. "I'm having another storeroom added on."

"Trucks cost money," Joseph said.

"Don't worry about the money. You'll have it — aplenty," Pete said.

Joseph made the second trip, signed a paper on the beach, the men in the motorboat went back out to their ship and Joseph went home, finally, exhausted. His back ached and Nettie rubbed it with castor oil.

The next morning Nettie remarked "I don't know why you're so tuckered out when all you have to do is help Pete at the card room."

"No, I'm all right. Just getting used to longer hours," he said.

Longer hours, and more1 money. He liked the money. A dollar a box, free and clear, he made. Pete got three and handled the money: paid off the Judge, the big boss who owned the ship, and made sure that Hank Lewis got his cut. Pete also made sure that Hank was on coastal patrol duty on the critical delivery nights,

Joseph got curious once. Just once. "Who is that guy? The big boss — the guy who owns the ship?" he asked.

Pete just looked at him and didn't answer for a moment. "Don't ask." he said finally. "You don't want to know. It's better that way."

Joseph never got a close look at the ship. It was usually shrouded in fog and on clear nights it stayed about a mile off shore. The men who came in the motorboat with the boxes of bottles never talked except to count the boxes and tell Joseph when he had to make an extra trip.

Joseph had always been an honest man, and at first, he was uncomfortable with his new business. But three ten dollar bills at the end of the first week made him feel much

better about it. That is, until he turned the money over to
Nettie, without thinking.

She looked at the bills, then she looked at him. "What
are you doing down there at the card room to make all this
money, Joseph?"

"Worked extra hours," he mumbled. "Helping build a
new storeroom."

However, it was plain to see that he would have to be
more careful. Nettie was getting curious. And she wasn't
stupid. She knew it would take a hell of a lot of penny ante
games to bring in that kind of money. So he began holding
out a good portion of the booze money. He couldn't bank it.
Nettie had the bank book. So he started stuffing the holdout
bills into the pockets of an old overcoat he seldom wore.
But when Nettie began her spring housecleaning, he realized
that was a precarious hiding place. She cleaned the clothes
closets too and sometimes gave away or threw out worn
garments. As she worked in the house one weekend with
her mop and broom and dust cloth, Joseph's desperation
grew. When she wasn't looking, he slipped into their
bedroom closet and removed the wad of bills. He stuffed
them into an old wool sock, hid it under his jacket and
started out the back door.

"Where you going?" Nettie asked. "I may need some
help moving furniture."

"Thought I'd start cleaning out the back shed," Joseph
said.

"Don't you go and work too hard out there," she said.
"You been looking kind of peaked lately, Joseph. Oughtn't
be working such long hours."

"Well, it helps with the extra money," he said.

"Tain't worth it if you get sick. And we got along all
right without it before," she said.

He escaped without answering. Nettie would be in a
hell of a pucker if she found out about the booze business.

Out in the shed, he looked around. He needed a hiding
place. A good one. Nettie seldom came out to the shed where
they kept stove wood and tools. He picked up an empty

paint can. No lid but the sock full of bills fit neatly into it with plenty of room to add more bills. Some day he'd have enough for a new truck. A bigger one. He found a hammer and a nail and climbed on a box and drove the nail high into the wall. Directly beneath a beam. Kind of dark back there. Nettie wouldn't see it. And if she did, she couldn't reach it. Way over her head. By stretching and standing on his toes, Joseph could drop a bill into the paint can. His worries were over. Satisfied, with his mind at ease, he went back into the house to help Nettie.

A few weeks later Joseph and Pete had a bad scare. A storm was blowing in and Pete had arranged for a pickup out at the cliffs.

Joseph was worried. "What if the ship don't come in? If the weather turns real bad.... I could get the truck stuck out there — muddy as hell when it rains."

"You'll be outta there before the weather hits the coast," Pete said.

Later, as Joseph waited on the clifftop he could hear the waves crashing below in the usually calm cove.

"I don't like it," he muttered to himself.

Finally, the ship's signal light flashed and jumped over the rough water. He answered with his flashlight, and heard the motorboat coming ashore. Suddenly there was a shout from below. A crash. More shouts. Joseph ran down the path to the cove. The motorboat had grounded on a submerged rock at one side of the inlet. The two men in it were struggling to get it off the rock. Joseph plunged in to help. The three of them got the boat free, but in the struggle a box of liquor fell into the surging water and sank. In the darkness, the confusion and the growing storm, they didn't miss it. The loss didn't come to light until Joseph was back at Pete's storeroom getting dry pants while Pete tallied up the boxes. By then it was too late. Seven bottles of booze from the broken box had washed ashore; two were broken but the others were intact.

The bottles were discovered a few days later by a group

of high school kids on a beach outing with their teacher. The news spread through town.

The Santa Catarina Daily Wave ran a bold black headline clear across the front page: RUM RUNNERS ON OUR COAST?

The Temperance Ladies went in a body to pound on the Sheriff's desk and demand action. The Sheriff announced that he was putting extra deputies on the coast run.

Pete wasn't pleased. "Hell, Joseph, we got us a pretty kettle of fish! Maybe if we lie low for a few weeks it'll blow over. But we gotta be extra careful. I'll pass the word along. No more deliveries till the coast's clear."

Privately, Joseph felt relieved.

Nettie got curious again. "Joseph, you haven't worked at the card room this week."

Joseph mumbled. "No, things slacked up. But it'll pick up again."

"It's real nice to have that extra money," she said. "But I'm kinda glad you aren't working so hard." She looked at him critically. "Your color's better."

Later, glancing at the Weekly Wave she said "Well, would you look at this! Bottles of liquor washed up on the beach and youngsters found them. Why, that's terrible! Bootleggers right here on our beaches!"

Joseph said something like "Yes—, terrible," and escaped out the back door. He shuddered, thinking what would happen if Nettie ever found out. He hadn't counted his hidden money or looked at it for weeks. He just dropped the bills into the bucket.

He opened the shed door. It smelled musty and he thought he should probably air it out once in awhile. He closed the door, just in case Nettie came out into the back yard. He reached for the paint pail and got it down. *Dark in here,* he thought. *Should have brought a flashlight.* He looked into the pail.

"My God!" He plunged his fingers into it. Small scraps of green paper bills fluttered to the floor. Shreds. He dumped it all out. The wool sock was in strings and every greenback was torn, chewed, ripped and mixed with rat droppings. He just stood there in shock for a few minutes. Stunned. Then he sighed and went back into the kitchen where Nettie was mixing bread dough.

"You know, Nettie, I been thinkin'," he said. "What you said — about me not feelin' so good lately and all. I think I'll tell Pete he better find somebody else. That is — if it's all right with you not gettin' the extra money...."

She wiped her hands on her apron. "Now you're talking sense," she said.

A NEW LIFE

Del Austin was running away when he drove into Santa Catarina one June day in 1922.

He had come from Seattle, Washintgon, in his Nash automobile. He was a total stranger in Santa Cat, as the natives called it, and that was the way he wanted it. He knew no one, no one knew him. He was twenty-eight years old, a high school teacher who was running away from his job, his life in Seattle where he had been born and had grown up. He never intended to go back there and he didn't want anyone in Seattle to know where he was. That included his mother, Lucy Austin, and his father, Graham Austin.

Del's full name was Delbert Graham Austin. Oldest of two boys, he was bright, tall, with slender fingers, brown hair, brown eyes. Honor student in college who graduated into a promising career in teaching.

He was walking out on all of it to make a new life in a new place and he had been driving down the coast almost aimlessly, not caring where he was headed, with a spare gasoline can strapped to the running board because gas pumps were few and far between.

Then he came to Santa Catarina. There was something about the small town on the curving shoreline of the Pacific Ocean that appealed to him. He drove through town a bit, exploring the business and residential streets, and finally located a rooming house where he rented a room. After several days he decided to stay in Santa Cat but he had to get a job. His money wouldn't last more than a month or two. He made discreet inquiries of the elderly landlady and learned that the lumbermills were hiring. No good for him. He looked at his hands. Long, slender fingers. Smooth skin. Hands that had always held books, pens, pencils. Besides he knew nothing about the lumber business.

Then, in conversation with the landlady, he learned that the school had lost a teacher. "Moved back East," she said. "But you'd need a paper — you know — a — a —"

"Certificate," Del finished for her. Then he added, almost too quickly, "No, I can't teach." He knew he would never teach again.

She wanted to be helpful; she handed him the Daily Wave which had recently expanded from four pages to eight. "Here. Sit down and look through the paper. You might find something."

Newspaper. A light went on in Del's brain. He'd like that. He could write. If it didn't work out, he'd move on.

The next day he went to the newspaper office. He could see that it was a casual operation. Four untidy desks with typewriters. Two reporters at work, one plunking away with two fingers, the other with a hat pulled down over his eyes, leafing through a notebook, frowning. There was the smell of printer's ink and well-oiled machinery. A tiny glassed cubicle in one comer held another desk piled high with papers and an older man that Del supposed was the editor. Through an open doorway beyond the cubicle, Del could see two linotype machines and a printing press.

He approached the cubicle. The door was open and the editor was bent over some papers, busily writing. Del knocked, then said "Mr. Bush?" He had noticed the editor's name in the landlady's newspaper.

"Yes? Come in, come in." Editor Bush sounded testy.

Del decided to get it over with. "I'm looking for a job."

Jeff Bush looked up, his eyes were sharp behind his glasses. "You a linotype man?"

"I'd like to write," Del said.

"Oh. A reporter, eh? Had any experience?"

"No, but I have a college degree. And I can write."

"Hmph. I've had those before. Most of 'em don't know sic-em. What's your name? Where you from? Do you drink?"

"Drink?" Del was mystified for a moment. "No — maybe once in awhile. But I'm not a boozer if that's what you mean."

"That's exactly what I mean, young man. It's an occupational hazard that goes with the job. Lost my last two reporters that way." He motioned to the chair that was squeezed into the corner across from his desk. "One in jail down in Salinas — the other gone God knows where. Just walked out."

He looked Del over. "Maybe I can use you. Now, let's get down to business."

An hour later, Del left with the promise of a job, starting in a week. And that evening he made a long distance phone call to Seattle, to his brother, Paul.

"Paul — little brother — it's me. Can you hear me? This is a terrible connection.... Yes, I'm all right. Where? In a little place called Santa Catarina — on the coast. California. Yes, I just got one — reporter. Newspaper. No.... I'm not coming back." He paused. "I can't." He was silent for a moment, listening. Then "Yeah, maybe I am running away. You think I am, don't you. But Paul, you always understood and no one else — Mother — Father — it's no good, Paul. I'm the way I am. Nothing can change that. But I can try. I've got to do it, Paul. Make a new life here. If it doesn't work, I'll move on."

He gave Paul his address before they finished the conversation. "I don't want anyone but you to know where I am, Paul. I trust you. You're the best friend I have, little brother."

Then he hung up and buried his face in his hands. The painful memories came flooding back: his father shouting at him, "What kind of a man do you call yourself!" His mother crying, moaning "The disgrace — it's not normal."

His father's words again: "A damned fairy in the family!"

It wasn't that he had actually flaunted anything, Del thought. He hadn't. It was just that he knew in his heart that he was different. Ever since he was a child, he had known. And he had tried to talk to them about it. His mother was always trying to pair him up with an eligible young lady. His father couldn't understand why he was closing on thirty and not married yet.

Growing up, as a high school student, Del had done the usual things — gone to dances and parties. But he had always felt out of place around girls. He had avoided them. Then, once a girl had kissed him. He could smile now, remembering his surprised shock and the swift rush of distaste he felt.

College was different. The first year, he roomed with a couple of carefree fellows who could care less what he preferred in his sex life. By the second year, he had made a contact — Bob. They roomed together, graduated together and taught together in the same school. They shared an apartment in Seattle — that is, until the principal called him in one day for a talk. A talk that centered about his influence on young people. Young men. High school students. There was something nasty about the whole discussion, he felt afterward. He knew he had taken care to avoid any of the attitudes and influences the principal was talking about so carefully. That conference was the beginning of the end of his teaching career. And now, here he was, in Santa Catarina. Leaving it all behind him. Except the wakeful nights and the dreams. The nights when he would get up, get dressed, and go out to walk for hours in the dark.

But could he leave it all behind? Change?

Paul didn't think so. "You have to be what you are, Del," he had said, when Del was packing up to leave Seattle.

"Then I'll be it some place else," Del had answered.

The newspaper job worked out. He liked it. The independence, the casual atmosphere except when deadline time rolled around. Then all hell broke loose if there was an important story — a fishing boat sinking or lost out on the ocean, or a rum-running ring caught red-handed up the coast, or a rare robbery or a murder — almost unheard of in Santa Catarina, which was a quiet little town. Del liked the click and clack of the linotype machines, the smell of hot lead, the roar when the old press went into action. And there was the pleasure of seeing his byline: *Del Austin, Staff Writer.*

He rented a cottage that looked out over the ocean, he made a few friends, both male and female. But deep inside, he was lonely; he felt incomplete.

Then, one day, he got into a backyard fence conversation with his neighbor. A girl. Not an ordinary girl. An ambitious girl. Lena Perelli rented the house next door and intended to go — eventually — to Hollywood. In the meanwhile she worked as a bank teller, saved her money and acted in the plays produced by the Santa Catarina Little Theater group.

"You should come down to rehearsals," she suggested after they had exchanged basic information.

She put down her pruning shears and ran her hands through her shoulder-length dark hair. Then she looked him up and down critically. "You're about six feet — maybe they could use you. We're starting rehearsals for *Charlie's Aunt* next week."

Del was surprised. "Little Theater?"

"Yeah. It's great. I love it. And I'm learning how to act. When I get enough money saved up...."

"What?"

She laughed. "I'll be off to Hollywood! But a girl's got to eat. So I'm working and saving."

Somehow, Del felt comfortable with her. She wasn't interested in him as a man — at least not yet.

"I don't know anything about acting," he said. "I'm a...." He almost said schoolteacher but changed it to reporter.

"You don't have to know anything, not at first. You start as a waiter, or a butler — or a spear carrier —

something like that. That's an old theater joke — the spear carrier. You just sort of stand around — maybe have five or six words to say." She laughed. "Don't look so serious! It's fun!"

That was how Del got involved with the Little Theater group. He found himself attending weekly meetings and rehearsals; he found himself moving stage props and painting scenery, and he liked all of it. He liked the people. He liked being busy. Best of all, he liked the feeling that he fit in. Between his reporting job and his activities with the theatrical group, he felt he was making a life he could be comfortable with. He called Paul one evening.

"Paul. How are you? How are the folks?" He paused. "I'm fine. Got a job. Newspaper down here. Reporter — I like it. And hold your hat — you'll never believe what I'm doing." They talked for twenty minutes while Del told him about the theatrical group. Finally Del said "I miss you, little brother." He paused. Then he said slowly, "The damned dream still comes, but not as often now," and hung up.

The theatrical group began meeting at Del's house after rehearsals, for drinks and talk. Del had never been a drinker, but he was finding that a couple of highballs helped him sleep, and the dream, when it came, didn't seem so ominous. He felt happy at times. Almost at peace with himself and his world, even though that world included Mort Packer.

Mort was a talented older actor who often took senior lead roles. His dark hair was graying at the temples, giving him a look of distinction. And in some unfathomable way, he seemed to know about Del. Other members of the cast thought that Del and Lena Perelli had something going, but Mort knew better.

They were painting a backdrop one evening in Del's garage, which had become a kind of theater workshop. Lena had just gone home.

"You ever think about being yourself?" Mort asked, wiping his hands on a rag.

"Being yourself?" Del was surprised, then silent.

Mort went on: "It's hell to do that in a town this size. Better to keep it private. They'd ride you out of town on a rail." His cool glance slid over Del, taking in the slender length of his arms, the brown hair curling slightly over his shirt collar. Del had been too busy to get a haircut lately. "If you decide to do anything ...." Mort's words trailed off. Del didn't answer.

That night Del was haunted by the dream that had recurred many times during his adolescence. He was trying to swim in an ocean so vast, so endless, with waves so fearful, that he was gasping for breath, struggling and getting nowhere. The shore was a faint line in the distance. He knew he would never make it. He would drown.

He awoke shivering, cold, miserable. He dressed and walked out to the edge of the cliffs. There he stood a long time, looking out over the dark ocean. Then he went home and poured himself a stiff drink.

At the newspaper office one morning Editor Bush called Del into his glass cubicle. "I hear you're acting these days, Austin."

Del smiled. "Yeah. It's kind of interesting. I paint scenery, mostly, and help set up. Things like that."

Bush put down his pen. "Think you could do a weekly column on the arts for us? Theater, art, that kind of stuff? We've never had much of that in the paper. There's an art club. You could include that." He leaned back in his chair. "Think about it."

That was the start of Del's career as a columnist. The column soon became a popular and well-read part of the newspaper and Del's reputation was made.

Month's passed. Mort had said no more but his knowing eyes followed Del when they were working together. Del was aware of it and his thoughts tortured him at times. How did Mort know? What was it about him that was different? What showed? Was it the way he walked? Or talked? Or blew his nose or picked up his knife and fork? He wished to hell be knew.

Busy as he was, Del still had trouble sleeping. The dream came more often now. He would awaken and go out to the cliff to sit in a sheltered place he discovered in the rocks. He would stay there for hours, listening to the soothing sound of the surf below, until the ocean damp seeped through his wool jacket into his bones. He had no idea that anyone observed his night vigils until Lena Perelli mentioned it one evening.

"You're a real night owl," she said, and when Del looked surprised she added "Sometimes I see your light go on and then I hear your door. It squeaks a little."

"Oh, I'm sorry. I had no idea I was disturbing anyone."

"Forget it," she said. "Sometimes I have trouble sleeping, too."

"There's a damned dream," he said suddenly, surprising even himself that he would mention it. "It wakes me up." There it was out. He felt better for saying it.

She was curious. "A dream? What kind of dream? I know it's none of my business, but maybe if you talk about it...."

He looked at her and felt she must be like the sister he never had. "I'm swimming — drowning. It's a weird dream. So real that sometimes I can hardly breathe after I wake up." He continued to describe it.

Lena closed her eyes for a moment. "You are struggling with a decision," she said. "Something that really is bothering you. It haunts you. You're fighting something in your life, Del."

Surprised, he looked at her. "What are you? A fortune teller or something?"

She opened her eyes. "I see things sometimes. Second sight. My grandmother had it too. I don't tell everybody. They think you're a nut — loose in the head. You know. But yours — that wasn't hard to figure out. Struggling to swim. You're swamped in something that's bothering you."

"And I can't change it," he said bitterly.

She reached out to touch his hand, then drew back.

"I'm not blind, Del," she said softly. "I see Mort looking at you."

"Good God! Is it that obvious? I haven't encouraged him...."

"Whatever you do, it's your own business," she said, walking away. "And no one else's," she added over her shoulder.

After a couple of drinks he slept better that night. Maybe Lena was right. Talking to her — getting it out. What was the term Mort used? "Being myself." Lena was a great girl. He almost found himself wishing — no. Forget it. It wouldn't work. He wished he could be like Paul, little brother Paul. Chasing after all the pretty girls and now he was engaged to be married. He'd have children, lead a normal life. Wasn't that what his mother had called it?

"Why can't you be normal like other people and get married and lead a normal life?" That's what she had said.

He had struggled to explain but his parents hadn't wanted to hear it. They had condemned him without any understanding of his feelings of guilt and misery.

Del tried to avoid being alone with Mort but one late evening he answered his doorbell and Mort was standing there. Del could hardly tell him to go away. Mort was blunt.

"You probably are not delighted to see me, but I had to come. Del, you look like hell lately."

"And you know why," Del said. "Come in. At least we can talk. Do you realize there aren't many people I can even talk to honestly?" Del's words were bitter.

"I know, I know."

"What the hell is it? Why am I a freak?" Del burst out.

"God only knows, and he isn't telling," Mort said wryly. "Maybe some day the docs will figure it out. In the meanwhile boy, you are tearing yourself apart."

Del poured them each a drink and sat down. Mort moved next to him and put his arm around Del's shoulders. "You can't run away from it," he said.

"I wish to hell I could! I tried. I came down here to

start over. Left everything behind — my teaching job — a good friend — and my brother. He's the only one I give a damn about. Good kid. He's straight as an arrow but he understands."

"You're lucky you've got a brother like that," Mort said. "My sisters won't have anything to do with me." His arm tightened around Del's shoulders. "You're not alone, Del. There are others like us. Most of them sweep it under the rug — keep it hidden."

"Yeah. In order to exist in a normal world," Del said. "A normal world! Normal! God how I hate that word."

They had another drink. Mort stayed the night. And the next morning Del hated to look at himself in the mirror.

After a week of sleepless nights, Del's job at the newspaper began to suffer. He slipped up on a couple of stories and Bush called him in one morning.

"Austin, you look real bad. What's the matter? You sick? I had to send Joe out on that railroad story you missed. It was your beat, you know." He looked at Del sharply. "Been drinking?"

Del mumbled something about a few parties and finally escaped to his desk. Bush was no fool. He would figure things out, sooner or later. And the drinking — yes, he was drinking. Every night a couple of stiff ones to help him get to sleep and another good shot when he awoke in the middle of the night. Del got up from his desk and went to the men's room to look at himself in the mirror. God! He did look terrible. Dark circles. His face was gaunt. He hadn't weighed himself lately but he'd noticed his pants were looser around the waist and he'd taken his belt up a couple of notches. He stood there looking at himself for a long time that day. His life was falling apart. His running away hadn't done any good. Not really.

The next day Del went to see a doctor. He related his problems matter-of-factly: couldn't sleep, losing weight, nerves on edge. The doctor examined him. Blood pressure within the normal range, heart sounded o.k., eyes, ears and throat all apparently normal.

"But I can't sleep. Or else I wake up in the middle of the night and can't get back to sleep," Del said. "It's wearing me out. Can't you give me some sleeping pills?"

The doctor considered, then prescribed a sleeping pill after warning Del not to take alcohol while he was taking the pills.

That evening, after a lonely dinner, Del phoned Paul. "Hello little brother. How're things going? How's the engagement? Made any wedding plans yet?" He sounded light-hearted, happy.

Then: "Oh I'm fine. Good job. Friends in the little theater bunch — good people. We're going into rehearsals for *Charlie's Aunt* — it's a kick." There was a pause. Then Del said "No, I just wanted to call and tell you you're the best brother a guy could have. That's all. I think about you often. Sure — sure. I will. Well, Goodnight, little brother."

He hung up. He opened the pill bottle and counted them out. Twelve. He poured a glass of whiskey and swallowed the pills with it. Then he undressed and got into bed.

They found him there the next day.

THE HOTEL TYCOON

When the hotel tycoon arrived in Santa Catarina and announced that he was going to build the town's first *real* hotel, everybody sat up and took notice. They couldn't very well not take notice. He and his wife came from Southern California, driving into Santa Cat in a classy red Studebaker — the chrome would put your eyes out.

His name was F. W. Volak. No one ever learned what the initials stood for although several years later a town wag made some lewd suggestions. And for a long time no one in town forgot the year 1922 and what followed.

The first thing Volak did was buy a hunk of downtown property and have a couple of perfectly good wood buildings on it torn down. Paid cash for everything. He had lots of money. No one in Santa Catarina had ever heard of him before, but by that time a couple of the town fathers had checked up on him and they welcomed him with open arms. Rumors flew through town like confetti in a hurricane — he was a millionaire — his hotel was going to be the biggest and best ever planned for Santa Cat — six storeys with a coffee shop next to a plush lobby and an elevator. Santa Cat's first elevator. And even more impressive — a bathroom for every room instead of a community facility at the end of each hall. There was even to be a two room 'suite' on the rooftop, although not much was said about that.

It was a big step into the 20th Century for Santa Catarina which was, after all, mainly a summer resort town with its beaches and bath houses at the edge of the sand. Not that there hadn't been hotels and rooming houses. Lots of them had come and gone, a couple of dollars a night, handy for traveling drummers. The Pacific Wave House, a three-storey Victorian, was the most elegant in its day with a saloon next to the lobby and outdoor priveys, one for men, the other for women and children. Large and small holes in the women's, so the little kids wouldn't fall through. The Pacific Wave House had just recently installed pull-chain toilets in cubicles at the end of each hall in an effort at modernizing.

There was nothing distinguished looking about Volak. He was a short fellow with a round face, kind of red and shiny, and he smiled a lot. Thin hair on top, no special color to it. The story circulated that he had grown up poor in one of those small European countries with an unpronounceable name where rich people lived in castles.

"He'll probably build something like that," the town fathers speculated. "Wouldn't hurt to have something a little fancy on Main Street," commented Ed Ferris, who owned property next door.

But Volak did not build a castle. Instead he picked a plain, square kind of building and the only fancy decorations, if you could call them that, were four curlicues at the tops of four panels that ran up the front side facing Main Street. They were up so high they could hardly be appreciated from the sidewalk. The hotel was plastered, then treated to look like stone and painted a dignified gray. It was a handsome building.

"Kind of plain, but it's still the tallest building in town and it's real modern inside," the Judge said.

The natives all pointed it out with pride; it became the town's show place where the Board of Trade met for lunch and everyone ignored the fact that it looked out of place because it didn't match anything near it. On one side it rubbed elbows with a one-storey haberdashery built in

1889, on the other side there was the old Foley Building, a Victorian from the 1880s.

The new hotel caused a brief spurt of activity in the Pacific Wave House up the street. New red plush upholstery appeared on lobby chairs and settees. But its former prestige was gone. Nothing could change the fact that the new hotel, plain as it was, was the star of the show. The Pacific Wave House began to slide into the kind of rooming house where old people with canes and walkers shuffled around and sat out on the front porch in good weather.

Volak was a busy man. He. not only had built the town's most prestigious hotel and ran it profitably, he also built a handsome home for his wife out on the edge of town. Mrs. Volak was a thin, faded blonde who wore her hair in perfect marcel ripples flat to her head, after a current movie star style, and she had the biggest and most expensive rose gardens in town. More than one hundred rare and expensive varieties where she spent hours every day with a hired gardener who worked full time. She also. had some exotic and unusual plants from other parts of the world, among them the Castor Bean from Asia, which thrived and provided a showy background of big leaves. Many of her plants were a rarity in Santa Catarina and as word got around, other amateur gardeners came to see them.

Although Mrs. Volak was not a friendly, open kind of woman, she was generous with rose cuttings and she also gave away the large brown seeds of the Castor plant to those who wanted to start a plant in their own garden. Her next door neighbor, Effie Layton, started half a dozen from seed.

"It's nice she has the garden," Effie often remarked. "The Mister is so busy downtown."

Effie Layton tried to get friendly with her, mainly to find out more about them, but Mrs. Volak was what Effie described as 'stand-offish'. It was said by those who knew Effie well, that she could usually find out a person's life history in five minutes right down to how many fillings they had in their teeth, but she never got very far with Mrs. Volak.

Indeed Mr. Volak was busy. The whispers didn't start

for almost two years, and by then he was an honored officer of the local Board of Trade and an officer in several of the town's prominent lodges. It was rumored that Judge Fantham, who was mayor, was even considering him for that post when the Judge stepped down.

Volak spent most of his time at the hotel and everyone accepted that as natural. A man should look after his investments and his business, shouldn't he? Especially when that investment soared into the one-hundred thousand area. Volak also had what the natives called 'pull'. He knew several big political figures who could persuade conventions to some to Santa Catarina and stay in his hotel and spend money. All the town's merchants appreciated that.

What most people didn't know was that he spent much of his hotel time in the two-room private suite on the top floor where his office also was located. The suite was Volak's private version of a penthouse and in addition to a view of the Pacific Ocean it bad a small bar, kitchenette, white velvet sofas and drapes in the living room, a huge bed in the bedroom and Ruby Inglehoff to keep him warm. Ruby was blonde, verging on plumpness like an overripe peach, and she had given up her struggle to break into the movies when she met Volak in Southern California. She was working in Hollywood as a waitress when she met him and she followed him to Santa Catarina discreetly — at his request. She felt it was easier to lie back on the big antique bed and give him what he wanted. In return he provided her with this fancy place to live in a manner she was unaccustomed to, a couple of fur coats and a small diamond necklace.

There was only one thing Ruby was unhappy about. She didn't care for Santa Catarina. Too small for her taste, no place to go, no place to wear her furs and necklace, except in the top floor suite. She much preferred Los Angeles and Hollywood. Once in awhile Volak could arrange an escape outing to San Francisco where they would meet, but it was always a risk because the more prosperous Santa Catarina natives occasionally went up to 'the city' to shop, dine and attend the opera or theater.

So, being utterly bored with life in Santa Catarina cooped up in the two-room suite, Ruby went back to waiting tables in the hotel coffee shop. Volak didn't mind as long as she was upstairs when he wanted her there, preferably without clothes on except for a fur coat and the diamond necklace. At least that was what she was wearing when the Judge knocked. They didn't hear him and he waited a second, then opened the door to what he thought was Volak's private office. A desk clerk new to the job had directed him only too well.

When the Judge found him, Volak was down on his knees doing something with Ruby that the Judge couldn't describe even if he had wanted to. Judge Fantham was a pillar of the Methodist Church and his vocabulary was very limited when it came to things like that.

After one unbelieving look, the Judge shut the door, took the stairs at a gallop, not waiting for the elevator, and never set foot in the hotel again. Not even in the coffee shop where he had been accustomed to taking his morning coffee break. Especially not the coffee shop where Ruby worked. His sensibilities had been shattered. After all, he was a deacon in the church and this was something so monstrous that he couldn't even tell Mrs. Fantham about it.

The new hotel clerk who gave the unfortunate directions was fired and left town. Another desk clerk was hired in his place with clear — very clear instructions about where Mr. Volak's private office was located.

Word of the Mayor's untimely visit got around discretely, the way things like that do in small towns, concerning prominent citizens. Volak gradually dropped some of his civic duties, not all at once, and rumors began to circulate that he was too busy with the hotel and also that he suffered from poor health.

Ruby disappeared. Went back to Hollywood with an offer of a bit part in a movie, according to the local weekly, The Santa Catarina Wave. It never appeared on the social page with all the club ladies and the church doings, but was just a brief mention on a back page between a couple of ads. Two lines. But it was enough. The people who mattered in Santa Cat saw it.

Some months went by, the hotel was doing fine and people noticed that Volak was spending more time at home.

"Finally came to his senses," muttered Judge Fantham.

Then word got out that Volak was suffering from a strange and rare disease. He complained of his mouth — a burning feeling. But the dentist couldn't find anything to cause it. Then Volak oouldn't eat. If he did, he lost it almost immediately. Mrs. Volak was seen less often in her rose garden, trowel in hand, sun hat covering her marcelled waves, working alongside the gardener. The Volaks began going for Sunday auto rides and Effie Layton's husband was hired to drive the Studebaker touring car.

Effie reported that her husband observed Volak having some kind of fits. "He acts real funny — gets all stiff and makes faces and Mrs. Volak has to hold him. It's awful. Sort of like epileptic attacks, but worse," she said.

The two doctors in Santa Catarina were puzzled. They tried various remedies and for awhile Volak seemed to improve a bit. He even talked about going to San Francisco to see a specialist. But before he could go, be died in his sleep. 'Heart attack' was the official verdict.

Although hardly anyone had got to know Mrs. Volak well enough to say 'Good morning' or 'How do you do', condolences poured in. Her husband had been a prominent member of the Santa Catarina business community and the town rallied to his memory with all sins forgiven by those who knew, even Judge Fantham.

Effie got a couple of women from the Baptist Church to call and bring baked beans and an apple pie.

The Santa Catarina Wave played Volak's death big on the front page the day of the funeral, with stories about him being a far-sighted developer who had done much for the town and would be missed by all. One smart-alec reporter who knew the whole story (from Ruby, no less), wrote a tongue in cheek piece about how hard Volak had worked at his hotel and that was where his heart was. The piece got past the editor and was printed to the great amusement of those who had known of Volak's dalliance with Ruby. Certain city fathers greeted each other with grins after reading it and remarks like "He sure wore himself out down there, didn't he" and "Worked himself to death." Editor George Ferris was not amused and he informed the reporter of his displeasure. The editor threatened — out loud in the news room — to skin the guilty reporter alive and nail his hide to the wall.

The funeral was impressive. The city fathers were well represented among the pall bearers, all except the Judge who pleaded a bad back. Mrs. Volak was in black from head to toe and at a dramatic moment in the service she stepped forward and placed a sheaf of roses on the casket before it was lowered into the grave. Volak went to his maker in style.

Things quieted down after that. Mrs. Volak went back to her rose garden, and the gardener was seen working there daily. Speculation circulated about what the widow would do with the hotel.

"She's in her fifties if she's a day," Effie said. "She never did a thing with the hotel business — he did it all. And they have no relatives in this country."

Before long, the town found out. Mrs. Volak had been approached by a group of local businessmen who made her an offer which she accepted. A month later Effie heard that she also was selling her house and planned to move away. Effie was stunned and she went over almost immediately early one morning to learn what she could. She hoped it wouldn't be a family with half a dozen noisy, bothersome kids. And what was Mrs. Volak going to do with all that money?

No, Mrs. Volak told her. It was an older couple who wanted to open a florist shop downtown. Her rose garden had attracted them to buy the place and they were going to raise most of their own flowers and plants.

Effie was thankful for that. She was in the kitchen

talking to Mrs. Volak, just getting around to asking a few more questions, when down the hall a bedroom door opened and the gardener came out. He was buttoning his shirt. Effie was so shocked that she forgot to ask the name of the people who had bought the place. But she knew, without asking, what Mrs. Volak would be doing with herself and her money.

There was one more thing. Strange it was, too. A minor thing. The new people moved in and almost immediately their cat died. A horrible death according to Effie Layton who witnessed its final moments.

"It kind of had fits — awful!" she said.

The cat had been chasing a mouse in the cellar when it knocked over a bottle of some kind of liquid sitting on a shelf. The bottle broke and spilled.

"The cat must have licked up some of it," Effie said later, telling her husband about it. "There were a couple of those castor beans in the stuff. The new owner — a man who knows a lot about plants — he said that those beans are a deadly poison. And he said it was lucky a human being didn't get any of it."

THE NEW YORK WOMAN

She came without any fanfare, slipping quietly into Santa Catarina to live on a quiet street in a modest house. It was all done so privately, so smoothly and so quietly that hardly anyone knew she was in town until the moving van arrived.

That was the whole idea. Quiet. Private. There had been so much publicity, especially back East, not so much in California — big black headlines in the newspapers, even reports on the radio. Radio was just coming into its own in 1923 and TV hadn't been invented yet.

The headlines spelled out the latest about El Papa. A trial. A famous criminal lawyer defending him. The jury's decision. A prison term for El Papa who headed one of the country's most powerful underworld operations. Gangsters. Murder. Payoffs. Kidnappings and torture. All that and more.

As soon as her immediate neighbors became aware of their newest resident, they labeled her The New York Woman, although as yet, they didn't know who she was or why she was in Santa Catarina. She just looked different. Not like the women of Santa Catarina. More like a movie actress. Exotic. Strange. Dead white face with a thick layer of powder. Almost Oriental looking. Eye makeup — eyes outlined with dark pencil — something that was never seen in Santa Cat. Not on the street in daylight, anyway. Black hair. As shiny black as the lumps of coal that were delivered to her basement in the early fall for winter heat.

She not only looked different. She dressed differently. Black. Long, narrow skirts, straight tailored jackets with just a touch of white collar showing from underneath and a close-fitting black hat.

"It's called a cloche, I think," commented her closest neighbor, old Mrs. Hervey.

The black clothing made the New York woman's stark white face even more startling.

"Who is she? Why did she come here?" Mrs. Hervey fumed. "She doesn't look like she belongs here at all."

The neighbors on both sides were curious and willing to be half-way friendly, but the most they got was a nod and once in awhile a 'Good Morning'. Mrs. Hervey lived on the west side in a similar dark brown cottage. She was a widow, eighty-two years old and seldom went out. Relatives brought her food and did her housework. On the other side, in a larger house, Mrs. Moroni and her bachelor son lived. She was in her sixties, he was forty. They had a lot of Italian friends and relatives who came for noisy visits to drink red wine and feast on Mrs. Moroni's ravioli. The Moronis tried a few friendly greetings toward the New York woman, shrugged, and gave up.

Across Jeffry Street in another, larger house, a grandmother was raising two grandchildren, a boy and a girl. The girl, who was eight, was bursting with curiosity about this different-looking woman. Was she an actress? One day the girl slipped out of the house, crossed the street, climbed the four steps to the front porch and peeked in a window. She could see the New York woman sitting on a pillow on the floor. The floor! But that wasn't all. She was smoking a cigarette. Smoking! And drinking tea or something. The teapot was on a low table in front of her. Real low. Funny.

"The table looked like its legs were cut off," she reported to her grandmother. "She held the cigarette in a funny long thing. And there was a curtain of colored beads. All long strings. And she has a big old piano — an old one sort of like ours."

After digesting that unusual information — the pillow on the floor, the smoking, the bead curtain, not the piano — the grandmother cautioned the girl never to go sneaking around there again. "You know better than that! Mind your manners." But word spread from the grandmother to other neighbors and the peculiarities of the new neighbor branded her in their minds as "The New York Woman."

After a month or so, the neighbors' curiosity deepened. A man appeared. He visited the woman about once a week and obviously was not a native. He dressed in what the Santa Cat residents referred to as 'city clothes'.

"He looks like a furriner," Mrs. Hervey reported to her old lady friends. "And I don't like the way he sneaks around. Never got a good look at his face. Wears a black hat pulled down low. Never knocks at her door. Goes right in. Like she's waiting fer him. Door's not locked." Mrs. Hervey nodded knowingly. "Something's going on. Maybe that's why she's so stand-offish. She hardly says good morning to me. The man drives a fancy ottymobeel," she added.

The New York woman's neighbors didn't pay too much attention to stories from New York and Chicago which occasionally made their appearance on the back pages of the Santa Cat Wave, days late. Mrs. Hervey read the local paper for the personals: who was going to head the next church social, or who was traveling to San Francisco on business. So she skipped over the short piece announcing that 'El Papa', big city crime boss recently convicted of extortion and murder in Chicago, was now residing in the new prison at Arroyo Blanco. Chicago was millions of miles away as far as Mrs. Hervey was concerned and a crook named El Papa meant nothing to her, even if he was being sent to Arroyo Blanco which was only twenty miles from Santa Catarina. She also skipped a small article announcing the sale of Hugus Court to an East Coast businessman, Sam Pagetti, who planned to live in the Victorian mansion recently vacated by the last heir of a well-to-do Santa Catarina family. Normally, the story would have been all over town. But Mayor Elmer Crawford killed it dead after a private meeting with the "town fathers." Crawford got his orders: Sam Pagetti was the brother-in-law of El Papa. Sam was going to run things from Santa Cat, near the prison, until El Papa got out.

"They're working on that — got the smartest lawyers in Chicago. They'll get him out for sure," Crawford told his group of police and town leaders. "In the meanwhile we got to keep it quiet or we can be in big trouble."

"Why do we have to toady to that gangster?" Sheriff Charlie Winkle asked.

"It's a free country, isn't it?" someone else said.

"Not only is it a free country, but these big boys play rough ball when they get mad. Not much we can do about it if El Papa's girlfriend moves here and his top man buys the Hugus Estate and wants to live there for awhile. A short while, we hope!" Crawford said, lighting a cigar. I for one don't want to rock the boat. We got enough troubles as it is, without stirring up more."

"Girl friend?" the Sheriff was surprised.

"Yeh. She moved in up on Jeffry Street. Modest little place. On purpose. Nothing fancy. She don't want to attract any attention, I guess. But that Pagetti fellow — he's got to have the best. Paid cash, too."

"What's she look like? The girl friend?"

Crawford laughed. "You'll know her when you see her. All black and white — black clothes — white face — a lot of makeup — sticks out like a sore thumb in this town. I heard she's from New York and El Papa is set on tying the knot when he gets out of prison."

Several of the men groaned. "We sure didn't need this," one of them said.

Up on Jeffry Street life was going on as usual. Church on Sunday, Mrs. Hervey to the Methodist Episcopal, Mrs. Moroni to Santa Catarina Catholic Church. Short walks to the grocery store. Visits to nearby neighbors and friends. Mrs. Hervey and three of her widowed lady friends got together once a week for a game of Hearts or Old Maid, feeling slightly wicked as they sat sipping tea and shuffling the cards. The Methodist Episcopals frowned on card games. "Pasteboards of the devil," they called them.

Mrs. Moroni had a bunch of relatives who took turns at each other's homes every Sunday for a feast of ravioli, wine and spaghetti. The men played Bocci Ball out on a backyard court while the women did the dishes and visited in the kitchen. The Moronis were naturally curious about the New York Woman, but they decided if she didn't want to be friendly, that was all right with them. They had plenty of friends. So they nodded politely when they saw her.

With Mrs. Hervey it was different. Her curiosity nagged at her constantly. She often stood behind her lace curtains at the parlor window facing the New York Woman's cottage, to see if anything was going on. Anything different, that is.

"What does she do all day?" one of the card-playing cronies asked.

"Heaven only knows," Mrs. Hervey said. "She does play the piano — I hear it in the evenings. And she takes those long rides with that man who comes to see her. About once a week. Sometimes they're gone for hours. All day. And she gets a lot of mail. Her box is always pretty full. And she sends out a lot, too. Puts it there for the mailman to pick up."

"You live next to a mystery," one of the card players remarked.

"An unfriendly mystery," Mrs. Hervey added. "She hardly speaks. Even when I say 'good morning' or 'good evening' to her."

"Maybe she's a famous actress or something — all that makeup and those clothes you said she wears. I'd like to see her. It must be lonely here for her if she's somebody like that — actress or maybe an opera singer."

"Humph. If she's lonely, it's her own doings," Mrs. Hervey snorted. "I'd like a dollar for every time I've said 'good morning' to her and tried to be friendly."

"She must have a family somewhere — and she goes out riding with that man. Do you think they're married?"

Mrs. Hervey shook her head. "No. They don't act like married folks. Not at all. And if they were, wouldn't he be living here with her?"

"Well, she must have relatives somewhere if she gets all that mail. Come on, whose play is it?"

The game of cards continued but the seed of an idea had been planted in Mrs. Hervey's brain. Mail. A lot of mail. Both incoming and outgoing.

On Friday, the New York woman's regular grocery shopping day, Mrs. Hervey went into action. She watched from behind her window curtains as the New York woman put several letters in her front porch mailbox for the mailman to pick up. The Post Office was downtown, too far to walk, especially in the fancy high-heeled black patent leather shoes the New York Woman wore. Mrs. Hervey watched until the New York woman disappeared down the street with her shopping bag over her arm, then she slipped out her back door, went through the geranium bushes, looked up and down the street to make sure no one was coming, and crept up the steps to the New York Woman's porch.

The metal mailbox was nailed to one side of the front door. Mrs. Hervey opened the lid, slid the letters out, scanned them quickly, gasped, then put them back and fled from the porch to her own back door. She was pale. She went to the telephone and called her best friend, Minetta Olds.

"Minetta! You'll never believe what I just found out!" She got out the awful news. "A common criminal — he's in prison, no less! Whatever should I do? With her living right next door to me — I could be in danger myself!"

When she had exhausted all her adjectives and unburdened herself, Mrs. Hervey hung up and followed Minetta's advice: she called the Chief of Police. She considered him practically a personal friend. After all, she had gone to school with his mother.

Chief Lon Emery was concerned, but also somewhat

puzzled by Mrs. Hervey's garbled message.

"You say your neighbor is a criminal of some kind?" he questioned. "Now calm down, Mrs. Hervey. Are you in any immediate danger? I'll come out right away — sure. Just stay in your house. Lock your doors. I'm coming."

Mrs. Hervey, still pale and breathless, followed orders and had to slide the bolt open to let Chief Emery in when he arrived. He listened as she again related her story.

"And she's writing letters to some convict at the prison — his number is on the envelope — down at Arroyo Blanco Prison — the address and all, right on the envelope. I knew there was something going on, Chief. She's not friendly at all — hardly says good morning. Heavens! If I had only known — I wouldn't have bothered to say good morning to her. She's mixed up in something bad — takes those rides with that man who comes here to see her. Just think — all this right next to me!" She stopped for a breath. "Do you think she's married to one of those criminals in that prison, Chief? No telling what kind of people will be coming here to see her. It's downright dangerous!"

The Chief listened patiently until she ran down, then he said. "You took her mail out of the box and read it?"

"Just the outside of the envelopes, Chief."

He looked solemn. "You probably shouldn't have done that."

"I didn't open anything!"

"Well, I'm sorry you did that. And I think you'd be wise not to tell anybody what you did — not any of your friends."

"But — but — she's probably a criminal — living right here next to me! No telling what could happen — I'm not sure I'm safe!"

The Chief, who knew more than he let on, tried not to smile. "You are perfectly safe, Mrs. Hervey," he said. "I'll keep a close eye on the whole situation. Believe me! Just go on as usual. There's nothing I can do unless you are actually attacked or harmed in some way. It's a free country, you know. She has a right to live there."

"You mean you can't arrest her and make her move away. Away from here? I have to live next door to a criminal?"

"She probably isn't a criminal," he said.

"But the letter ...."

"Could be her brother," the Chief said. "Or her uncle, or her husband."

"Husband!" Mrs. Hervey shuddered at the thought.

The Chief left after spending a few minutes soothing Mrs. Hervey's wounded nerves.

She spent the rest of the day rearranging her parlor furniture. She moved her favorite easy chair from its accustomed place near the gas heater to a move favorable view out the side window. That window looked over at the New York Woman's front porch. She figured if she sat there she could see well enough through the lace curtain to keep track of who went in and out next door. Then she called a handyman she hired for occasional jobs, and had him install slide bolts on the back door and smaller ones on the windows. That took several days. When he was finished, she paid him and went to sit in her parlor easy chair, satisfied that she had done everything possible

Well, not quite everything. She was not only upset and worried, she was beginning to feel a sense of rage that she had to live next to a criminal — or a criminal's wife or sister or cousin, whatever it was. The ugly fact remained. A criminal — or someone related to a criminal — had moved in next door to her in a perfectly respectable neighborhood. It was just too much.

Sitting there fuming, behind the lace curtains, she got another idea. Maybe — just maybe — she could get the New York Woman to move out. It would be doing the whole neighborhood a favor. But how should she go about it?

"I'll call Minetta and talk to her — there ought to be some way to scare that woman out of here," she said to herself.

The two women talked at length with Minetta, suggesting that Mrs. Hervey do something to frighten the New York Woman. Mrs. Hervey turned down one idea.

"You mean dress up in a sheet like a ghost or something? I'm not going to do that. Someone might see me. No, it's got to be something that looks natural but something she won't like."

"Put spiders in her mailbox — a lot of them," suggested Minetta.

"Ugh. I won't handle spiders — I don't like them."

"I'll come over and bring a jar of spiders — I've got hundreds in my woodshed," Minetta offered.

"But how can you get them to stay in her mailbox?"

"Dead flies," Minetta said. "They eat them. I'll start collecting flies and spiders today. It'll only take a day or two."

"She goes out to market on Thursdays," Mrs. Hervey said.

On the following Thursday Minetta appeared with spiders and dead flies in glass jars. The two women sat in the parlor and watched through the curtains until the New York woman left for her usual shopping trip.

Mrs. Hervey almost got cold feet. "Oh Minetta — do you think we oughtta do this? It sounds crazy — it may not work at all — maybe we could think of something else...."

Minetta took her by the arm. "Come on! We can try it anyway."

They ran over quickly, after looking up and down the street to make sure no one was coming. Then they climbed the porch stairs, dumped the flies and spiders in the mailbox, shut the lid firmly, and went back to the parlor to wait.

What they had failed to consider was the mailman. He came up the street with his leather mailbag over his shoulder, stopping at houses along the way. He put a couple of ads in Mrs. Hervey's mailbox, then climbed the steps next door. When he opened the New York woman's mailbox, he hesitated for a moment, then swept it out with one hand before putting the mail inside. Spiders, flies, all on the porch floor.

"We timed it wrong," Minetta said sadly. "I shoulda

thought of that."

The following Thursday, Minetta arrived again with her jars of freshly caught spiders and dead flies, and this time they waited until the mailman had passed by.

"Now we gotta hurry," Minetta said. "You carry this — I'll take the flies."

Mrs. Hervey reached for the jar of spiders just as the lid fell off and a stream of insects fell to the parlor floor. All except for a few that landed on her sleeve. She screamed and danced up and down and waved her arms frantically. Minetta, who was much braver, stepped on them — or most of them.

"They won't hurt you," she said reassuringly.

"One bit me! Right on my hand!" Mrs. Hervey cried. "And look at my carpet! Dead flies and spiders all over it! Look! There go some spiders — they're still alive! Minetta — do something!"

That episode finished the spider-fly project, but Minetta had a fertile brain and she was a stubborn woman.

"I ain't goin' to be licked by something like this," she said. "Next we'll try a mousetrap. That oughtta work."

"I never set a mousetrap in my life," Mrs. Hervey said. "The hired man does it if I need it done."

"She'll catch her fingers in it and she won't know who put it there," Minetta said. "I'll set it for you. I do it all the time."

The next Thursday they waited in the parlor until the mailman had passed, then slipped out the back door with Minetta carrying the set trap. Carefully. Mrs. Hervey opened the mailbox and Minetta slid the trap in on top of the mail.

"There," she said. "It has to face this way so it'll get her fingers."

But she didn't push it quite far enough

"The lid won't close now," Mrs. Hervey said.

"Hurry — push it in — I think someone's coming up the street. Close the lid!" Minetta whispered.

Mrs. Hervey pushed at it, the mousetrap went off and caught two of her fingers. She opened her mouth, started to scream, thought better of it and retreated to her own back door with the mousetrap still dangling from her hand. Minetta removed the trap at the kitchen sink and drew a pot of water for Mrs. Hervey's hand which was throbbing with pain.

"We had to hurry too fast," she said. "Let's see — maybe next Thursday...."

"Never mind," Mrs. Hervey said hastily. "I'll just write her a note and not sign my name to it. I won't threaten her or anything — just let her know she's not wanted here. Ooooh, my fingers hurt. Do you think they're broken?"

They weren't, Minetta reassured her, and offered to help her compose the anonymous letter.

"Tell her you know she's related to a jailbird," she suggested. "Tell her the whole neighborhood is going to hear about it. And be sure you print it. Don't hand write it. Tell her she don't belong in this respectable, God-fearing family neighborhood. Sign it with a skull and crossbones. That oughtta scare her good."

And that was what Mrs. Hervey did. The printing was a bit wobbly due to her sore fingers and the skull and crossbones were crude but recognizable. She sealed the note in a plain envelope and slipped over after dark to slide it into the New York Woman's mailbox. Then she went to bed with a hot water bottle on her throbbing hand.

She watched the next day, grimly satisfied, from behind the lace curtains, when the New York Woman took her mail from her box. Nothing happened for a day or two, but Mrs. Hervey wasn't expecting immediate changes. Then, several days later, her own doorbell rang one morning and Chief Emery was standing there. He removed his cap with the gold badge on it as he entered.

"Cup of coffee, Chief?" Mrs. Hervey asked as they sat down. "It's kind of early."

"Nope. Can't stay long, Mrs. Hervey. I got a complaint from your neighbor lady — seems someone's wrote her a threatening letter. You been bothered with any lately?"

Mrs. Hervey gulped and turned a shade or two paler

but her voice was steady. "Why no — my goodness, of course not."

"Seems it was someone who found out she's got kin in prison," Chief Emery said.

"Well — my goodness! Imagine that."

"I just thought you might have an idea," he said. "She's planning to move down the valley, end of the month, she told me. Closer to the prison and all. But I had to make an investigation anyway. Probably nothing to it. But you never know. But it's my duty no matter what."

"Yes, I guess so," Mrs. Hervey said faintly.

"My — what happened to your hand? It's all swoll up," the Chief said.

"Oh I caught it in the door," she said.

"Well, I'll be going." He got up and reached for his cap. He started to put it on, then stopped and swatted vigorously. "A spider," he said. "Take care of that hand," he added as he went out the door.

THE RED DRESS

She was strikingly beautiful as she stood there in her flaming red dress. A scarlet tulip, slim, elegant, with shining dark hair piled high above her slender throat. Clyde Burrows saw all that — and the little half-smile she aimed at him. Or was it someone standing behind him? The perfect figure under the snug silk dress, the blue eyes. Clyde couldn't take his eyes off her.

The occasion was Santa Catarina's annual charity fete to which wealthy citizens donated objects of art they were tired of, to be auctioned, with the proceeds going to the County Hospital and Orphanage. The event always took place in the spacious ballroom of the Santa Catarina Hotel.

Clyde was one of the town's most eligible bachelors in 1925. The Burrows family controlled the beachfront hotel and amusement park which brought thousands of vacationers — and thousands of dollars — to the small California coastal town each summer. Clyde would, one day, inherit it. all. He had just graduated from college — a small, obscure one, not the prestigious University at Berkeley, or Stanford Univesity, both of which required top grades for entry. He was home now, he was beginning to think about marriage and settling down. And there she was.

He nudged his friend, Charlie. "Who is she?" he asked.

Charlie shook his head. "You got me. Never saw her

before, Clyde. She's sure a knock-out."

"I'm going to marry her," Clyde said suddenly, then wondered why he had said it. But he had no doubt that he would. Clyde never believed there was anything in the way of his getting what he wanted. Anything he couldn't manage, somehow.

But this time, there was. She was already married. Her name was Zennola Pruitt and the reason Charlie and Clyde had never laid eyes on her before was because she lived down on the wrong side of the tracks. The tracks divided Santa Catarina society into two major groups. The modest and squalid homes on mostly dirt streets were on the east side of the railroad line that ran through town. The Victorian mansions and better homes stood on wide avenues which were paved and lined with trees, or sat on winding drives which overlooked the river or the Pacific Ocean.

Zennola had grown up in the shabby cottage where she now lived with her husband who worked occasionally at stripping logs in lumber camps. Two years of marriage and Zennola was bored to death with her life and determined to change it. That was how she happened to appear at the Santa Catarina charity benefit. She had borrowed the red dress.

Zennola walked slowly through the crowd, past the tables loaded with china and crystal works of art, pausing now and then as if admiring a certain piece. She knew Clyde's eyes were following her.

"I'm going to find out who she is," he said.

"I guess you'd better, if you plan to marry her," Charlie said with a laugh.

Clyde followed her almost to the hotel entrance before he spoke. "I beg your pardon," he said. "You're not leaving so soon?"

Zennola turned. "I don't believe we have met," she said. She had done housework for the 'swells' as she called them, and she had observed how they spoke and behaved.

"No, we haven't," Clyde said easily. "But that's my fault. I've been away at college."

"Indeed?"

"Yes. I would like to introduce myself — Clyde Burrows. And may I ask your name?" As he asked, Clyde held his breath. Would this beautiful creature answer him or would she be insulted at his boldness? The old ways took a long time to die in Santa Catarina, and the roaring twenties with their short skirts, beads, bobbed hair, Charleston kicks and Black Bottom shimmys hadn't arrived — yet. Prohibition was in full force but there was booze if you knew where to get it, as well as other pleasures of the flesh.

She smiled and Clyde relaxed. "Pleased to meet you, Mr. Burrows."

"Shall we sit here and become acquainted," he suggested, motioning toward chairs flanked by potted palms.

For a second or two Zennola appeared to hesitate, then she said "Why yes, of course. I have a few minutes."

Later she was to marvel at how easy it had been. They chatted for the better part of an hour and he was fascinated by everything about her, even her name.

"Zennola — it's a lovely name. Unusual. So exotic," he remarked.

"Yes, she said demurely. I believe it's been in the family for ages." Actually, her mother had got it out of a penny dreadful — one of those cheap novels of the 1800s.

Zennola knew how to play the game. She had to be careful — she would pretend she was visiting family friends in Santa Catarina — older people who were not well; she couldn't invite him to their home.

She glanced up at the wall clock in the hotel foyer and murmured she must go.

Clyde got up. "When can I see you again?"

"Oh dear — let me see. I will be here for several weeks. Maybe next week?" She mustn't sound too eager.

"I was hoping it would be sooner," he said. "Perhaps for lunch?"

She appeared to be thinking. "All right. I'll meet you here. When?"

"How about day after tomorrow?" Clyde didn't intend to waste any time. "Noon," he added. "We'll drive up the coast. I know a roadhouse up there — good food and drinks. The sheriff hasn't shut them down yet."

She got up and moved away, toward the door. Clyde took her arm and his hand lingered on it when they reached the door. "I've got to go back in there." He gestured toward the ballroom.

She smiled up at him and nodded. She had him hooked. A Burrows. One of the richest, most influential bachelors in town. Now — if she played her cards right ...

That was how it started. With a red silk dress she had borrowed from her sister Zena, who was a prostitute in San Francisco. She walked slowly home to the shack, remembering the day she chose it.

"It can't be cut too low," she said. "It has to be flashy, but — flashy in a ladylike way. You know what I mean? The swells in Santa Cat like things to be ladylike."

That was when Zena held up a long, red silk dress. "I was going to give this away. It's too old style for here now. The girls are all going for the short dresses — the new styles. If you don't show your knees no one's going to look at you up here in Frisco. And I gotta get my hair cut off — short bobs they call them. Its all the rage."

"No one is doing that yet in Santa Cat," Zennola said.

Zena laughed. "All right big sister, have it the way you want. But all the swells I do business with up here like it bare-ass naked. Who're you setting your sights on, anyway? The preacher's son?"

Zennola shook her head. "I don't know yet but there'll be somebody. I'm sick and tired of Grant. He never works. He never takes me out. All he does is drink rot gut — he's got some cooking now in tubs in the bathroom. I never should have married him."

"What about that? Being married already?" Zena asked.

"Doesn't matter — I'll do something. When the time comes — I'll work it out some way."

"Well, just remember if things don't work out, you can always come up here and work with me," Zena said. "Its easy. I do most of it lying on my back and it pays good."

That was how Zennola got the red dress.

She had made her plans carefully. The big charity event of the year. All the important people in Santa Catarina would be there in the hotel ballroom. She wouldn't go as a quiet little mouse. On the other hand, she wouldn't look like — a slut either. And she didn't. With her dark hair piled high on her head, and dressed in red silk, no one would recognize her as the grubby girl who worked in the back of the fish market, trimming heads and tails. In the market she hid her dark, glowing hair under a tight cap and her shapely curves under layers of warm clothing and an ugly waterproof apron. Protective garments were necessary not only for the cold, but for the spatter of fish blood and guts.

Zennola decided she never wanted to see another fish as long as she lived. She also was aware that styles were changing. Women were bobbing their hair and wearing knee-length dresses with no waistlines. But it cost money to re-do a whole wardrobe and she didn't have much of one anyway, just a few skirts and worn dresses and a shabby coat.

That evening she looked her wardrobe over with a critical eye, and finally settled on a gray wool skirt and the best blouse she had. But what would she do for a jacket? She had only the bulky rainproof she wore to work. And she didn't have time to borrow one from Zena who was a hundred miles away.

Then she happened to recall seeing a dark red jacket downtown in the department store window. She had stopped to admire it, as one might admire the moon and stars on a perfect night. Completely out of her reach, she knew. It would be perfect with the gray skirt, but she had no money. Where could she get enough money to buy the jacket? Her whole future could hinge on something as simple as a red jacket, she felt.

She walked restlessly back and forth through the two-room shack where she and Grant lived. Nothing. There was nothing worth selling. Everything was old and worn out. Even the quilt on the bed — the quilt her mother had pieced together so many years ago. Double wedding ring pattern. Now stained and worn. It was the only thing in the house that Zennola cherished. She sighed. Might as well forget the whole thing. Without decent clothes, without money, she was doomed. Then she saw them. Grant's tool box. He hadn't worked for weeks and he wouldn't miss them for ages. By then she hoped to be gone.

On the day of the luncheon date, Clyde arrived at the Santa Catarina Hotel exactly at twelve noon. He looked at his watch nervously. Would she show up? When she said yes, did she mean it? He wished he knew where she was visiting. When he entered the hotel lobby, Zennola was sitting in one of the Victorian chairs behind a potted palm and he could see she was wearing a red jacket. Red must be her favorite color, he thought. She's a sophisticated woman. Knows how to wear it. It's my favorite color too. She'd soon find that out.

"You look great," he said, and daringly he gave her a small hug. "Come on, let's go."

He led her out front where he had parked his new, red Stutz Bearcat roadster. He opened the door for her. "Be my guest, pretty lady."

Zennola could hardly speak. "It — it's gorgeous, Clyde. I've never seen an automobile like it. What is it?"

"Stutz Bearcat," he said proudly. "Brand new. Only one in Santa Cat. It's called a roadster. See? The black leather top can fold down and you're right out in the open driving along. I think I'll leave the top up today — don't want to blow you to pieces when we go up the coast. Might be windy."

"It — it's really beautiful," she said as she sank into the leather seat.

"We're going to a special place for lunch," he said.

"Special place for a special lady." He got in and tromped on the starter.

"Don't you have to crank it?" she asked.

"Not this one. It's got an automatic starter."

"Why — that's wonderful!" she said.

It seemed to her that they almost flew up the coast road, leaving a trail of white dust clouds behind. The Pacific Ocean had never seemed so blue, the day so bright, the hills so green with spring grasses and wild flowers.

"Forty miles an hour!" Clyde called to her above the engine noise. "This baby really goes!"

"It's awfully exciting!" she called back.

To herself she thought *at last, my life is changing. I'll get rid of Grant and marry Clyde. Then I'll have everything. Life will be wonderful.*

She wasn't sure yet just how she'd manage the part about already being married but she would work it out. Maybe go to Frisco and Zena would help. If she did it up there it could be kept secret.

A few minutes later Clyde slowed the Bearcat and cruised into a small fishing settlement. He stopped in front of a rustic looking building with a sign that said FISH DINNERS — FRESH DAILY. He pulled on the brake and turned off the engine.

"Here we are. It sure doesn't look fancy but just wait until you get that dinner — best on the coast. It's the best bootleg joint too — the cops haven't shut it down yet. We can get a drink with our meal."

Zennola tried to smile. To look enthused. She was thinking *FISH. UGH. Maybe there would be something else.*

The dining room was almost empty. Clyde chose a table for two at a window overlooking the ocean. For a moment Zennola almost forgot her role as a 'swell' and started to pull her own chair out. Then she remembered in time to let Clyde seat her.

A waiter in a grubby apron brought menus. Zennola took one quick look and waved hers away. "You choose, " she said to Clyde with a smile. She wasn't going to make any more mistakes and she was going to have to eat fish if it killed her.

Clyde ordered cocktails — whiskey smashers — Zennola had never heard of them — and double-thick salmon steaks, baked potatoes, biscuits and pie for dessert. "All my favorites," he said. "I really appreciate you letting me order."

She looked at him through half-closed lids. "I like a man who knows what he likes."

He lifted his cocktail glass. "I like what I see. Here's to us."

She took a sip of her drink and almost choked but caught it in time.

"It's a Smasher — made of the best bootleg whiskey on the coast," he said.

"A Smasher," she repeated. "First one I've ever had."

He was concerned. "Too strong for you? I started drinking them at college."

"Oh no! It's fine." As she sipped it she could feel the warmth spreading through her body. Down her legs. It was a sensation new to her. She wasn't used to drinking. She hated it when Grant came home drunk after a visit to one of his home brew friends.

Clyde downed his drink and ordered another for each of them. "For the pretty lady who likes to wear red," he said, clicking his glass against hers.

Zennola found herself sipping another Smasher and she hoped the food would come soon. Her head was beginning to feel funny.

At last, the waiter set their dinners in front of them. Large plates with buttered baked potatoes and thick slabs of pink salmon. Fish. Zennola looked at it and knew she had to eat it. Worse, she had to pretend she was enjoying it.

"It looks wonderful," she said, hoping the words sounded right. Her tongue felt queer, like it wasn't working right. She took a large segment of fish on her fork. *Might as well get it over with*, she thought. If she married Clyde she would never touch a bite of fish again as long as she lived, she promised herself. She would see to that.

The forkful of fish filled her mouth and she began to wish she had taken a smaller piece. She tried to chew and swallow. Too late, she realized there were bones in it. She didn't want to spit it out. She struggled to swallow and got it part way down, then she began to choke. Clyde put down his fork and looked at her.

"You all right?"

Zennola nodded. She couldn't speak. She was trying to swallow and she couldn't. The glob of fish and bone was caught in her throat. She reached for the glass of whiskey and tried to swallow a mouthful. It spilled down the front of her jacket. She fought to breathe and couldn't. Her lungs were bursting. She staggered to her feet, then fell to the floor.

Clyde tried to lift her up. She was limp.

His yells for help brought a circle of waiters, the cook, two helpers and the other diners. "Phone for a doctor!" he shouted. "Hurry!"

Zennola lay there on her back on the floor, not moving, not breathing. Someone brought a blanket and they put it over her. Clyde paced the floor, waiting.

The closest doctor was at Santa Catarina. He arrived thirty minutes later, felt for a pulse, put his stethoscope on her chest, then shook his head. "She's gone."

In a weak voice Clyde said "You mean — you mean — she's dead?"

"I'm afraid so. From her appearance it would seem that she choked on food," the doctor said. "Food that lodged in her throat. Then she regurgitated some of it. She couldn't get air — couldn't breathe."

In a dull unbelieving voice Clyde said "We were just eating fish."

A PASSION FOR POLITICS

When Lottie Carston's husband died unexpectedly in 1926 no one dreamed that she would take up politics as her main interest in life. Some thought she might re-marry. She was still attractive in middle age; she had her hair tinted every two weeks, a pale blonde that set off her pink and white complexion. She dressed well, she was careful about too much makeup and she kept her petite figure. There had been no children. Altogether, she didn't look like she was in her late forties.

She also considered herself a member of one of Santa Catarina's better families. That small California coastal town was one where family status was on a par with England's Peerage — at least in the minds of its residents. Society's stratas were rigid. If you were somebody, you were somebody. If you weren't — well, forget it.

Lottie's uncle had been a lawyer — "Attorney at Law" as she put it. She put it often, in her conversations, reminding everyone subtly and not so subtly that she was Somebody.

Widows in Santa Catarina in the early nineteen hundreds were expected to take up membership in the flower arranging club, or the group that met weekly to embroider and do petite point pillow covers. They also did a lot of afternoon entertaining of other widowed ladies at bridge parties. But there was none of this for Lottie. She got hooked on politics. The Democrat Ladies' Circle, no less. People accepted it because her late husband, Herb Carston, although only a clerk in a drygoods store, had always been a staunch Democrat.

"She's doing it in his memory...." they said almost reverently.

Lottie had never really paid much attention to the Democrats when Herb was alive. "It's all so boring," she would say when he urged her to take more interest. "All they talk about are those Bills and electing somebody or other."

But her life, and her views of politics changed drastically with an afternoon visit to her modest home by Garrison Pruitt. He came to extend his condolences to the widow of his old friend, Herb Carston, who had helped elect him to one of the more important committees.

Garrison was middle-aged, with a distinguished mane of gray hair and calculating eyes, and he was thinking of running for Supervisor of his district.

"Sorry I couldn't attend the services for Herb," he explained. "I had to be in Sacramento."

Lottie was flattered. "Do sit down," she said. "I was about to have a cup of tea. Or would you prefer something stronger? There's brandy." She remembered that most of her husband's male political friends were not tea drinkers.

As Garrison settled on the sofa he looked at his watch. "Don't mind if I do. The sun's over the flagpole."

He sat down and she poured a generous splash of brandy and handed him the glass. Their fingers touched momentarily. There was an awkward silence. Garrison Pruitt took a sip and wondered what he ought to say next. Express more sympathy? She didn't look particularly sad, or like she was in mourning, he thought. In fact she was wearing a brightly colored blouse that was unbuttoned low enough to show the beginning of cleavage. He wished his wife looked that good. That sexy.

Lottie came to the rescue: "Tell me about Sacramento. There must be exciting things going on up there. The State

Capitol and all."

Garrison smiled. "I didn't realize you were interested, Lottie." Then, realizing how that sounded, he continued smoothly "I knew you were active in other areas. And of course Herb was the political member of the family. He was always very helpful to me, Lottie."

"I'm glad to hear that," Lottie said thoughtfully. "You know, Garrison, I've been thinking about things, now that I have more time and all. I believe I would like to take a more active part in it — politics, I mean. What do you think?" She looked at him with appealing eyes.

He smoothed his gray mane with the hand that wasn't holding the glass. "Why, that's great, Lottie! We need all the help we can get. And with your background — I can't tell you how pleased I am!"

Lottie came over and sat down next to him with her cup of tea. "Will you — advise me how to go about it? I know you're terribly busy and all, but I'd be pleased to volunteer for anything I can do to help — your campaign maybe? I think Herb mentioned you might run for supervisor?" Her voice was as soft as her eyes.

Garrison Pruitt looked at her. "That's an offer I can't refuse." His voice was even but his thoughts were churning. Was this attractive woman, widowed just three weeks ago, coming on to him?

He cleared his throat and put down the glass. Then, tenatively, he put his hand on her arm. "Lottie, it must be very lonely for you now and I just want you to know I am there if you need me — any legal matter...."

She put her hand on top of his. "Thank you, Garrison. It's nice to know you are close." She looked up at him. Their eyes locked. "It was lonely even before he died," she said. "We hadn't — hadn't lived together — not really — for about three years. I think his heart was failing then. He had trouble breathing." She looked off into space.

Garrison's hand moved slowly up her arm to her shoulder, then brushed her cheek. "Poor little girl," he said gently.

Lottie wiped away a tear.

"Dear girl, don't cry." Then his arms were around her and he was kissing her.

"Oh Garrison, it's been so long," she murmured.

His hand found the top button of her blouse, then the others, the silky bra beneath, and his fingers were busy. She moaned softly and collapsed against him. Then she stood up and led him down the hall to the bedrooms. At the end of the hall she hesitated for a second, then opened the door to the spare bedroom. The shades were drawn and she stood there for a moment looking at him in the dim light. The pulse in Garrison's ears became a roar. He closed the door and began to undress her.

Lottie became a dedicated member of the Santa Catarina Democrats Club. She worked tirelessly on committees, she attended luncheons, dinners and breakfasts. She was so busy with it that she set up a kind of office in her home. There, she answered phone calls at all hours and made arrangements for meetings, programs and visits by county and state dignitaries. Lottie's neighbors observed the comings and goings of men — mostly men — but they knew she was involved in politics and assumed it was business.

In the course of her work, over a period of years, Lottie accumulated a collection of autographed photographs of incumbents as well as political hopefuls. There were even a few national figures on her wall. She framed each one and lined her hallway with them. "To Lottie, a tireless worker" — "To Lottie who never lets you down" — "To Lottie, hope to see you again soon" and on and on.

"My rogue's gallery," she would say coyly.

In addition to the photographs, Lottie acquired a nickname she knew nothing about. The male members of the Party referred to her as "Lottie-pop." All a male member had to mention was "Lottie-pop" and his fellow members knew where he was headed and what for, or where he had been if he was looking a bit worn.

Lottie's extra-curricular career was the best kept

secret in Santa Catarina. At least among the men.

There were a few close calls. Once, when Lottie decided to have a goldfish pond, she discussed it with Garrison Pruitt. He recommended his nephew who was a landscape gardener. The nephew also was a tanned, macho fellow in his thirties who had bulging biceps and a hairy chest that showed above his open shirt. He was also newly married. When Lottie grasped the nephew's arm and started down the hall to the guest room with him, he suddenly 'remembered' a previous engagement and bolted, promising to telephone her later about the job. This incident might have passed quietly into oblivion if the Pruitts hadn't invited the nephew and his new wife to dinner one evening shortly after that incident. During table talk, the nephew began to relate his narrow escape from Lottie when he received a sudden sharp kick on the shin from Garrison, his uncle. He shut up and looked inquiringly at Garrison who looked back at him like a thundercloud and gave him another sharp kick.

Later, Garrison growled "You damn near spoiled my recreation, boy. Keep your mouth shut! We're just lucky the women weren't paying attention. They didn't catch what you said."

"You came near breaking my leg, Uncle." The nephew was rubbing his shin.

"Next time I will," Garrison said.

Lottie's days were full. Full of club activities and the related physical activities. On the day before an election she once entertained a state senator, a congressman and a local supervisor, separately of course, in her guest room. All within fourteen hours. She marked that day on her calendar with a big red circle.

"My red letter day," she said to herself happily. "I'll bet there aren't many women in Santa Cat who can make that claim."

She noticed a bit of fatigue that night after the supervisor left, and the next morning she pampered herself by staying in bed until nine. The ringing phone got her up.

It was Garrison Pruitt who had been out of town for a week.

"I'm coming right over," he said.

For the first time in their long relationship Lottie found herself wishing he wouldn't. "Garrison, I'm not even dressed yet."

"All the better. Hold off — don't dress. I'm coming over." He hung up.

Lottie sighed. She felt tired. She hadn't slept well. Or had she? She couldn't seem to remember. She went to the dresser and took out a skimpy red silk nightgown. She noticed a slight pain in her chest when she raised her arms to get into it. She combed her hair and added a touch of makeup and looked at herself in the mirror. "I even look tired this morning," she said to herself. "Must be catching cold or something."

Garrison arrived in a hurry. "Haven't got much time," he said. "Been a hell of a week." He looked appreciatively at the red nightgown. "Not much in the way, with that one on."

He pulled it up and over Lottie's head. "Lottie love, you've got the best pussy I ever had — and I've tried a lot of 'em."

Lottie closed her eyes and gave herself up to his violent love-making, his demanding thrusts, his mouth on her breasts, his tongue in her mouth. "God I've missed this," he gasped.

Suddenly Lottie went limp under him. She could feel herself going and she tried to tell him — to say something. She groaned. She was so tired. So damned tired.

Garrison stopped. Looked at her. "Lottie — Lottie girl...."

Her eyes rolled back in her head. She gave one long, shuddering sigh and she was still. Still as death.

Garrison gave a half-hearted thrust and stopped. He raised his head to look at her again. Her mouth had fallen open as if she was trying to say something. She wasn't breathing. Garrison Pruitt said "My God" softly and pulled himself off her. For a moment he almost panicked. Then he got himself together. Dressed. Pulled the bedclothes up over Lottie and went out a side door. Hoped no neighbors had seen him. He had parked down the street because of the early hour. He went out the side door, through the garden. Drove to his office in a stupor. Muttering to himself over and over — "I can't believe it —" and sat at his desk, his mind in a fog. After an hour or so he phoned, half hoping it wasn't true. Maybe she'd answer the phone. The ringing — no answer. He waited another hour then reported to several people in his office that Lottie was not answering her phone.

Garrison Pruitt couldn't eat his lunch. The food tasted terrible. His favorite soup and sandwich. That afternoon he called Lottie's house again several times. Then he decided he had to do something. Anything. Anything but go there and find her the way he last saw her.

He called his secretary in. "She was to contact me today about that dinner next week — she was arranging the speaker. I wish you'd drop by her place and check on her — she may be ill or something. It's not like Lottie, to fail to show for an appointment."

The secretary was the one who called the police and the coroner. Then she returned to Pruitt's office to break the bad news to him.

He took it bravely. "She was such a reliable person," he said sadly. "This is terrible. So sudden. A heart attack — is that what they said? A real tragedy. She was such a hard worker for the Party. Absolutely dedicated. We will all miss her."

Margaret Koch was born and raised in Santa Cruz County, fourth generation descendent of early settlers to the county. As a child being raised by her grandparents, she always had her nose in a book but her ears were wide open as she listened to their stories and gossip.

Margaret graduated from Santa Cruz High School and attended the University of California at Berkeley. Several years later she wrote extensively about Santa Cruz County history for the *Santa Cruz Sentinel*, and published a number of books including *Santa Cruz County, Parade of the Past*, which is the standard reference work on that topic.

Margaret currently lives in Sedona, Arizona, where she continues to write and paint watercolors.